PRAISE FOR

Funny You Should Ask

"You will absolutely devour this book. It's filled with delightful banter, hot romance, and a love story that's worthy of the big screen. To put it bluntly, I freaking loved it and couldn't put it down."
—Kate Spencer, author of *In a New York Minute* and host of *Forever35*

"*Funny You Should Ask* is a smart, sensitive story full of love and longing—and not to mention a totally swoonworthy hero. It's also a page-turning peek into the celebrity machine. Framed by one infamous weekend and its fallout, the book goes beyond the glossy surface to thoughtfully tackle questions of perception versus reality, and which can hurt more: the limitations other people place on us, or the ones we place on ourselves."
—Heather Cocks and Jessica Morgan,
bestselling authors of *The Royal We* and *The Heir Affair*

"*Funny You Should Ask* is the kind of fascinating, intimate character study that feels like reading about real people. A breezy, addictive romance—I couldn't put it down!"
—Rachel Lynn Solomon, author of *The Ex Talk*

"Elissa Sussman's adult debut promises a glamorous celeb romp, but offers a double-whammy with thoughtful, emotional depth. As the narrative jumps back and forth in time, the truth of what happened between Gabe and Chani unfolds and a romance blooms—cautious, sweet, and sizzling with tension. . . . A beautiful, fun, heartfelt love story that I couldn't put down."
—Maurene Goo, author of *Somewhere Only We Know*

"I loved this book! Smart, funny, and crackling with the most delicious sexual tension, *Funny You Should Ask* is exactly the kind of book I am always wishing there were more of. I've already recommended it to all my friends."
—Katie Cotugno, *New York Times*
bestselling author of *Birds of California*

DELL

NEW YORK

Funny You Should Ask

A NOVEL

Elissa Sussman

Funny You Should Ask is a work of fiction. Names, characters, places, and incidents are the products of the author's imagination or are used fictitiously. Any resemblance to actual events, locales, or persons, living or dead, is entirely coincidental.

A Dell Trade Paperback Original

Published in the United States by Dell, an imprint of Random House, a division of Penguin Random House LLC, New York.

Dell and the House colophon are registered trademarks of Penguin Random House LLC.

LIBRARY OF CONGRESS CATALOGING-IN-PUBLICATION DATA
Names: Sussman, Elissa, author.
Title: Funny you should ask / Elissa Sussman.
Description: First edition. | New York: Bantam Dell, [2022] |
Identifiers: LCCN 2021014019 (print) | LCCN 2021014020 (ebook) |
ISBN 9780593357323 (trade paperback; acid-free paper) |
ISBN 9780593357330 (ebook)
Classification: LCC PS3619.U84 F86 2022 (print) |
LCC PS3619.U84 (ebook) | DDC 813/.6—dc23
LC record available at https://lccn.loc.gov/2021014019
LC ebook record available at https://lccn.loc.gov/2021014020

Printed in the United States of America on acid-free paper

randomhousebooks.com

9 8 7 6 5 4 3 2 1

Book design by Barbara M. Bachman

For John

All my stories are love stories

because of you

"The course of true love—"

"—gathers no moss."

—THE PHILADELPHIA STORY

Funny You
Should Ask

Prologue

"HE REQUESTED YOU," ALEXANDRA SAYS.

It's a good thing we're on the phone because I'd bet the editor in chief of *Broad Sheets* magazine would not appreciate the death glare I'm giving my screen. And I *know* she wouldn't understand why.

"Bullshit," I say.

I'm half hoping she'll prove me wrong, and I'm embarrassed to realize that I'm holding my breath while I wait for her answer.

"Okay, okay," she admits. "His people requested you."

That makes sense. The article I did on Gabe Parker ten years ago had been a PR team's wet dream. It gave Gabe the kind of publicity that people would buy if they could. Which is, in essence, what they're attempting to do now.

I can't blame them. Hell, I'm sure my own publicist is kicking herself for not thinking of it first. Stars aligning and all that.

That article is the reason that ten years later, no matter what I'm promoting, no matter what I'm being interviewed for, I still get asked the same, exact question.

And I always offer the same, exact answer.

"Nope, nothing happened," I'll say with a big smile. "Don't I wish, though."

My ego still takes a hit when people accept that answer with an easy, relieved nod. But I get it. That's my brand. Being the kind of woman who spends a platonic weekend with a Hollywood heartthrob in his prime. Readers didn't have to be threatened by me. Instead, they could sympathize with how I—a "regular girl"—had gotten a chance with someone like Gabe Parker and whiffed it.

It also helped that Gabe's immediate reaction to the article's release—running off to marry his gorgeous, former-model co-star—proved emphatically that I wasn't his type.

A bruising but necessary public rejection. One that had done wonders for me professionally.

It made me lovable. Accessible. Relatable.

It sold articles.

It sold books.

It made *my* career.

"They want you two to re-create as much of your weekend as you can," Alexandra says. "He arrives in L.A. in a few hours."

I mentally scoff. I've never had an interview like this happen when it was supposed to. Even that first weekend had been rescheduled at least twice. Still, it's surprising how quickly they're trying to pull this together. It doesn't give me any time to research, to prep.

I guess they assume that, to a certain extent, I've been preparing for this for ten years.

They're not wrong. Because the truth is, I've spent those years simultaneously profiting and running from that Gabe Parker interview.

From Gabe Parker.

"You have the paperback coming out," Alexandra says. "He has a movie coming out."

She didn't need to remind me of either.

The professional benefits are clear.

The personal ones . . .

It's impossible to ignore Gabe, and his career trajectory. The adage about car wrecks and being unable to look away has been true of him for the last five years or so. Everyone knows that he got fired after his third Bond film. Everyone knows that his marriage to

Jacinda Lockwood reached an embarrassing, pedestrian conclusion. Everyone knows that he's been in and out of rehab centers.

Everyone says that this new movie could either revive his career or end it for good.

"I can send over the screener," Alexandra suggests. "See what you think."

I bite my tongue, holding back what would have probably been a caustic, unwelcome response. I know Alexandra is being helpful. I know she wants this interview to be as successful as the first.

I know I'm being ungrateful to even consider turning it down.

But the thought of sitting across from Gabe Parker after all these years, pretending I haven't replayed that weekend over and over in my head, pretending I don't *still* think about the moments we shared, pretending that what I tell everyone is the truth and that nothing really happened between us . . .

Well. It makes me feel more than a little unsteady.

"I've heard the movie is good," Alexandra says.

It's a remake of *The Philadelphia Story*. My favorite movie. One of ten dozen things Gabe and I had talked about.

Back then, Gabe would have been perfect as Mike Connor, the struggling writer vying for the heart of socialite Tracy Lord. Now, at forty, he's playing the ex-addict ex-husband, C. K. Dexter Haven.

There have already been a dozen think pieces about the choice—about how it's so close to Gabe's real life that it's not really acting at all. How it's nothing more than stunt casting. How Gabe is washed up and doesn't deserve another chance.

No one thought he deserved to be Bond either.

I don't need to see the movie to know he's probably perfect in it. Just like I know that trying to fight my editor, Gabe's management, and (if I told her about it) my therapist would be futile.

"He'll be waiting at the restaurant at one," Alexandra says. "But if you really don't want to, I can send—"

"I'll do it," I say.

I've chickened out on only one interview in my career—I won't do it again.

Instead, I swallow back the taste of impending doom. It tastes a lot like a really good burger and a perfect sour beer. It tastes like Jell-O shots and popcorn.

It tastes like expensive mint toothpaste.

I know that by accepting this assignment, I'll get the answers to every unasked question I've had for the last ten years.

No matter what, everything that Gabe and I started that weekend a decade ago in December will *finally* get a proper ending.

Friday

BROAD SHEETS

GABE PARKER:
Shaken, Not Stirred—
Part One

BY CHANI HOROWITZ

GABE PARKER IS SHOELESS, SHIRTLESS, AND HOLDING A puppy.

"I'm sorry," he tells me. "This place is a rental. Do you mind holding her for a moment while I deal with this?"

The *her* in question is his ten-week-old black rescue mutt. The *this* is the mess she's made on the floor, which he's now mopping up with his T-shirt.

I'm standing in his kitchen, holding a squirming fluffy dog, watching Hollywood's biggest heartthrob clean up puppy pee.

It's not a fantasy. It's real life.

Usually, I'd have to pay twenty bucks (plus another forty for popcorn and a soda) to get this good of a look at Gabe Parker's abs and lats. Today, however, *I'm* the one getting paid to spend a couple of hours with those body parts—as well as the rest of him.

"Gabe is just so *likable,*" his co-star Marissa Merino has been quoted as saying.

"A guy's guy," Jackson Ritter, another co-star, claims.

That's the company line—that Gabe Parker is exactly as gregarious and charming as he appears on the big screen.

I know you're reading this secretly hoping that I'm going to tell you it's all a lie—that it's the Hollywood machinery working overtime—that Gabe Parker is a womanizing creep who has an exceptionally effective PR team to build this image of a man so good that he can't possibly be real.

But he's real. And he's spectacular.

He finishes cleaning up after his pooch, dropping his shirt into the trash before coming over to me, taking the puppy's face in his hands, and cooing at her.

"It's okay, honey," he says. "It's not your fault. I love you so very much."

Have I mentioned I'm still holding her? And he's still shirtless? He smells amazing, by the way. Like lumber, and peppermint, and the backseat of the Ford Focus where you had your very first kiss with the guy from Jewish summer camp who you knew had already kissed all of your friends, but had an eyebrow piercing and turned out to be really, really good with his tongue.

We're only five minutes into our interview and I'm already at a disadvantage.

Unfortunately, Gabe puts a shirt on and the three of us—me, him, and the puppy—head out to grab lunch. He has a favorite place nearby. It's not too crowded, he says, and no one really bothers him. Reminds him a little of home.

I brace myself for what I know is coming next—a big-time star rhapsodizing about the small town where he grew up and how he loves Los Angeles, but aw shucks, he really misses his hometown, where no one cared about fame or money.

This is not my first rodeo, after all.

He says it, of course, but the power of Gabe Parker is that I actually believe him.

Speaking of rodeos, I'm sorry to say that on our way to lunch, Gabe himself shatters part of the Montana Man fantasy by informing me that he'd never actually been on a horse before his role in *Cold Creek Mountain*—the first time that audiences saw him without a shirt.

"No ranches, no riding," he tells me. "I grew up in a small town."

Gabe looks like the kind of guy that should be a movie star. Heads turn when he passes, and it's not just because he's six foot four and holding an adorable puppy. He has that ineffable quality that we'd all bottle and sell if we could.

And yes, ladies—he is actually six foot four. Not Hollywood's version of six foot four, which is closer to five foot ten, but actually a towering, tall hunk of a man. I know this for a fact because *I'm* Hollywood's version of six foot four.

We get a table in the back where there's a patio for the dog. It takes us fifteen minutes to get there, but it's mostly because Gabe himself keeps stopping and talking to the waitstaff.

You see, they all know him. He's a regular.

"Madison, honey, you look gorgeous," he says when our waitress comes to take our order.

She's radiantly pregnant, and waves off the compliment.

"I mean it," Gabe says. "Your husband should say that to you. Every. Single. Day. On his knees."

I'm pretty sure that if *I* were pregnant, my water would have broken at that exact moment.

But Madison just laughs and takes our order, giving Gabe's puppy a pat on the head before floating off to the kitchen with more grace then I could have ever managed, pregnant or not.

We each get a beer and a burger.

We talk about his childhood in Montana. How close he is with his family, especially his sister, Lauren. She's older by a year and Gabe's best friend.

"I know it's cliché," he says. "But she really is."

We talk about the bookshop. The one he bought for Lauren and his mom when he got his first big break.

"It's a bookshop/craft shop," he makes a point to say. "Lauren gets mad if I don't include that as well."

It's called the Cozy. They have a website. Gabe recommends books on it, even though he's said in past interviews that he was never much of a reader as a kid.

"My mom was an English teacher, so having a kid that didn't like books was so embarrassing," he says. "But I was just a late bloomer—I'm a big reader now. The bookstore was her dream. And Lauren's always been good at making things—baking, crafting, that kind of stuff. She still knits me a sweater every Christmas."

I bite my tongue to keep from making the obvious joke: "What are they made of? Boyfriend material?"

In case you're wondering, he *is* single.

"Rumors," he tells me when I ask about Jacinda. "We're co-stars and friends."

Jacinda Lockwood—the newest Bond girl for the newest Bond. She and Gabe have been photographed numerous times coming out of restaurants, standing close to each other on dark sidewalks in Paris, even holding hands a few times.

"She's a sweet girl," Gabe says. "But there's nothing there."

He orders a second beer. I'm a lightweight so I decline.

Remember this detail later, friends. Two roads diverge and all that.

I ask how he feels about taking on such an iconic part—about being the first American to step into the role.

"Nervous," he tells me. "Anxious. I almost said no."

That's the narrative his people and the film's producers have been pushing, and I was skeptical when I heard it. But Gabe's entire demeanor changes when I ask. He's been open and cheerful, answering questions eagerly.

Bond puts a somber hush on the conversation. He's not looking at me, staring down at his napkin, which he's twisted into a tight knot. He's silent for a long time.

I ask if the backlash bothered him.

"I'm beyond lucky," he says. "All I care about is doing the part justice."

He shrugs.

"But do I worry that they're right? Yeah, sure. Who wouldn't?"

"They" are the fans writing angry articles and blog posts detailing all the reasons why Gabe is the worst possible choice for Bond. Because he's American. Because he's not Oliver Matthias. Because audiences are used to him playing hunky, dim-witted himbos.

And then there's the whole *Angels in America* thing.

He orders a third beer.

"My publicist would have my head if she saw this," he tells me. "I'm supposed to stop at two, but it's Friday! Hey, what are you doing after this?"

Twenty minutes later, with puppy in tow, we're on our way to look at a house in the Hollywood Hills.

I want to ask him more about Bond, specifically if he had anything to do with leaking the audition footage online, but it's around this point, dear readers, where I embarrassingly lose control of the interview.

It's the moment when Gabe starts interviewing *me*.

"You're from here, right? Wow, that must have been wild. I can't even imagine what it's like to grow up in Los Angeles. It was Los Angeles, right? I know a lot of people say L.A. but they really mean Orange County or Valencia or Anaheim and I know that real natives don't consider that to be L.A. at all. Right?"

He's correct on both counts. That I am from Los Angeles and that we get very testy about folks from neighboring cities trying to claim residence.

"This place still feels magical to me," he says. "Been here almost five years, made almost eight movies, and it's all still magic. Bet that makes me seem like a sap."

It doesn't. It makes him seem inhumanly charming.

The puppy is asleep on his lap.

"I haven't named her yet," he tells me. "I'm waiting for it to come to me."

We pull up in front of a gorgeous white-stone mansion.

Gabe lets the puppy explore the backyard while we get a tour of the amenities. The real estate agent is bending over backward trying to make this sale, but unfortunately for her, Gabe has decided that my opinion matters a great deal.

And although the house is beautiful, it's not really my style. Which means that today, it's not Gabe's style either.

We bid the real estate agent goodbye and begin our own farewells. Gabe has given me several hours of his time and yet, I'm not ready to say goodbye. I've been fully charmed by the future Bond. That's the only excuse I have for what happens next.

Gabe mentions that he has a premiere to go to the following night and as I hand his adorable sleeping puppy over to him, I somehow manage to finagle an invite to the afterparty.

—

Then

Chapter 1

I ARRIVED EARLY AND DAMP. THE BLUE COTTON BLOUSE THAT HAD looked professional and flattering in my apartment mirror was now stuck to my armpits in dark, wet half-moons. Lifting my arms, I blasted the AC in my car, hoping both to dry my shirt and shock the nervousness out of my system.

I'd interviewed celebrities before.

I'd even interviewed supernaturally beautiful celebrities before.

This was different.

Gabe Parker wasn't just any celebrity. He was my number one, heart-fluttering, palm-sweating, thigh-clenching celebrity crush. I'd entertained multiple extensive, detailed fantasies about him. I'd done numerous searches for paparazzi pictures of him. Until this morning, a shirtless photo of him had been the lock screen of my phone.

I had zero chill when it came to Gabe Parker.

If Jeremy and I were still dating, there'd be a major possibility he would have tried to veto this interview. He knew how I felt about Gabe. When he'd insisted on us declaring our "free pass" celebrities, I'd chosen Gabe. Jeremy had pouted.

It was ridiculous, of course.

Gabe would probably be charming and kind and amiable. It wouldn't be because he liked me, or thought I was interesting, or because we had any sort of deep emotional connection. It would be because it was his job to charm me. And it was my job to be charmed.

His management had been very, very clear about the kind of profile they were expecting me to turn in. What they wanted in exchange for the access *Broad Sheets* was getting to Gabe before he started shooting.

They wanted a story that would counter the bad press his casting had caused. They wanted a story that would convince the naysayers that he was the best choice for Bond. They wanted me to sell him to America. To the world.

I wanted a story that would keep getting me work.

I blogged and sent short stories to literary magazines like I was tossing rocks into the ocean.

I'd only gotten one published, and then, just when I was considering that maybe I should give up trying to be a writer, I'd gotten the gig at *Broad Sheets*.

I'd been recommended by a former professor who had once called my writing "mainstream"—as much of an insult as one could get in an esteemed MFA program but apparently exactly what *Broad Sheets* was looking for.

Jeremy called the stuff I was doing "puff pieces," but we'd still celebrated when I got the job—spending a good chunk of my first paycheck on bottomless fries and happy hour beers.

The editors at *Broad Sheets* seemed to like my writing—at least, they kept giving me work—and every month I could pay my bills with the money I made off my writing felt like an accomplishment.

I knew that this interview was an opportunity to show that I could take on more high-profile, better-paying articles. It needed to go well.

Even though I'd just checked it five minutes ago, I scanned my bag again to make sure that I had a pen, my notebook with the questions I'd written out last night, and my tape recorder, which had a new set of batteries. I was as prepared as I was going to be.

My armpits were now cold *and* wet. I realized, with horror, that I wasn't one hundred percent sure I'd put deodorant on. I gave myself a sniff, but couldn't tell.

It was too late now.

I glanced in the rearview mirror one last time, grateful that at least my bangs had chosen to be obedient.

Gabe was staying in a rental house in Laurel Canyon. I'd expected something grand, with a massive gate and intense security system, but I'd been sent to a modest bungalow set back from the street with nothing more than an unlocked, waist-high gate to keep people out.

But even though it was small, I knew the place had to cost at least four times more than the apartment I shared with one stranger and one half-friend.

I could feel my heart ricocheting up and down my throat as I walked through the gate and down the pathway. A heart attack or a panic attack or some other sort of attack seemed extremely likely.

"He's just a person. He's just a person," I said to myself.

I lifted my hand, but before I could even knock, the door swung open and there he was.

Gabe. Parker.

I'd done enough interviews like this to know firsthand the difference a camera and a crew could make in someone's appearance. Actors were usually shorter than they appeared, their heads often bigger. Round cheeks could make someone look chubbier than they were, just as chiseled features could come off as gaunt in real life.

A part of me had been praying that Gabe Parker's good looks were mostly manufactured.

I was swiftly and immediately proven wrong.

He. Was. Glorious.

Tall, knee-bucklingly handsome, and backlit by the best sunlight California could muster on a brisk winter day. His dark brown hair was mussed, a wavy lock flopped onto his forehead in a way that looked both boyish and rugged. He had a dimple in his left cheek—which I already knew about, but it was on full display as he greeted me with a smile that made my heart stop so abruptly that I put a hand to my chest.

He was so beautiful.

I was *so* fucked.

"It's you!" he said.

As if he had been waiting for me. The truth was that I had been waiting for him. Literally. This interview had been scheduled and rescheduled several times already.

But none of that mattered now.

I felt fluttery. All over.

I didn't like it.

It was deeply unprofessional and a complete cliché. The world already assumed that all female reporters slept with—or were trying to sleep with—their subjects. I was here to do my job, not get all hot and bothered over a sexy celebrity.

It was enough to keep those tingly feelings at bay.

Gabe was still blasting me with that full-force grin. It was so powerful that it took me at least ten seconds to realize he was holding a puppy in his arms. And I *loved* dogs.

"Can you take her for a moment?" he asked.

I was apparently incapable of speech so I just nodded and held out my arms. His fingers brushed mine as the wiggling, furry bundle was passed over. My heart stopped again, and the tingly feelings returned.

Dammit.

At this rate, if he shook my hand, I was likely to pass out at his feet.

After giving me the dog, he turned and headed back into the house. The puppy shifted in my arms, craning her head so she could take a swipe at my chin with her soft, pink puppy tongue. I inhaled deeply, breathing in her puppy breath. Pure. Unfiltered. Good.

It stabilized me.

"Come on in!" Gabe said from inside the house.

I followed his voice, taking in the beautiful rental with its wood-paneled walls and warm, cabin-like feel. The back of the house was open—glass sliding doors pushed to the side—and I could see a big, grassy lawn with a pool and hot tub. The rental itself had maybe two bedrooms, but the property was spacious. It was exactly the kind of Laurel Canyon home where you could easily imagine the Mamas and the Papas or Fleetwood Mac doing drugs, having sex, and making music during the seventies.

I walked into the kitchen and found Gabe on his hands and knees. Without a shirt on.

"Sorry," he apologized, using his cotton T-shirt to wipe the floor. "I still have no idea where any of the rags are, and we've been having a hard time with house-training."

He looked up at me, and I realized I was holding the puppy in front of me like a shield.

Standing, Gabe looked down at the pee-stained shirt in his hand and winced before tossing it in the trash. Then he came toward me.

"It's okay," he said to the dog. "I still love you."

"Unngh," I said.

He took her from me, cuddling her against his bare chest. It was smooth and sleek—all those muscles perfectly defined—exactly how it looked on the big screen. Well. Not exactly. He was actually a little thinner than I had expected.

Not that I minded.

He still looked good. Beyond good.

I laced my fingers behind my back to keep from reaching out and touching, but my imagination did not hesitate in envisioning how his skin might feel beneath my palms. Because if I was going to touch—even if it was just a fantasy—I was going to be putting my whole hands on him. Maybe my mouth too.

If I had the time, there was a long list of *my* body parts interested in touching *his* body parts.

It was completely inappropriate, but it *was* just in my head. What harm could there be in that?

"Sorry about that," Gabe apologized again.

We both stood there for a moment. He made no motion to indicate he was going to put a shirt on, and I wasn't going to prompt him to do so.

As far as I was concerned, this was a once-in-a-lifetime opportunity to ogle one of the hottest up-and-coming stars of our time and I was going to ogle my brains out. Silently. Covertly.

I knew I was justifying my unprofessional thoughts, but the truth was, I wasn't sure I could help it. He was just so handsome and my pulse was racing like I was being chased.

"Wow," he said, almost under his breath. "Your eyes."

I blinked.

"They're very big," he said.

It was the last thing I expected him to say.

And he said it as if he'd never seen eyes before. As if he might take my face in his hands and try to examine them close up, like an archeologist would with a fossil. I tilted my chin upward, my eyes—my *very big eyes*—meeting his straight on.

My heart felt a little like a live wire, jerking around in my chest, throwing off electrical currents. Could these currents be mutual? Did *he* believe the stereotype about female reporters? Did he think I was going to try to sleep with him? Did he *want* me to try to sleep with him?

"Can I ask you something?" he asked.

Anything, I thought.

"Mmhmumph," I said.

He tilted his head, his hair sliding across his forehead. I wanted to brush it to the side. Wanted to run my fingertips down the side of his face and trace the line of his jaw. Wanted to lick—

"Has anyone ever told you that you kind of look like one of those cat-clock things?" he asked.

When I didn't answer, Gabe put his hands on either side of his face, opening his own eyes wide.

"You know—tick tock, tick tock?" He looked from side to side.

I knew what he was talking about—it was a decent impression—and felt a weird sort of relief at being compared to a plastic, kitschy clock. It made more sense than Gabe Parker, movie star, complimenting me. Or wanting to sleep with me.

It threw some much-needed cold water on my rampaging libido.

"How do you pronounce your name?" he asked, not waiting for a response.

I'd barely said one fully formed word since I'd arrived, but he didn't seem to notice.

"My manager said *Han-ni,* but I wanted to make sure."

My name was confusing for a lot of people. During my last interview—with a breezy starlet—she'd spent the entire time alternating between "Hannah" and "Tawney." It made a weird sort of sense as my name was basically a combination of the two, and I hadn't bothered correcting her.

"That's fine," I said.

Gabe frowned at me. "But I'm saying it wrong, aren't I?"

"It doesn't bother me," I said.

"It bothers me," he said. "It's your name. I want to be able to say it correctly."

Well.

"Like 'knee,' but with a *ch.* Chani," I said, using the back of my throat to get the proper half-hacking, half-rolling sound.

As I did, a tiny bit of spit popped out of my mouth and arched in the air between us. Thankfully it fell before it came into contact with any part of Gabe's person, and he was gracious enough not to comment on it.

I wanted to die.

"Chani," he said. "Chani. Chani."

He got it right on the second try, though I could have listened to him say my name all day long. Because he said it as if he was tasting it.

"My makeup artist on *Tommy Jacks* was named Preeti," he said. "But everyone on the crew said *Prit-ee* instead of *Pree-tee*."

He gave the puppy a good scratch under her chin and she snuggled up close, tucking her head against his chest. *Lucky dog*.

"She told me that she used to correct people but it never seemed to stick and after a while, she just got tired of trying." Gabe shrugged. "I always think about that. How much it must suck to have your name constantly mispronounced."

He wasn't wrong—I'd just learned, like Preeti, that most people didn't care.

Gabe obviously did.

We stood there for a moment—him shirtless and holding a puppy, me with my crush on him growing exponentially larger with every second. And me helpless to do anything about it. I felt like a teenager again, with hormones I couldn't control. It was disorienting.

"What were you saying before?" he asked.

"About my name?"

He shook his head. "No, when you were coming up the walkway—it looked like you were saying something."

My face got prickly and warm. Getting caught talking to myself wasn't exactly the first impression I'd hoped to make.

"Sorry," he said. "Guess I just revealed I was kind of spying on you through the window."

He gave me a sheepish smile, even though I was the one who was beyond embarrassed.

"It's okay," I said. "I was, uh, I was just talking to myself."

There was no way in hell I was going to tell him what I had actually been saying. Between that and being compared to a clock, this interview was already awkward enough.

Gabe looked at me for a long time.

"Do you do that a lot?" he asked.

"Talk to myself?"

He nodded.

"Um, sometimes?" I squirmed a little under his penetrating gaze. "I guess it just helps me sort out my thoughts? It happens when I get stuck on things, sometimes. Like, saying them out loud makes them real? Or, I can organize them better than if they're just in my head? Almost like a list? Or not really a list, but a documentation of my ideas? For posterity?"

I was rambling about talking to myself. Wonderful.

Gabe leaned back on his heels and let out a whistle, as if I'd just said something profound.

"A documentation of your ideas," he repeated. "You *are* a writer."

Suddenly I got this horrible feeling that there had been some huge, weird mix-up and he didn't know I was here to interview him. Or I was being pranked.

"Yes? *Broad Sheets* sent me?" I hated how my voice kept going up at the end of my sentences, making everything a question.

"Yeah, I know," he said, as if *I* was the one who wasn't making any sense. "You write other things too, right? Like, fiction?"

"Yes?"

He grinned at me as if I'd just told him I had the cure for cancer.

"That's awesome," he said. "I love books."

I didn't know what to think. On one hand, it seemed that all the people who had thought that Gabe was too much of a himbo hick to play Bond might have had a point. On the other hand, he was so damn adorable, it was hard not to find him and his "I love books" comment utterly charming.

"Should we get started?" I realized that I'd been in his house for almost ten minutes, seen him shirtless, and still hadn't asked him a single serious question. "Where's the best place to talk?"

"I thought we'd go to lunch," he said. "There's a great pub on Ventura. Do you mind driving?"

"Uh . . ."

"But first," he said, walking past me. "Let me show you something."

I didn't have any choice but to follow.

Broad Sheets had said I'd be getting more access than other interviewers. Gabe's management really wanted to counter the anti-Parker narrative coming from Bond fans.

But when Gabe showed me into his bedroom, I stopped in the doorway, knowing that there was access and there was *access*.

"Check out this view," Gabe said, throwing open the curtains.

It was *quite* the view.

The puppy sat at Gabe's feet, the two of them a gorgeous, film-worthy tableau, bathed in the December sunlight. He still wasn't wearing a shirt. His back was incredible. All smooth muscles and sleek lines. I wanted to stand behind him, wrap my arms around his waist, and press my cheek against one of his shoulder blades.

The desire to do so was so strong that I could practically feel his hot skin against my face. Or maybe that was just because my own skin felt warm. Very warm. I pressed my cool hands to my throat and looked away.

Enough was enough.

I took in his room instead, searching for something I could use in my article.

It was a nice bedroom—big and simple. Pleasant, but impersonal. Very clearly a temporary living situation.

The furniture was pale wood, the furnishings all neutral. There was enough space that I could have fit most of my own bedroom between Gabe's bed and his built-in fireplace.

The only signs of individuality were the haphazard stacks on almost all the available surfaces. He hadn't been lying when he said he loved books. Or his publicist was really working overtime to hammer home this new narrative.

I spotted a few recognizable spines from my safe space in the doorway. Fiction. Nonfiction. Poetry. Plenty of recent bestsellers and book club books, but also a few that surprised me.

bell hooks. Katherine Dunn. Tim O'Brien. Aimee Bender. James Baldwin. Alan Bennett.

Books that I had on my shelf at home. My hands itched with the desire to run my fingers along their spines—something familiar to center me in an unfamiliar environment where I felt completely out of my element.

Instead, I tucked my hand into my bag, once again checking. Pen. Notebook. Tape recorder. Everything I needed for this interview was there, and yet . . .

Maybe I couldn't do this.

Ever since Jeremy and I had broken up, that thought had been circling in my head like an un-swattable fly. It hadn't helped that my motivation had apparently walked out the door right after him.

I hadn't written anything in weeks.

While all of my former MFA classmates were out there signing with agents or having short stories published or getting book deals, I was stumbling through the kind of assignments they all would have sneered at.

I didn't really blame them. Not because I was ashamed of the work I was getting, but because I knew that the *writing* I was doing was, at its best, boring.

At its worst, it was just bad.

What if that was the kind of writer I was? The kind of writer I'd always be?

But now wasn't the time for an existential crisis.

I pushed aside my doubts, and focused on the room. On the piles of books. There were movies too—a stack of them on the credenza next to the ridiculously oversized and completely expected flat screen TV.

Even though I knew it was probably more professional for me to stay in the doorway, I ventured toward the DVDs. A familiar one stared up at me from the top of the pile.

I don't want to be worshipped. I want to be loved.

"Sorry?"

Gabe turned back toward me, and I realized I'd said that out loud.

I blushed and held up the DVD. *The Philadelphia Story.*

"It's from the movie," I said.

"Oh yeah, that's what I wanted to show you. Ryan sent these over the other day," Gabe said. "For research."

Ryan Ulrich, the director of *The Hildebrand Rarity*.

I looked at the rest of the pile. All older movies—most in black and white. *Arsenic and Old Lace, The Thin Man, Holiday,* and *My Man Godfrey*.

"I've only seen one or two," Gabe said. "But I have to watch them all before we start filming."

I nodded.

"Is it good?" he asked.

"Is it good?" I looked down at the DVD, at the cozy threesome of

Katharine Hepburn, Cary Grant, and Jimmy Stewart, all smiling up at me. "It's only one of the best romantic comedies ever made. One of the best comedies ever made." I knew most of it by heart.

"'I don't want to be worshipped. I want to be loved,'" Gabe repeated.

He had a good memory.

"Is there a difference?" he asked.

"I think so?" I said. "You can worship someone you don't know, but you can't love them."

Gabe looked at me. I looked back.

I was a little startled by the sincerity of my words. If Gabe was too, well, he bypassed that awkwardness quickly.

"I think Ryan wants our Bond to be a combination of Cary Grant and William Powell," he said.

I could see it. Could see the angle they wanted to take.

Because even though Gabe's on-screen persona—and apparently his off-screen one—wasn't necessarily known as sophisticated, he had shown a talent for humor. If Ryan Ulrich could channel that into the same cool, dry humor that Powell and Grant excelled at, then Gabe's Bond could be something unique.

"That's a good idea," I said, more to myself.

Gabe came over to me, taking the DVD from my hand. Once again, our fingertips brushed against each other, and once again I did everything I could to ignore the tight, scratchy feeling the contact gave me.

"It's good, huh?" he asked.

"It's amazing," I said.

I should have stopped there, but I didn't.

"Except for one gross story line that almost wrecks it for me every time."

Gabe raised an eyebrow.

"I don't want to ruin it for you," I said.

"My sister already told me the plot," he said. "She was so outraged that I'd never seen it that she spoiled the ending for me. I already know who ends up with who. What's the story line you hate?"

"It's not a big deal," I said. "Just some stuff that would never fly if they remade it now."

Shut up, shut up, shut up.

"Like what?" Gabe asked.

Jeremy had once called my rants a "feminist monologue hurricane." Once I got started, I could go on and on and on. Blowing hot wind, he said. Everyone should take cover.

He was *such* an asshole.

But he wasn't wrong, because I opened my mouth and let the hurricane fly.

"It's just that the whole thing that sets the plot in motion is Katharine Hepburn's father cheating on her mother with a chorus girl. And Tracy Lord—Hepburn's character—is the only one who thinks there's anything wrong with that. Because she criticizes her father for cheating, she's considered cold and uncaring—and a hypocrite because of one night where she got drunk and climbed on the roof of her house naked."

Gabe was suddenly looking at the DVD with interest.

"Katharine Hepburn is naked in this movie?"

"No," I said. "It's just something they talk about."

I kept going. Mostly because Gabe looked curious, not completely bored and/or horrified. Yet.

"Her father has this whole terrible speech about how basically the only reason he cheated is because his daughter didn't worship him unconditionally and he had to go seek out the approval of a younger woman. Instead of Katharine Hepburn calling him a lecherous old man, she ends up *apologizing* for how she wasn't a good enough daughter to him. *She* asks *him* for forgiveness. It's a crash course in gaslighting and it's gross."

I was panting now, the way I always did when I really got caught up talking about something that needled me.

Gabe didn't say anything for a while.

"So, you hate this movie."

"No!" I tossed the DVD onto the bed. "I love this movie. It's funny and romantic and has amazing banter. But it's not perfect and I think it can be better."

Jeremy had said that was ridiculous.

"It already exists," he'd said. "It's done. You can't improve on something that was made over fifty years ago. You have to take it as it is."

Maybe he was right.

Gabe looked thoughtful. "My sister didn't mention any of this," he said.

"There's a lot more to the movie," I said. "A lot of it is good."

Gabe seemed doubtful. "You like the movie even though it has this horrible subplot."

"I guess you could say that I love it, but I don't worship it," I said.

It had sounded extremely clever in my head but out loud it didn't really make sense. Which, in a way, was the story of my life.

"It's a good movie," I said.

Gabe looked completely confused. I couldn't really blame him. Jeremy had often said I didn't make sense on the best of days.

Not that he didn't have a point. Occasionally.

Gabe did seem like he regretted showing me the DVDs.

This wasn't going well. I wasn't supposed to be lecturing Gabe about misogynistic themes in classic films—I was supposed to be asking what he thought about the big-budget feature he was about to do.

Before I could, though, Gabe slapped his hands together, making me jump.

"I'm starving," he said. "Let's eat."

SERIOUS_CINEPHILES.COM

FIVE REASONS WHY GABE PARKER WILL BE THE WORST BOND EVER

By Ross Leaming

IT WILL COME AS NO SHOCK TO OUR LOYAL READERS THAT the team here at Serious Cinephiles is extremely disappointed with the latest Bond news. Here we break down all the reasons we think director Ryan Ulrich is making a huge mistake with the casting of his new leading man.

1. He's American. Yes, I know that it's been confirmed that Parker will be tackling a British accent, but why make him go through the trouble when you could just cast someone with a more appropriate background?

2. He's not Oliver Matthias. I don't know about you, but I call absolute bullshit on the claim that Parker was the production's first and only pick. Presumably the producers saw him in *Tommy Jacks,* which is a fine enough movie but certainly doesn't display any reach on Parker's part. Especially not in comparison to his co-star WHO ACTUALLY HAS A BRITISH ACCENT. BECAUSE HE'S ACTUALLY BRITISH. That anyone could pick Parker over Matthias indicates that they shouldn't be in charge of casting Bond. Ever.

3. He's a hick. Look, I'm sure Gabe Parker is a perfectly nice person. He might even be somewhat intelligent. But we all know that his on-screen (and in-interview) persona is the polar opposite of what we expect from our Bond. The man with the martini needs to be sophistication personified. He shouldn't be played by someone whose most famous talk

show moment involved him playing *beer pong* with another guest. And winning.

4. He's already sleeping with his co-star. They haven't confirmed it, but anyone who saw those pictures of him and Jacinda Lockwood in Paris can tell that they are definitely knocking boots. But, Ross, you might say, doesn't that speak to why he would be a good Bond? He's already proven he can get the girl. Yes, exactly, I would say to you. Where's the excitement, then? The chase? The anticipation? It just seems like Gabe Parker is a bro who can't keep his dick in his pants. Plus, it's just another sign that Parker is forever getting his co-star's sloppy seconds.

SIDE NOTE: Is anyone surprised that Lockwood dumped Matthias for Parker? The Black British-born model has gotten quite the reputation for doing whatever it takes to get her movie career off the ground.

5. He's too soft. I'm not talking about his body—we've all seen the shirtless pics from *Cold Creek Mountain,* a beefcake photo shoot parading as a serious movie—but there's something undeniably tender about him. And Bond is NOT tender. He's tough. Maybe it's all Parker's experience in the theatre, particularly his leading role in *Angels in America.* You all know what I'm saying.

Chapter 2

I DROVE US TO THE RESTAURANT. ANOTHER INTERVIEWER MIGHT have been able to use the extra time in a small space to her advantage, but being a generally nervous driver and having a huge movie star and his new puppy in my passenger seat kept me focused on the road. Instead, it gave *Gabe* the opportunity to pepper me with questions, which he did almost nonstop. As if I was the subject and he was the interviewer.

"You're from L.A., right? Like, *Hollywood* Hollywood? Wow. It must have been cool growing up here."

"I guess?" I hated that I couldn't stop responding in a questioning tone. "I mean, it felt normal to me when it was happening."

"Crazy." He drummed his fingers across the top of the glove compartment.

There was a slight manic quality to him that seemed more noticeable in the car—like he was literally overflowing with excess energy.

"And you've lived here your whole life, right?"

I nodded, white-knuckling my way down the narrow Doñas, praying that we didn't encounter another car needing to go the opposite way.

He rolled down the window, which seemed to temper his eagerness but did little to help calm me. Now all I could think about was the possibility that his dog, who was now standing on his lap, paws on the armrest, nose twitching in the breeze, might leap out of my moving car and then I'd be the person who killed Gabe Parker's puppy.

"It's nice here in the winter," he said. "I'm usually in Montana with my family around this time, or filming somewhere else. But you probably get bored of all the sunshine, right? I always miss seasons when I'm here. Fall. Spring. Do you miss seasons?"

"Sort of," I said. "I'm used to it, I guess."

He nodded, his whole upper body rocking forward with him.

"Yeah, yeah, yeah, that makes sense," he said. "Have you ever been to Montana?"

"No," I said. "But I've heard it's beautiful."

"Beautiful? Naw. It's stunning. Unlike anywhere else," he said. "We'll have to get you out there sometime."

I nodded, as if that was something that might actually happen.

The pub was nice, with brick-lined walls and naked lightbulbs jutting out above each booth. Gabe led me past the bar and out to the back, where there was a table waiting for us and a little bowl of water for the puppy.

"You must love it here," he said.

I looked around. "I've never been here before," I said.

"Not here." He tapped the table. "Here." He gestured broadly. "L.A. You must love it if you came back after college."

"I do," I said.

"It's not what I expected," he said.

I stiffened.

"Yeah, well, a lot of people think L.A. is just Hollywood. That it's this vapid, superficial town full of vapid, superficial people, but it's really so much more. People say there's no culture in L.A., but we've got culture coming out of our ass—and all kinds of culture. There's Chinatown, and Little Armenia, and Little Ethiopia, and Alvarado Street. We've got amazing museums and gardens and parks. It's *beautiful* here. Sometimes, in the morning, the mountains are pink and gold, like these perfect cutouts against the sky. There's tons of history here—not just Hollywood, but there's architecture and art and music. It's a great place to grow up. A great place to live. And you can't beat the tacos."

I sounded like an extremely aggressive marketing campaign. But I couldn't help it. My hometown was constantly maligned—Jeremy had certainly made it clear that he thought L.A. was trash—so when I went on the defensive, I *went* on the defensive.

Gabe leaned back.

"I totally agree," he said. "The tacos are great."

I couldn't tell if he was making fun of me, but before I could suss it out any further, our waitress appeared.

Gabe was on his feet immediately, giving the beautiful redhead a hug and a kiss on the cheek.

"How are you feeling?" he asked. "You look like you're going to pop."

She was extremely pregnant, and rubbed her stomach.

"I'm gonna tell your momma you said that to a pregnant woman," she teased Gabe.

He winked at her. "You wouldn't dare." He glanced over at me. "Madison, this is Chani."

He said my name *perfectly*.

"Y'all ready to order?" Madison asked. She had a thick, charming Southern accent.

"Give us a moment with the menu, okay, darlin'?" Gabe asked, tossing the accent right back at her as he sat across from me.

Madison blushed beautifully. "You just holler, okay?"

"The burgers are great," Gabe said once she'd gone. "But if you get one, you have to get a beer. That's the rule."

I knew it was unprofessional to drink on the job, but I could handle a beer. I *needed* a beer. Because so far this interview had consisted of me ranting about both the intrinsic sexism of *The Philadelphia Story* and presumptive stereotypes about Los Angeles. It had not consisted of me doing the actual job I was hired to do.

"What's their best sour beer?" I asked.

Gabe's eyebrows went up and he met my gaze.

"Sour beer, huh?"

"Yeah," I said, like I was issuing a challenge. "Any suggestions?"

The grin returned, and with it, my improper tingly feelings.

"Why don't I order for us? Do you trust me?"

"Yes," I said.

He looked down at the menu with the childish glee of a kid on the night of Hanukkah when you actually got real gifts, not socks or chocolate gelt.

"I've got it," he said. "You're gonna love this one."

Madison returned and he gestured for her to lean toward him. He held up the menu between us, his gaze alternating between what he was pointing at and back at me. As he did, the puppy sauntered over, nudging her wet nose against my hand. I reached down and gave her a scratch, which was apparently an invitation for her to flop onto her back, showing me her stomach. I rubbed that, reveling in the velvety softness of her skin.

"She likes you," Gabe said after Madison left with our orders.

"Puppies like everyone."

He shook his head. "Not this one—she's afraid of her shadow, the birds in the backyard, and paper bags."

"Me too," I said.

Gabe laughed. I liked making him laugh.

The puppy's tongue was out; that pink ribbon—bright against her black fur—seemed almost too long to fit back in her mouth.

"Should I be worried?" I asked. "About what you ordered?"

"I don't know." Gabe leaned back, linking his hands behind his head. "Are you someone who likes to take risks?"

I stared at that startlingly intimate line of muscle running from his biceps to under his arm, disappearing into his shirt.

"No," I said.

He laughed.

"Then maybe you should be worried." He wiggled his eyebrows at me. "But just a little."

Was he . . . flirting?

Of course, he was flirting. The same way he had flirted with Madison. It wasn't personal. He probably didn't know how to talk to a woman without flirting in some way. Madison and I were just people in his orbit and therefore we were going to be charmed by his very existence.

That was the nature of celebrities. Of fame.

There were times that I imagined what it might be like to be famous. That *I* might like to be famous. When I craved the attention and the interest that the spotlight afforded. When I longed for the validation that fame implied.

Gabe was probably good at being charming the way I was good at observing. They were skills that both of us had a natural inclination for but had no doubt honed over the years as they were required for us to do our jobs.

It was a good reminder that the only reason I was here right now, sitting across from Gabe Parker, trying not to stare at his gorgeous armpit, was because it was my job. A job I desperately needed to do well.

I took out my tape recorder.

"Do you mind if I ask you some questions?" I asked, placing it on the table.

He froze for a second, for a blink, his whole body going so still that it felt like a glitch in the matrix. Then, as if he was rebooting, he smiled at me. A shallow, empty kind of smile.

I wasn't expecting that.

"Of course," he said. "That's why you're here, isn't it?"

It almost sounded like he had forgotten.

But just as quickly as that apparent glitch had appeared, it was gone.

"Okay." Gabe cracked his knuckles. "Hit me."

I looked down at my notebook.

I'd spent all of yesterday preparing. I'd read existing profile pieces, I'd watched old interviews.

But I realized, sitting here, in front of Gabe, looking down at my notes, that what I'd really done was research *him*.

My questions—painstakingly written out—were ones that *I* could answer.

I stared down at my notebook, dread sitting heavy in my stomach.

Gabe cleared his throat.

"Or we could just talk," he said.

I couldn't tell if he was being nice or condescending. Either way, it indicated that he didn't think I could do my job.

It was going to be okay, I told myself. When I'd interviewed Jennifer Evans, I'd started the interview asking about her hometown and she'd ended up talking nonstop for almost twenty minutes.

"Cooper, Montana," I said.

Gabe raised an eyebrow. "That's where I'm from, yes."

"Good place to grow up."

"Yep," he said.

"You went to college there."

"Yep," he said.

"Did theatre. At JRSC."

"Yep," he said.

There was a slight curve to his lips, just the hint of a smile, as if he was enjoying this. Enjoying my completely incompetent attempt to interview him. Because so far, I hadn't asked him a single damn question.

This tactic might have worked on Jennifer Evans, but it certainly wasn't working now.

My ship was sinking and I needed to do something to right it. And quick.

The puppy shifted beneath the table, letting out the kind of sigh that was usually reserved for those contemplating the meaning of life. It was exactly the kind of sigh I had sitting at the back of my throat.

"What's her name?" I asked.

Gabe looked down and a full smile bloomed.

"Haven't decided yet," he said. "I'm going to wait for it to come to me."

"She looks like a teddy bear," I said.

"She does." He glanced up at me. "Were you the kind of kid who had a teddy bear?"

I blushed for no reason.

"Maybe," I said.

He leaned back. "I knew it," he said. "What was your teddy bear's name?"

"Teddy," I said.

He raised an eyebrow.

"I wasn't a creative child," I said.

"I don't believe that."

There was that sparkly, hot, live-wire feeling again.

"Were *you* the kind of kid who had a teddy bear?" I asked.

It was the first decent question I'd asked, and technically it was one I'd stolen from him. Unfortunately, before Gabe could answer, Madison returned with our drinks.

He waited as I took a sip of my beer.

"So?" he asked. "Did I get it right?"

I wasn't a big fan of beer, but I did love a good sour. And he had gotten me a really, really good sour.

"I think this is my new favorite beer," I told him honestly.

He beamed and my heart thumped out of rhythm.

"Cheers," he said, lifting his glass and clinking it against mine.

Then I watched as he drained almost a third of it in one gulp.

"Thirsty?" I asked.

It sounded a lot more accusatory than I meant it.

"Answering questions is thirsty work," he said.

Touché.

Gabe Parker might have been a hick, but he was a hick with a finely honed sense of irony.

"Why did you audition for *Angels in America*?" I asked.

This time Gabe was the one who blinked.

A-ha, I thought triumphantly. *A question. A good question.*

"Because it was a class requirement," he said. "I'd taken theatre because I thought it would be an easy A. I didn't realize that part of the deal was auditioning for the winter performance."

I deflated.

It was almost exactly the same thing he'd said in the *Vanity Fair* interview he'd done after *Tommy Jacks*.

"You must have been surprised to get the lead."

"Yep," he said.

He drank his beer.

I wanted to bang my head on the table. He knew why I was here—why we were doing this interview. This article was meant to help fix the public perception around him being chosen for Bond. It was supposed to help *him*.

"Did it bother you?" I asked. "The material?"

"No," he said.

"Did it bother your family?"

"No," he said.

"They didn't care that you were kissing a man onstage?"

"My sister thought it was hilarious," Gabe said. "But only because I'm her baby brother. She thinks everything I do is hilarious. Usually unintentionally."

"You and your sister are close."

Gabe downed the rest of his beer, and signaled for another.

My pen froze above my notebook. *Two* beers?

Gabe was a big guy and two beers was nothing to some, but I started to feel nervous. For him. It was ridiculous, of course. It wasn't my job to protect him from himself. He was an adult. He knew his limits. Besides, if he ended up drinking enough to make him more talkative, all the better for me.

Right?

"She's my best friend," Gabe said. "We're only a year apart, so we're basically like twins."

It was—almost verbatim—what he'd said in an interview with *Entertainment Weekly*. And *The Hollywood Reporter*.

"And you have a niece?" I asked, even though I already knew the answer.

"She's three," Gabe said. "And she's the love—"

"—of your life," I finished for him before I could think any better of it.

He'd said that in the *Vanity Fair* article too.

"You've done your research," Gabe said.

It wasn't a compliment.

"It's my job," I countered.

I knew I wasn't doing great with the questions, but he was an actor. I didn't expect him to spill anything surprising or shocking, but I had expected him to say *something*.

But it was quiet on the other side of the table. For a moment.

"I did my research too," he said. "Both of your parents are teachers. You have a younger brother and a younger sister. They all live locally. You usually have Shabbat dinner with them. You went to Sarah Lawrence for undergrad, Iowa for grad school. You met your boyfriend there. In the campus bookstore."

"Ex-boyfriend," I said.

Gabe ignored me. "You started out in fiction, but mostly write nonfiction now. Your writing has been described as sharp. You're from L.A. You hate New York."

"I don't hate New York." I was unnerved.

I *did* hate New York.

I stared at him. He stared back.

"It's weird, isn't it?" he asked softly. "When someone thinks they know you."

The whole thing reminded me of the time I'd tried to learn how to skateboard in some ill-advised bid to get the attention of a guy I knew in high school. I'd been floating along, when suddenly I leaned too far back and the skateboard had come shooting out from under me. I was airborne for half a second before hitting the ground—tailbone first—hard. The pain had made me cry and the tears had made the boy disappear.

It felt a little like that now, like Gabe had yanked the skateboard—something I had been arrogant to even try to ride—right out from under me.

I was used to asking a simple question and sitting back, letting my subject monologue until I got some decent pull quotes. I was used to celebrities being excited to talk about themselves.

"It's my job," I repeated lamely.

"I know," he said.

Do it better was what was implied.

I flipped through my notebook as if a life raft would suddenly appear.

"Have you always been a Bond fan?" I asked, floundering.

"Sure," he said. "What man isn't?"

"Did you watch them with your dad?"

Gabe's face went blank.

If this interview was a sinking boat, I'd just blown out the bottom.

Because there was one thing I'd been told was off-limits.

Years ago, some scummy online tabloid had dug through Gabe's proverbial trash and written a piece about the person that Gabe never spoke about.

It had been called "Gabe Parker: Without a Father Figure."

The piece had been poorly written, thin on details, and yet it said more than Gabe or his management ever had. I was ashamed that I was one of millions who read it—discovering that Gabe's father had died when he was ten.

The whole thing might have gone away if Team Parker hadn't threatened to sue the tabloid. Instead, it just made people more curious. After all, if Gabe and his late father had had a good relationship, there would have been nothing to hide. Clearly there was something to hide. Abuse or estrangement or something equally horrible and juicy. Exactly the kind of information the public seemed to feel entitled to.

The kind of information that any interviewer would kill to have access to.

Looking at Gabe now, I could guess what he was thinking. That I was the kind of interviewer that would do whatever it took to get what I wanted—that I wasn't above pushing his buttons to get a reaction. To get a story.

I wanted to get a story, just not in that way.

"I'm sorry," I said. "I know the rules."

If I had to grovel, I would.

"I didn't mean—"

He waved a hand. "Let's just move on, okay?"

Fuck. When I'd thought about all the ways I could mess up this interview, I hadn't really considered that I would unintentionally and thoughtlessly lob a "gotcha" question at him.

"I won't include that," I said, knowing he probably wouldn't believe me.

"Uh-huh," he said. "What about your father?"

"My father?"

"Is he a Bond fan?"

His arms were crossed.

"Sure," I said. "What man isn't?"

I was trying to be playful, tossing Gabe's words back at him. I had no idea if my father liked James Bond movies. The only things I'd ever seen him watch were Lakers games.

Gabe didn't say anything, just cast a cynical look down at my notebook. I put a hand over the page. As if he could read it upside down and from across the table.

"I—"

But before I could finish my sentence, Gabe stood abruptly.

My stomach plummeted.

"Will you excuse me for a minute?" he said, scooping the puppy off the ground.

His tone was cold and polite.

I nodded.

He left the outside patio and I watched him go, those wonderful broad shoulders, that narrow waist, that very, *very* nice ass. I was one hundred percent sure that this was the last I was going to see of Gabe Parker, so I might as well take a long look.

When he was out of sight, I drew a line through the condensation on my beer glass, knowing that our food would appear soon and it was going to be very, very embarrassing when Madison arrived at the table with two burgers and only one person to eat them.

My boat had sunk to the bottom of the lake.

I put my head down, my forehead against my notebook.

I thought about all the stories I wanted to write. I thought about Jeremy and his book deal. I thought about my student loans.

I thought that I might just take that second burger to go because who knew when I'd be getting another job.

Suddenly my ankle was wet.

I looked down through the glass of the table to find the puppy licking the exposed skin between my shoe and my jeans. Lifting my head, I discovered that Gabe was sitting across from me, his expression neutral. He had another beer in front of him. One that was already half gone.

"Well?" he asked. "Shall we continue?"

THE_JAM_DOT_COM .BLOGSPOT.COM

BREAK UP/BREAKDOWN

IT'S OVER. THE NOVELIST PACKED UP HIS DRAWER LAST NIGHT, and this time I didn't cry.

He's going to move to New York where people are creative and wild and interesting. Not like the people here who only care about smoothies, exercising, and watching bad TV.

I'm pretty sure people in New York watch bad TV. They just do it in smaller apartments.

I told him I'd never move to New York. He said that was the problem. That because I wasn't the kind of person who would move to New York with him, then I just wasn't the kind of person he could be with.

Depending on who you ask, we've done this dance half a dozen times since we've been together, but this time I'm certain it's going to stick.

Mostly because that's what the Novelist said when he slammed his car door, right before he drove off.

I'm single again.

I didn't cry but I did eat a lot of ice cream.

Heartbreak is supposed to be good for inspiration, but besides this post, I've managed to write absolutely nothing. All my plans, all my goals, have been swept away by this latest personal riptide.

The Novelist always said I had trouble with focus. No doubt he is sitting in front of his typewriter with his glass of gin, typing furiously away, turning this matter of personal growth (his words) into creative fertilizer (mine).

I'll be deeply resentful if he turns this experience into a book and it becomes a bestseller.

xoChani

PS: Before all this, I wrote a piece on up-and-coming starlet Jennifer Evans. You can read it in this month's *Broad Sheets*.

Chapter 3

"YOU KNOW, YOU HAVE SOMETHING HERE . . ." GABE SAID, gesturing toward his own face. "I think it's ink."

My skin was hot against my hand as I looked down to find that the words written on my notebook were smudged. Of course. Knowing my luck, I probably had "Bond" imprinted on my forehead.

I gave it a furious scrub.

"Jesus," Gabe said. "Hold on."

He took his napkin and dipped it into his water glass. I expected him to pass it over, but instead he crooked his finger in my direction. I leaned toward him, and he gently dabbed at my forehead. I did not breathe the entire time, crossing my eyes in an effort not to stare.

"There," he said, and withdrew.

Thankfully before I could do anything else embarrassing, our food and Gabe's third beer arrived.

In addition to his own burger, Gabe had also ordered a plain patty for the puppy, which she ate with enthusiasm punctuated with several happy snorts. As he observed her, I arranged my burger the way I liked it, dipping my fries in ketchup and laying them across the patty in a crisscross pattern.

I looked up and found Gabe watching me.

"I don't think I've ever seen someone eat a burger that way," he said.

"I've done it since I was a kid," I said.

"Huh," he said, and then opened his burger and did the same. "Like this?"

I nodded, wordlessly, and watched as he took a bite.

"Oh yeah," he said, a soft moan escaping. "That is fucking delicious."

Heat spread through my body as if I had swallowed something spicy and wonderful.

I watched him eat for a moment. He savored each bite, licking his fingers, his lips, even the palm of his hand at one point. He was clearly a man who enjoyed his food.

Wow. Even when I was single-handedly torpedoing my career, I was still very, *very* horny for him.

"It's going to get cold," he said.

Not a chance, I thought.

It took me a moment to realize that he was talking about my food.

"I've read your articles," Gabe said as I took a bite of my burger.

"You have?" I asked.

"Of course," he said.

It was as if the whole slipup with his dad had never happened. Gabe Parker was clearly someone who rolled with the punches.

He dipped a French fry in ketchup.

"I like your blog."

I choked on my drink.

It was one thing for Gabe to have read my articles—unusual, but still, those pieces were well researched, edited, and vetted. They weren't all that dissimilar to the type of interview we were doing right now.

My blog on the other hand . . .

At least I now knew where he'd gotten all that information about me, like where I went to school and the fact that I hated New York. For better or for worse, my blog had become somewhat of a de facto journal these days. Mostly because I thought that no one was reading it.

"You're funny," Gabe said. "Your writing. It's funny."

My brain was going a mile a minute, trying to remember what kind of embarrassing personal shit I'd word-vomited recently.

Jeremy had read my blog once.

"Is there something worse than navel-gazing?" he'd asked during a fight. "Because that's what it is."

I wondered what Jeremy would think about Gabe Parker calling my writing "funny."

"How's the burger?" Gabe asked.

"Good," I said. "It seems like you come here a lot."

He nodded. "Yeah," he said. "People are nice and the food's great." He looked at the remainder of our fries with a deep longing in his eyes.

I pushed them toward him. He hesitated.

"I've had enough," I said, and since he hadn't walked out of this interview, I didn't have to worry about hoarding food like a chipmunk. Yet.

"It's not that," he said, though he took a few and dipped them in ketchup. "I'm really not supposed to be eating this in the first place."

I tilted my head questioningly.

"James Bond can't have love handles," he said, leaning back and patting his stomach.

"I'm sure that's not a problem for you," I said with a laugh, thinking he was joking.

It became immediately clear that he wasn't.

I knew that actors and actresses made sacrifices to look the way they did, but I'd never really thought much about it. I just enjoyed looking at the results. Gabe moved the fries away, and I felt a little guilty for all the ogling I'd done.

"My trainer will be pissed," he said.

He looked so sad that I was momentarily speechless.

"When can you have a burger and fries again?" I asked.

He glanced down at the tape recorder as if it was a snake ready to strike. "After Bond," he said. "Unless we start shooting the second movie right away. Then it's protein shakes and lettuce until we're done."

He held up his almost empty beer glass and gave it a loving look.

"Farewell, friend," he said before finishing it.

There was a long silence and then he smiled—but not a real smile. It was funny how I could tell them apart already.

"Not that I'm complaining," he said.

His voice was a little lower, a little slower. Not drunk, but on his way.

"Are you excited?" I asked. "About Bond?"

"I'm lucky," he said as if that was the same thing.

"It's the role of a lifetime," I said.

"I was their second choice," Gabe said. "They wanted Ollie."

I froze.

Now we were getting somewhere. I knew that this was what I needed—what I'd come for—yet I couldn't ignore that extremely icky feeling knowing that I was possibly, maybe taking advantage of the fact that Gabe was more intoxicated than he should be.

But this was a job—to me and to him—and if anything, this had leveled the playing field. Plus, if I were a guy, I might not even have these guilty feelings, let alone acknowledge them. I'd probably be ordering him another drink or offering to buy him shots.

I couldn't let my crush on Gabe keep me from getting a good story.

"Ah," Gabe said, leaning back. "You'd prefer Ollie too."

"No."

"No?"

"I don't have a preference," I said.

It was a lie. Because of course I had a preference. In life—in my fantasies—it was always Gabe.

But I knew what critics had been saying. Because while Gabe was gorgeous, he wasn't a natural fit for Bond. Not the way that Oliver was.

Oliver Matthias was sophisticated. Cultured. It was the accent, of course, but he was an intellectual as well. An Oxford grad. Someone who had performed in the West End, doing Shakespeare and Beckett. He had years of experience, starring in a BBC teen comedy version of *Pride and Prejudice* when he was sixteen, then returning to the small screen to do a miniseries version of *Cyrano de Bergerac* after university. Even a prosthetic nose had done nothing to dim his appeal with his female fans—myself included. I might have even had a poster of him as Darcy when I was a preteen.

He was a proven leading man.

But according to interviews with Ryan and the Bond producers, Oliver hadn't even been considered for the role. My journalistic senses, as immature as they were, were now the thing that were tingling.

"My mom prefers him too," Gabe said.

"No, she does not," I said.

He raised an eyebrow at me.

"My mom *loves* Bond," he said. "She said—and I quote—'Was Oliver not available?' "

I winced.

"I know what people are saying," Gabe said. "Contrary to popular opinion, I *can* read."

"No one thought you couldn't read," I said.

"They thought I couldn't read good," he countered with a thick, hick-like drawl.

I didn't really have a response because to tell him that wasn't true would be a lie. People did think he was a bit of a rube. It didn't help that his management had been pushing that version of him up until he landed Bond.

Interviews amplified his "good country boy" qualities—that he might have been a simpleminded community college graduate, but his talent was just as homegrown. While Oliver was someone who had been trained and cultivated, Gabe was all-natural. He was genuine.

But that also meant he was a harder sell in roles that went against that brand.

Bond *had* been a surprise.

"It's fine," Gabe said. "I've been working with a dialect coach, who promises me we'll keep my 'hyucks' down to a minimum."

"I think you'll be great," I said.

"You're the only one," he said.

There was clearly more to this. Everyone already assumed there was a rivalry between the two former co-stars. Jacinda Lockwood had been linked with Oliver before rumors of her dating Gabe emerged—was this all part of a longer, deeper competition between the two of them? If Oliver had really been the first choice, then why didn't he get the role?

"Have you seen his latest movie?" I asked. "Oliver's?"

It was a period piece—romantic and epic—and the thirteen-year-old me that had been enamored with Oliver Matthias couldn't wait.

"I'm going to the premiere tomorrow," Gabe said. "Looking forward to it."

"Jealous," I said without thinking.

It wasn't that I wanted to go to that particular premiere—it was that movie premieres still held an element of magic. I'd interviewed enough celebrities to hear plenty of stories about the parties they went to and it was hard not to feel a certain twinge of envy at spending a night dolled up and surrounded by beautiful people.

"They're pretty boring," Gabe said. "Premieres."

"Maybe to you," I said, wanting to refocus the conversation before either of us could get distracted. "You've stayed in touch? You and Oliver?"

"We're friends," he said.

There was something he wasn't saying, but before I could ask, he'd waved Madison over.

"Can I get another one?" he asked, gesturing toward his empty glass.

"Sure thing, hon," she said. "How about you?" she asked me.

I shook my head. That would be Gabe's fourth beer, and he was definitely more than a little drunk. He slouched back in his chair more, and his eyes were hooded, flitting around the room, unable to focus.

I saw my opportunity, swallowed my guilt, and took it.

"Still friends even after the Bond decision?" I asked.

Gabe looked up at me, narrowing his eyes. For a moment, I waited, breath held, bracing for him to react negatively. To yell, or throw something.

Instead he just laughed, and wagged a finger at me.

"Nu-uh," he said. "I see what you're doing."

I said nothing.

"We're friends," he said, enunciating each word. "And he said he didn't care."

"He said he didn't care about the part?" I asked, sensing I was getting close to something really interesting.

But then, as if she had appointed herself the bouncer of Gabe's wayward tongue, Madison reappeared with his beer.

"Y'all need anything else?" she asked.

If I didn't know any better, I would have sworn she shot me a warning look.

"We're fine," I said, answering for the both of us.

But she waited until Gabe nodded, waving his hand at her.

"We're fine," he echoed. "Chani here is just raking me over the coals."

Even tipsy, he could still get that perfect *ch* at the beginning of my name.

"He's a good man," Madison said.

I hadn't been imagining it—that *had* been a warning look.

"I'm sure he is," I said.

"It's fine," Gabe said, grinning at both of us, definitely sauced.

He took another long drink.

"It's fine," he said again, this time to Madison, his voice soft.

"Okay," she said, and walked away, but not before tossing her beautiful hair over her shoulder in a very pointed manner.

"They're protective of you here," I said once she had left.

Gabe shrugged.

"You and Oliver . . ." I tried again.

"Are. Friends," Gabe said, and then crossed his arms as if he was a child about to throw a tantrum.

It was clear he wasn't going to say any more—not even drunk. I was disappointed but not defeated. I changed tactics.

"You're working with a dialect coach," I said. "Have you decided what kind of accent you'll be using?"

"A posh British one," he said. "With a hint of Scottish. A little homage to my favorite Bond."

"Connery."

"Connery," he confirmed.

"Is that the biggest challenge with a role like this?" I asked. "The accent?"

He looked at me and drank his beer. He took his time.

"The biggest challenge with a role like this is doing it even when you know you don't deserve it."

Film Fans

TOMMY JACKS REVIEW

[EXCERPT]

By David Anderson

WORLD WAR II FILMS ARE A DIME A DOZEN. EVERY DIRECTOR seems to think that the shortcut to an Academy Award is making a movie where handsome young men in period clothes and dirty faces stare up at a sky full of enemy planes and then run through a muddy field as shells explode around them.

Annoyingly, most of these directors are correct. These movies are, without a doubt, Oscar-bait. If they are actually deserving of the award, however, remains to be seen.

Tommy Jacks has all the trappings of such a film. You have the handsome young men, you have the dirty faces, and the running through the mud. There's the requisite love story between an earnest soldier and his blushing bride-to-be. There's enough patriotism to make an American flag cry.

And if those were the only things it had, it would be as cliché and forgettable as most of its brothers-in-film.

But *Tommy Jacks* has something that those other movies don't have. It has Oliver Matthias.

As the titular Tommy, Matthias wants out of the small town, a place where he is constantly butting up against his family's expectations. It's clear, immediately, that he's too clever for his own good—that he believes he's destined for better things.

Gabe Parker plays his younger brother, his opposite in every way. He's not smart; in fact, he dropped out of high school to join the family dairy farm, where he apparently spends his days shirtless and glistening in the golden-lit fields behind the house. He joins the army because "I think I might be able to make a small sort of difference."

There's a love triangle—I know, I know, but trust me, please—with the two brothers in love with the same girl. She lets Matthias's character romance her with poetry and promises of a life outside their podunk town, but she accepts Parker's ring before they ship out, because, as she says, "He ain't much to think about, but he sure is a lot to look at."

It's clear that this has always been the case—Matthias's Tommy is too intense, too intelligent, too *much* for everyone—while his sweet, simpleminded brother might not be the right choice, but he's the easy one.

Of course, that means he has to be sacrificed at the altar of war.

This isn't a spoiler—Parker's Billy is lost within the first twenty minutes of the film.

A lesser writer and director could have turned this story into one about Tommy's redemption—about him leaving behind the ambition on the battlefield where his brother dies. It could have been about him stepping into his brother's shoes and learning that maybe Billy was right all along—that it's the "small sort of difference" that truly matters.

But that's not the story of *Tommy Jacks*.

Chapter 4

GABE NURSED THE LAST FOURTH OF HIS BEER. IT WAS STILL sunny out, but had gotten colder. Enough that I'd needed to pull my sweater out of my bag. I knew that we were reaching the end of the interview—that it was likely that once this beer was finished, Gabe would call for the check and it would be over.

I had wanted this article to be something special. Not just to impress my editors and get more work—though that was part of it—I wanted to impress *myself*. Wanted to prove something.

I wanted this article to be something special, because *I* wanted to be something special. I wanted to be the kind of writer that could take a subpar interview and spin it into gold.

At this point, I'd be lucky if I didn't just regurgitate every other story that had already been written about Gabe.

To put it mildly, I was fucked.

I couldn't even really use Gabe's assertion that Oliver *had* been the production's first choice. It wasn't enough to prove anything, Ryan Ulrich could just deny it, and I'd look foolish.

But while my attempt to interview Gabe had been a complete and unmitigated disaster, Gabe's interrogation of me was going swimmingly.

"You and the Novelist are done, huh?" he asked.

That's what I called Jeremy on the blog when I wrote about him.

And since we'd just broken up—again—I'd written about him recently.

"Yep," I said, looking down at my notes, praying I'd thrown a secret Hail Mary in there somewhere. "We're done."

The Novelist. What a dumb non-pseudonym. Maybe Jeremy *was* right about my writing skills.

After all, he was actually a novelist, with a highly anticipated first novel under contract. I maintained a navel-gazing blog and interviewed celebrities. Badly.

"Our sensibilities are too disparate," he'd said when we broke up this time. "We're going in opposite directions."

"Good," Gabe said.

My head popped up.

Gabe shrugged. "He seemed like a jerk."

"He had his moments," I said.

I didn't know why I felt I needed to defend Jeremy when all I'd done recently was defend *myself* to him.

"Sure," Gabe said.

Weirdly, it didn't make me feel better that Gabe Parker thought my ex-boyfriend was a jerk. After all, Jeremy had broken up with *me*. So what did that say about me that I dated and got dumped by a jerk?

Probably that I was pathetic and naïve.

I shifted uncomfortably in my seat.

Who did Gabe think he was, judging *my* relationships?

"What about you and Jacinda?" I asked, knowing that everyone and their mother had been trying to get confirmation that they were dating.

Gabe might have been the unexpected choice for Bond, but no one had blinked an eye when Jacinda Lockwood had been announced as his leading lady. The British-born model was elegant, glamorous, and pursuing an acting career. Though the press hadn't been surprised, they had definitely been snarky, declaring her "overly ambitious."

"Jacinda and I are just friends," Gabe said too quickly and flatly to be even remotely believable.

"Sure," I said, and took a bite of a cold fry. We both knew he wasn't being entirely truthful.

I didn't get it. If Gabe and Jacinda were dating, why keep it a secret? There was nothing the tabloids loved more than two beautiful people sleeping together. Even if they were both single.

If I could get confirmation of their relationship or some quote acknowledging that they'd been more than just friendly, then *that* could make the article. It wouldn't be special but it would have something new, at least. It would make people read. It would probably get me another job.

"She's a friend," Gabe said.

I tried to remember all the times I'd been photographed with a friend's hand resting on my ass while we stumbled out of a bar in Paris. I'd also never wound my arms around a friend's neck, pressing my face against his cheek. Nor had I ever nibbled a friend's earlobe while sliding my hand into his shirt.

All of a sudden, I wasn't sure if I really wanted Gabe to confirm that he'd slept with her.

Still, I had to try. For the article.

"A *very* good friend, I've heard."

Unfortunately for me, Gabe was saved by Madison's impeccable timing and an extra glass of water he hadn't ordered. He finished his beer and drank the water in one long gulp.

The puppy had fallen asleep under the table—I could see her through the glass tabletop. She'd rolled around a few times, trying to get comfortable, finally resting her chin on the top of Gabe's right foot.

"Is she going with you to set?" I asked.

"Considering she's in the movie, yes, she'll be going with me to set," Gabe said.

It took a moment before I realized that he thought I was still talking about Jacinda.

I pointed through the table. "I meant your dog," I said.

He looked down, and his whole body, his whole face, relaxed.

"Yeah," he said. "She's going to be coming with me."

"Is that why you got her?" I asked. "I've heard it can get pretty lonely, being on set, away from family and friends for months."

"That's part of it," he said.

He stared down at his empty water glass as if it might refill itself.

I knew an opening when I saw it. "What's the other part?" I asked.

He picked the puppy up and set her on his lap. She was still snoozing, with her head cradled in Gabe's arm, her nose tucked into his elbow.

"I have this list," he said. "Of things I'd do if I became successful. Getting a dog was one of them."

He looked at me expectantly.

I looked back.

Because I'd heard about his list. Everyone had heard about his list. Every time he did an interview and it mentioned some new development in his life, it was usually connected back to the list. The seemingly endless list of Things Gabe Parker Will Do When He's Successful.

The bookshop, of course, was always mentioned in this context.

There were all the trips he'd taken with his family—to Hawaii, to Bali, to Cape Town, to Paris (where everyone thought Momma Parker might have gotten a formal introduction to Jacinda Lockwood herself).

He'd bought his mom and sister cars. He'd put together a college fund for his niece.

I didn't doubt that he had done all those things, but I also knew that it was very, very good publicity to talk about them. Personal, but not *personal*.

I also knew that he was expecting me to ask the same question everyone always asked—what else was on the list? And why wouldn't he? I'd shown thus far that I was a thoroughly unoriginal interviewer.

This was probably one of the last questions I would be able to ask him.

"Do you want to hear about the trip we're planning to Italy?" he asked politely. "I'm taking my whole family—my mom, Lauren,

Lena, and my brother-in-law, Spencer. He's never been out of the country before."

I knew that's what every other interviewer would ask him.

"How did you know that you'd become successful?" was what I ended up with.

Of course, it came out all wrong.

I flung it at him, like an accusation. Like I didn't believe he *was* successful.

And that's how he took it.

"You think I could do better than playing James Bond?" Gabe asked.

His tone was light, but it seemed like there was a hint of doubt underneath it.

Ridiculous. Gabe Parker did not need his ego stroked.

And it wasn't really the question I was asking.

I shook my head. "I'm trying to ask how you knew that it was time to start fulfilling the list?"

It still wasn't right, but at least it made a kind of sense.

Maybe not.

Gabe looked at me, visibly confused.

"I guess what I'm asking is what makes you—Gabe Parker—feel like a success?" I asked, continuing to blabber when his expression didn't change. "You know, for some people, success might mean honors and accolades. My ex, for example, said he would never feel like a success unless he'd won a National Book Award or some other big-name award like that."

"The Novelist," Gabe said.

There was a hint of a smile at the corner of his mouth.

I ignored it. "But for me, I mean, I think of success as being able to work whenever and as often as I want. Being able to support myself comfortably just through my writing."

Gabe leaned back in his chair, the puppy now propped up against his chest, the weirdest and most beautiful version of Madonna and Child that I'd ever seen.

"No one's ever asked me that," he said.

"I'm sure they all want to know what's on the list," I said.

He nodded. The puppy yawned.

"So?" I asked. "What does success look like to Gabe Parker?"

He looked at me and didn't say anything for a good long while. If it wasn't for the unwavering eye contact, I might have thought he'd fallen asleep or something.

But he was over there thinking. Thinking hard.

Then, without looking away, he raised his hand, indicating for the check.

"Want to get out of here?" he asked.

"Yes," I said.

THE_JAM_DOT_COM .BLOGSPOT.COM

I'M NOT GOOD. I'M NOT BAD. I'M JUST WRITE.

SOMEONE ONCE SAID THAT CHOOSING TO BE A WRITER WAS like choosing to be slapped in the face repeatedly.

Was it Salinger who said it? Hemingway?

No, it was a girl in my first-year fiction workshop who came to class drunk on peach schnapps, tossed her short story at our teacher, threw up in a trash can, and walked out of class.

I think about her often.

Because she was right.

It's also the reason I'm pretty sure that no one actually *chooses* to be a writer. It's a terrible choice.

Also terrible? The title of this post.

I hope Stephen Sondheim will forgive me for the egregious pun. I *really* hope Stephen Sondheim doesn't read Blogger.

I tried taking a lesson from him, and attempted writing while lying down.

I fell asleep before I could write a Tony Award–worthy musical. Before I could write anything.

One would think all the brilliant ideas swarming around my head would keep me awake. They didn't. The only thing that keeps me awake is the fear that I'm not a good writer. That I'm not even a bad writer.

No. I'm worried I'm just a boring one.

And that feels like the worst option of all.

xoChani

Chapter 5

THE HOUSE WAS BEAUTIFUL. AND ENORMOUS.

"There are eight bedrooms," the real estate agent said. "Plus a pool house that can easily be renovated into a two-bedroom guesthouse. Three acres with a pool and hot tub. Screening room in the basement, next to the gym. Four bathrooms. Kitchen. Wine cellar."

I had never been in a house as large as this one. The amount of space was obscene. Eight bedrooms? A gym? A sauna?

As far as I could tell, Gabe was one person. What did he need with all this space?

I glanced over at him, but he was being paid the big acting bucks for a reason—his face was inscrutable. I couldn't tell if he loved the place or was five seconds away from picking up a chair and throwing it through the glass doors because he wanted nine bedrooms, dammit!

Even though he'd gotten more than a little drunk during lunch, he didn't seem the type to throw a tantrum over the number of bedrooms available to him.

"Do you mind if I take a look around?" Gabe asked the real estate agent.

"Not at all," she said, taking the hint and leaving the room.

We were in the kitchen. It was clean and modern, with shiny chrome everything and big windows that opened up onto a yard that was truly gorgeous. Impeccably maintained, it looked like a museum lawn.

"What do you think?" Gabe asked.

"It's beautiful," I said honestly.

He looked at me and crossed his arms. "But?"

"How do you know there's a but?" I asked, immediately regretting the way I'd worded that.

He laughed. It was a great laugh, all low and dark and rich. If chocolate cake had a laugh, it would be that.

I kept moving my hand toward my bag, my fingers itching to pull out my tape recorder again, but I was worried that if I did, the happy, relaxed look on Gabe's face would disappear.

Instead, I just tried to remember as much as I could, hoping that I could use this in my piece.

"You're not in love," he said.

"What?"

He gestured. "With the house," he said. "I can tell."

The puppy was playing in the grass outside, her tail twitching as she flopped from side to side.

"What don't you like about it?" he asked.

"It doesn't matter," I said. "I'm not the one buying the house."

Why did Gabe care what I thought about a multimillion-dollar mansion that he might or might not buy? It's not like I'd be coming over to hang out at his pool on the weekends. I almost snarkily suggested that he call Jacinda and ask her, but I held my tongue.

"I'd still like to hear your thoughts," Gabe said. "Would you buy this house?"

I laughed. "There's no universe where I'd be in a position to buy a house like this. It's huge!"

Gabe nodded. "It is pretty large."

"Are your mom and sister going to move to L.A.?" I asked.

This time, he was the one who laughed. "I can get my family here for premieres and awards, but that's about it. There's no way either of them would consider moving to L.A. They love Montana too much to leave. Besides, they have the Cozy."

I nodded. I thought about telling him that I had ordered a few books from them online, which I'd received with a handwritten note thanking me for my business and a recommendation for another book based on the ones I'd just bought. The suggestion had been spot-on and I ended up ordering it from them as well.

Mentioning it to Gabe, though, felt a little teacher's pet-y.

"Do you visit them a lot?" I asked.

Gabe nodded, still looking around. "I bought a house for my mom and then helped my sister and brother-in-law with the down payment on theirs. I usually stay at an apartment above the store when I visit." He put his hands on his hips. "My manager said that it's a waste of money to keep renting a house here—that I should just buy something."

"You'd have plenty of space for your family when they come to visit," I said.

"I told them I wanted a pool and guest rooms, but now that I'm seeing it, I don't know if I need this much space." He looked thoughtful. "I like my current place a lot."

"It is really nice," I agreed. "Seems like it suits you."

He grinned at me as if I'd said something profound. "That's funny," he said. "Because even though I've never lived here before, the place feels kind of nostalgic for me. Almost like it's part of a collective memory about Los Angeles." He leaned back on his heels. "It has this great energy, you know?"

I did know.

"Sorry," he said. "That probably sounds pretty cheesy. It's just I can totally picture Brian Wilson hanging out by my pool, or Dennis Hopper rummaging through my fridge."

I nodded eagerly. "I know exactly what you mean. You can practically smell the weed and righteous rebellion."

He laughed.

"You should get a house like that," I said. "Not something big and grand like this. A home."

Unfortunately, I said that right as the real estate agent was walking back into the room.

"I think you're right," Gabe said before turning to her. "I might need to rethink what I'm looking for."

"Of course," she said with a smile, but the moment he turned away, she shot me a glare.

I couldn't really blame her. I'd be pissed too if I lost the commission on this house.

We drove back to his rental in Laurel Canyon. The puppy fell asleep in his lap, but rested her nose on the armrest between us, her hot breath tickling my elbow. Gabe didn't say much on the ride home, gazing out the window while I only got lost once.

"Hey," he said, as I stopped at a stop sign. "The mountains."

I glanced over to what he was pointing at. We were almost to his house, about to go around one of the many cliffside curves. The sun was beginning to set.

"Gold and pink," he said.

It was beautiful—a shadow across half of the Valley—the rest of it looking like it had been painted with vibrant watercolors.

Behind me, a car honked.

As I pulled into his driveway, I knew that I'd totally blown the interview. That I was going to have to go back to my little apartment that I shared with two people I didn't like very much and attempt to write an article that I knew was not going to be very good.

It would be functional and it would serve its purpose—I'd find a way to make Gabe seem like he was a perfect fit for Bond—but it wouldn't be anything more than that. It wouldn't be special, and I desperately wanted to write something that was special.

I shut off the car and turned to Gabe, planning to thank him for his time and make as much of a gracious exit as I could.

"I should probably have some coffee," he said before I could even open my mouth. "Do you want some coffee?"

"I don't drink coffee," I said.

It was such a dumb thing to say. If it meant more time with Gabe, I could drink coffee. I could choke down a whole fucking carafe of it.

"I have tea," Gabe said.

VANITY FAIR

GABE PARKER:
The Man Who Would Be Bond

[EXCERPT]

BY TASH CLAYBORNE

HE CAN'T STOP GUSHING ABOUT HIS FAMILY. PARKER IS THE youngest of two, though "we were practically raised as twins," he says. "We shared birthday parties, shared a room, shared almost everything until she started going to school. I know technically you're only Irish twins if you were born within the same year, but we're only thirteen months apart. Maybe you could call that Montana twins, or something."

He has equally loving things to say about his niece, who just turned two.

"She's the love of my life," he tells me, pulling out a picture of a chubby-cheeked child with dark curls. "I mean, she's way smarter than I am, but besides that we're actually pretty similar. When I go visit my family, it's usually just the two of us at the kids' table, laughing at how silly peas are. Because they're pretty silly, aren't they?"

We talk about his list—about the things he always wanted to do when he became successful—and how most of them ended up being gifts for his family.

"My mom was a high school teacher," he says. "We didn't have the kind of money that other families had to go on trips and vacations. I wanted to take her everywhere that she dreamed of going."

They've been to Bali, Paris, Argentina, and Kenya. Next on the list?

"She wants to eat her way through Italy," he says. "I think we're going to take the whole family for that one."

All that in addition to the bookstore he bought for her and his sister.

"The Cozy." He makes sure I write the website down. "They have everything. Books, crafts, everything. And if you aren't sure what you want, write them an email—they're great at recommendations."

—

Chapter 6

"I USED TO HAVE A GOOD RECIPE FOR CHAI," GABE SAID AS HE rummaged through his kitchen. "But I keep misplacing it."

"You have a recipe for chai?" I asked.

"From Preeti," he said. "She used to bring it to work every morning and it always smelled so amazing. She gave me the recipe on our last day."

He pulled his head out of the cabinet, revealing a box of pink tea bags in his hand.

"Is peach okay?"

I nodded, wondering who he had bought peach tea for.

"Why do you hate New York?" Gabe asked as we waited for the water to boil.

"I don't hate New York," I said, once I realized that he was recalling the part of the conversation we'd had at the restaurant where he had essentially handed me my ass for being presumptuous and unprofessional.

"I think you do," he said.

He was spooning ground coffee into a pour over. Jeremy had been big on coffee—very particular about what he drank and how he made it. I'd admired the ritual of it all. I liked rituals.

"It's just not for me," I said. "Like coffee."

Gabe nodded.

"It's nice to visit," I said, feeling like I had to explain myself. "And I liked going into the city to see shows when I was in college."

"At Sarah Lawrence."

"At Sarah Lawrence."

"Not an all-girls school," Gabe said, as if he wanted to prove that he'd done his research.

"Not an all-girls school," I said. "Not since the fifties or sixties."

"What kind of shows did you see?"

"Mostly musicals," I said. "I like musicals."

The kettle began to whistle. Gabe shut it off, but the kitchen wasn't quiet. It took me a moment to realize that *Gabe* had started whistling. And that he was whistling a familiar tune.

"You know *Into the Woods*?" I asked.

"Maybe," he said.

He had been humming "Last Midnight."

"You liked the theatre," Gabe said. "But nothing else."

"No," I said. "I liked the food. No one does bagels or pizza like New York. Their Chinese food is better too. I still can't find a place here that does a decent scallion pancake."

"And that's it," he said.

The smell of coffee filled the kitchen. It was a smell I loved—ironic because I didn't like the taste of coffee at all. Jeremy had kept telling me that it was something you had to get used to, but I never had. I was content just to smell it whenever he made a cup.

It always smelled cozy to me—and it smelled that way now—Gabe and me standing in his kitchen together while his puppy stretched out on her belly, looking a bit like a surfboard, chin against the floor.

"I guess it feels like you have to choose," I said. "Between New York and L.A. And I choose L.A."

"You're loyal to your hometown."

"Yeah," I said. "Especially because New Yorkers can be such jerks about L.A. They really think they have the cultural upper hand."

"But they don't have tacos," he said.

"But they don't have tacos," I said.

Gabe poured some hot water into my cup and I watched as it bloomed a bright, vibrant pink. I dunked the tea bag a couple of unnecessary times and left it, the water going fully fuchsia.

"When does he move?" Gabe asked. "The Novelist?"

I shrugged as I took an exploratory sip of my tea. It was weird that Gabe had read my blog. That he knew about Jeremy. Knew that he was moving to New York.

"Probably soon," I said.

I knew he thought he needed to ensconce himself in the literary scene in order to write the kind of book he wanted to write. The kind of book he had promised to his publisher.

"I think I'd pick L.A. too," Gabe said. "How's the tea?"

"Good," I said.

"You really should try that chai recipe," he said, before turning to search again.

"If you find it . . ." I said.

"I thought it was in here." His voice was slightly muffled from inside the cabinet. "You'll just have to give me your number so I can send it to you."

"Ha," I said, but when he turned around, hand outstretched, gesturing toward my bag, I realized he was serious.

"I'll text it to you when I find it," he said.

Wordlessly, I dug my phone out of my bag and handed it to him, extremely grateful I'd remembered to remove his photo from my lock screen.

He still raised his eyebrow at my ancient phone, but didn't say anything, typing in his number. There was a buzz, and he pulled out *his* phone—the highest-end iPhone that money could buy—and saved my contact information.

When he handed back my sad little phone with its cracked screen, I saw that he'd put his number in as *Gabe Parker (Team L.A.)*.

I smiled at that.

It was getting late. My tea was getting cold.

"I should probably go," I said.

Gabe nodded.

"I should probably watch *The Philadelphia Story,*" he said. "Even though someone told me it's sexist."

I opened my mouth to apologize, but he smiled, indicating that he was teasing me. The warmth I felt in the center of my chest was not a result of the tea.

"Just part of it," I said. "It is a good movie otherwise."

"Oliver likes it," Gabe said. "He said we'd talk about it after the premiere."

It seemed that the tabloids were completely wrong about Gabe and Oliver's so-called rivalry. Going to a former co-star's movie premiere was just good business, but planning to discuss a movie that was assigned homework for a role they'd maybe both been considered for? That seemed like actual friendship.

Maybe the rumors they'd both dated Jacinda were wrong too. Maybe all the rumors were wrong.

"I bet you'll have fun," I said.

He shrugged. "If you think standing around in uncomfortable clothes while everyone tells Oliver how handsome and talented he is sounds fun, then yeah, it will be a blast." His tone was light.

"At least you won't have to wear heels," I said.

"You don't know what outfit I've chosen," he said.

I laughed.

"You wouldn't have to wear heels," he said. "If you were free tomorrow night."

The rest of my laugh was snatched right out of my throat. Was Gabe Parker asking me to go to a premiere with him?

"I—"

Gabe's phone buzzed.

"What is it?" I asked, glad that I didn't have to respond to what was probably not really an invitation to Oliver Matthias's movie premiere.

"Just my manager," he said.

His expression indicated that whatever his manager wanted was not something Gabe was excited about giving.

"Can I ask you something?"

"Sure," I said.

Gabe put his phone away, shoving his hand in his pocket after it. "Have *you* seen *Angels in America*?"

"I've read the play," I said. "But I've never seen it."

"You know the story, though," he said.

"Yes."

Gabe looked down at the ground, and then up at me.

"Do you think it's a problem that I've kissed a man onstage?"

"No," I said. Quickly.

He lifted an eyebrow.

"No?"

"No," I said.

Gabe crossed his arms and leaned back against the counter as if he was settling in. I shouldn't have taken it as an invitation.

I did.

"*Angels in America* is a great play," I said. "Probably one of the best contemporary plays ever written. People should be using that as an indication that you're a really good actor, not obsessing over the fact that you made out with another man. Onstage. I mean, even if you had made out with another man in the alley next to the theatre, it shouldn't matter, right? If you're a good actor, you should be able to play Bond, and people who are freaking out because of one play you did in college have way too much time on their hands and are way too interested in your personal life. If their idea of masculinity is so fragile that the mere thought of you locking lips with someone of the same gender makes their head explode, then they have bigger problems than which actor should play James Bond in a movie."

I ran out of air and stopped, catching my breath, while Gabe stared.

"I'm sorry," I said. "I was on my soapbox again."

Gabe looked a little dazed, but not like I'd hit him with a baseball bat, more like I'd flashed him. Like, he was surprised but it wasn't necessarily a bad thing.

"I didn't think it was possible for so many words to come out of somebody's mouth that quickly," he said. "And I auditioned for *Gilmore Girls*."

"I can get a little worked up," I said.

"I like it," he said.

It seemed genuine, but I had a hard time believing that a movie star like Gabe Parker actually enjoyed being lectured by a lanky, loudmouthed Jew who was just supposed to interview him, not rant about systemic homophobia.

"I should go," I said.

He didn't argue, which basically confirmed my suspicions. I knelt to give his still-unnamed dog a scratch behind her ears. She rolled over and showed me her belly, so I rubbed that like a magic lamp before I stood.

"Thank you for your time," I said, realizing how formal I sounded.

It was how I should have conducted the entire interview, but it was a little too late for that.

The corners of Gabe's mouth quirked upward, barely hiding a smile.

"You're very welcome," he said.

"Okay, well." I started backing toward the door. "Bye, then."

"Bye," he said.

"Bye." I lifted a hand as I got to the door, finally turning away.

"Chani," he said.

Dammit, he was really good at saying my name.

"Yeah?" I twisted around quickly.

Too quickly to play it off as cool but I tried anyways.

"Yeah?" I asked again.

This time he did smile.

"Call me if you want to go to the premiere," he said. "We'd have fun."

GO FUG YOURSELF

THE FASHION AT THE *SHARED HEARTS* PREMIERE

True Blue

MATTHIAS'S FORMER CO-STAR GABE PARKER ATTENDED to lend his support, though he didn't come alone. Parker's date was unknown, but her sparkly blue number was a delight to the senses. Wonder if she wore it to match with Parker's favorite blue suit. As all Fuggirls know, the real way to show a man that you care is through your sartorial choices.

Now

Chapter 7

The restaurant is still around, which is an accomplishment in itself. Even though I've driven by this place on multiple occasions since I moved back to L.A., I've childishly averted my eyes every time I passed the block. And I've certainly never gone inside.

I would think about that beer, though, and my mouth would water.

I park on a side street, and check three things before I get out of the car. I check that my shirt—with its once and forever wayward middle button—is neatly clasped. I check that my notebook is still in my bag. And I check my chin for the little black hair that I'm always plucking and yet still manages to find a way to grow back at the most inconvenient times.

It has decided not to join me today, and for that I'm grateful.

The interior of the pub is the same. Jarringly so.

I find myself looking for the waitress—Madison—when I walk through. Part of me expects to see her—and for her to still be pregnant. It's ridiculous, I know, but the whole thing already feels surreal. It only becomes more surreal when I realize that even if Madison still works here, she's now the mother of a ten-year-old.

The passage of time suddenly feels real and oppressive.

It's been a year since I've moved back to L.A., and I keep waiting for it to feel like home again. Instead it feels like an old sweater I found in the back of my closet, one that I remember fitting perfectly, only when I put it on, it's stiff and plasticky, permanently creased from being forgotten. I wonder, sometimes, if this is my penance for leaving L.A. for New York in the first place. Then I remember that Jews don't believe in penance. Not like that, at least.

I duck into the bathroom before I head to the patio. I press my hands to the cold porcelain of the sink and tell myself that this is just another interview.

I've gotten good at lying to myself when it comes to Gabe.

The last time we met, we were young and brash and stupid. I remind myself that two people can experience the same exact thing in completely different ways. I remind myself that I now know better.

My phone buzzes.

It's a text from Katie.

You can say yes, she writes.

She'd read a book recently about saying yes to things. To life. To opportunity. To everything.

"I like saying no," I'd told her when she offered this advice the first time.

"Only because you don't know how to say yes," she'd countered.

Katie Dahn was someone who loved her mantras, celebrated the start of astrology seasons like people celebrated the start of baseball, and who I'd once seen swish mouthwash with her pinky raised.

She was the best friend I'd ever had.

"She's a kook," Jeremy had always said with affection. "She's the kind of person who would accidentally join an MLM scheme and somehow manage to either make money or take it over from the inside."

He wasn't wrong.

Katie was the only thing that Jeremy and I had really fought about during the divorce. Jeremy argued that he should have first dibs because he'd met her in undergrad. That the only reason *I* knew her was because of him. I had countered that Katie was an adult woman who could make her own choices when it came to friendship.

Katie had promised that she could remain friends with both of us, but in the end, she came to L.A. with me. We lived in the same building, like we were college students in a dorm. I'd come home some days and find a bag of crystals on my doorstep, or a note reminding me that Mercury was in retrograde.

It seems like Mercury is always in retrograde these days.

But Katie is a reminder that even though it had gotten bad the last year or so between Jeremy and me, there had been some good there too.

"You gave it your best shot," she'd told me. "But you were up against the stars."

That was her way of saying our astrological signs weren't compatible. I didn't believe it, not really, but I did take some comfort in the belief that someone else thought the end of my marriage was inevitable in some way. That it wasn't my fault.

Say yes, she texts again as if she might not have been clear enough the first time.

I roll my eyes and put my phone away.

There are several things she could be referring to, but it's probably in regard to the email I'd gotten from my agent after accepting this assignment.

She wants me to pitch another collection of essays. My editor wants to buy one. I know they're both thinking that this article would be the centerpiece of that theoretical book.

I keep telling them to wait.

I don't know what I'm asking them to wait for.

They're both thrilled I'm doing this interview. Everyone involved is looking to capture the same lightning in a bottle that happened the first time—when my article about Gabe made him a believable Bond and me a marketable name.

I don't want to be ungrateful, but I also know that the main reason I got my first book deal was because I was *that* writer. The one that didn't sleep with Gabe Parker (or did sleep with him, depending on what part of the internet you visit).

It's not exactly what I want to be known for.

But I don't really have a choice.

I step out of the bathroom and head to the patio.

Ten years ago, it was a sunny winter day. Today is overcast.

It's a good day for writing—for holing up inside with a cup of tea and working until your eyes are bleary and you've missed dinner.

I wrap my cardigan around me, second-guessing my outfit. I know that for the most part, I look the same. The changes are small—my jeans aren't as tight; my eyesight isn't as good. There are some witchy whites threaded through my hair, which is bang-less and has been for years.

I wonder what Gabe will think of it—of me—now.

I wish I didn't. I wish I didn't care. I wish this was like the other celebrity profiles I do these days—where I don't worry what the person thinks of me. Where I don't wonder what they remember about that weekend. About that night in New York. About that phone call.

I wish I didn't keep wondering *what if?*

Of course, *I* know what *Gabe* looks like now. I did my research. Technically, I never stopped doing my research, but it was nice to tell myself I had an excuse to look up pictures of him.

The last time he'd been photographed was a few months ago when he was filming *The Philadelphia Story*. He'd been clean-cut and groomed in a dreamy 1940s-modern mash-up reminiscent of his predecessor, Cary Grant. He'd looked good, his jawline still razor-sharp with just the right amount of salt peppered through his dark hair.

There are a few people scattered about, but that famous jawline is nowhere to be seen.

My heart is fluttering at the base of my throat, and I hate how nervous I am.

Does Gabe feel the way that I do—the way I wish I didn't—as if those three days ten years ago have been suspended in time? Perfectly frozen like a mosquito in amber.

I'm about to head inside, when I feel a hand on my elbow.

I turn, already knowing it's him.

"Chani," Gabe says.

He has a beard now.

But he still knows how to say my name.

Tell Me Something I Don't Know

REVIEWS

Horowitz's much-anticipated collection gathers some of her best works—including, of course, the infamous Gabe Parker interview—and includes some new pieces. Her writing sparkles with humor and wit. Reading it, you'll feel like you're talking to your best friend—if your best friend was the type of person who snuck out of the newest James Bond's house in the middle of the night. —*Broad Sheets*

Fans of Horowitz's profiles will love *Tell Me Something I Don't Know*. A fizzy, lighthearted read, it's the perfect book to toss into your beach bag. You'll tan while you giggle at her best hits—her Gabe Parker profile is of course the star of the collection—and grin at the new additions. —*Publishers Weekly*

Tell Me Something I Don't Know is a bubble bath in a book—soothing and calming, the perfect balm for the end of a long day. The collection revolves around her viral hit, "Gabe Parker: Shaken, Not Stirred," and readers will wince again with embarrassment as she recounts how she blew her once-in-a-lifetime chance with the Bond star after attending a house party of his and passing out in his guest room.

—*Kirkus Reviews*

Apparently, Horowitz is a fairly beloved celebrity interviewer. This reviewer could not say how or why—even the profiles included in her collection of essays are self-serving and self-centered. Everything is about *her*. It's kind of cute at first, the way it's cute when your child asks you a precocious question, like "Daddy, why is the grass green?" But when that question is asked over and over and over again, it doesn't seem cute.

Instead, it seems likely that something is wrong with your child and their intelligence. One only has to read her infamous interview with Bond star Gabe Parker to realize exactly why she's gotten any attention for her mediocre writing.

—Goodreads

Chani Horowitz is a slut. *—Reddit*

Chapter 8

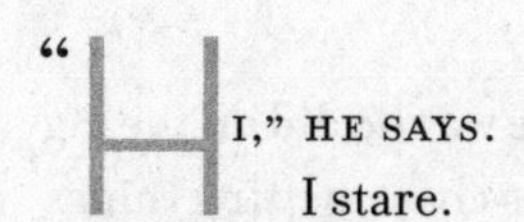

"Hi," he says.

I stare.

I'd been expecting a version of the Gabe from photos. A combination of that and who he'd been ten years ago. Boyish. Open. Carelessly handsome.

He's still handsome—breathtakingly so—but it isn't careless anymore.

There's the beard hiding the lower part of his face and the baseball cap which tries to conceal the rest of it. But he tilts his head back far enough so I can see his eyes. He looks tired and worn, but it suits him. Or rather, it suits me. It blunts his beauty a bit, makes him seem more real, more touchable, which in turn makes him seem more distant.

"It's good to see you," Gabe says.

He's still holding my elbow and I can feel the warmth of his fingers through my sweater.

"Unngh," I say.

And I know, right then, that all the growing up I thought I'd done, all the walls I'd erected around my heart after six years of marriage and what since then has felt like constant heartache, are damn near useless against this.

I also know the answer to my question. About what he remembers. How much he remembers.

Amber, meet mosquito.

We sit, and he takes off his hat.

He's had a beard before—a while back, seen briefly in the grainy photos of him being escorted into rehab. The first time. The tabloids had made a point to focus on his weight gain and the loss of the Bond six-pack, but plenty of people complained about the beard or the scruffy way he was wearing his hair. His hair has far more gray than I would have expected, far more than I saw in pictures. Contradictory bitch that I am, I prefer this look.

I don't mind that he's gained weight. Don't mind that I can see a curl of chest hair peering out from the undone top button of his shirt. Don't mind that he's gotten older.

I'd seen a hint of what it had cost to look the way he did on the big screen back then. Starving himself, waxing his chest, getting things plucked and shined and oiled. It had been part of the job and even then, he hadn't complained.

I like this version of him better.

I don't want to like him. Not the way I liked him back then—that starry-eyed girl who had fallen head—and heart—first into what turned out to be the generic trap of celebrity. Gabe is a movie star. An actor. It's his job to make people fall in love with him.

At least I hadn't fallen in love with him.

I *hadn't*.

Because that would have been truly ridiculous.

For years, I've been trying—in my way—to escape this magnetic pull he's had over my life and my career. And today I'm stepping right back into its force field.

Part of me wants to get up and run.

I don't like how my heart is racing. Don't like that my palms are sweaty. Don't like that I'm having almost the exact same reaction to him that I had ten years ago. I'd been so sure that I knew better by now.

Maybe my mind does, but my body sure as hell hasn't gotten the memo.

Gabe looks up and smiles.

And dammit if my heart doesn't skip a beat.

Fuck.

He sits there, across from me, and people are staring. He is, after all, impossible to ignore.

I smooth my hands down the front of my shirt, my fingers checking that button one last time. His eyes follow the gesture and they linger there for a moment.

At first, I think he might be staring at my boobs, but then I realize he's looking at my fingers. Specifically, at my ring finger.

The last time he did that, I'd been wearing my wedding band.

But I stopped wearing it after the party with Jeremy in Brooklyn. When I knew my marriage was over, even if we still managed to draw it out for almost a year with therapy and promises to change.

I pointedly return the gaze, staring at Gabe's hands. No ring.

Still, he holds them up, like a magician pretending he has nothing to hide.

But ten years ago, that hadn't been the case.

Gabe had lied to me about Jacinda.

When he flew to Vegas days after the interview went viral, he'd made me feel like a fool.

Not just because I'd repeated that lie about them to the whole world in my article, but because *I'd* believed him. If I had known . . .

I'd felt a lot of things when I heard the news, but mostly I felt angry and humiliated. It's what I allowed myself to feel. Because those emotions were powerful and protective. They helped keep Gabe and my memories of him at arm's length. It was easier to be angry at him.

I summon that anger again.

Gabe, of course, has no idea what is going on in my head. He's looking at me, studying me, but I'm doing everything I can to keep my expression neutral.

"It's you," he says.

As if he hadn't just had his hand on my elbow. As if he hadn't come across the room to get me. As if we haven't just walked over to this table and sat down together. As if it hasn't been ten years since I walked out of his rental house in Laurel Canyon, blinking in the sunlight, the ground beneath me somehow farther away than it had been the day before.

If I'm not careful, I'll crack. I'll smile at him. I'll melt.

It will be as if I've learned nothing.

Instead, I lean into my anger.

"Mr. Parker," I say.

He frowns.

"That bad, huh?" he asks.

I take out my phone. Set it to record.

"Shall we begin?"

THE RUMOR MILL

GABCINDA CONFIRMED . . . AND WED

JUST DAYS AFTER A *BROAD SHEETS* PROFILE CHAMPIONED the newest Bond, Gabe Parker surprised fans by leaving set to marry co-star Jacinda Lockwood in Las Vegas. The now viral article refuted any involvement between the two, but it's clear that reporter Chani Horowitz didn't get the whole story.

The marriage was confirmed by both Parker's and Lockwood's management, who then released a statement saying "Gabe and Jacinda's relationship—and their marriage—will remain private, but they appreciate the outpouring of love and support from their fans."

It's quite a reversal from their recent claims that they were just friends.

As for Lockwood, she's gained herself a reputation for being a heartbreaker and home-wrecker, having been linked to Parker's former co-star Oliver Matthias and more than one married director. She's continued to deny all rumors, even after she was named in a particularly scandalous divorce settlement.

"I was just as surprised as everyone else," Horowitz said when reached for comment. "I wish them nothing but the best."

Chapter 9

GABE GESTURES FOR ME TO ORDER FIRST.

They still have that same sour beer, which I get with my burger.

"Wait," I tell the waitress, after Gabe asks for a burger and water. "No beer."

His sobriety is one of the things we're supposed to talk about today. One of the things he's been very transparent in discussing.

"It's okay," Gabe says.

The waitress—not Madison, but a bracingly young brunette—pauses, pen poised above the order pad.

"Are you sure?" I ask.

"I'm flattered you still like that one," he says.

I'd forgotten how damn charming he is.

"Okay," I say. "Keep the beer."

I can already tell I'm going to need it.

The waitress nods, and if she's impressed by Gabe's celebrity, she doesn't show it. She leaves and I check the recording app.

"Shall we begin?" I ask again.

"If you'd like," Gabe says.

"That's why I'm here," I say.

He gives me a long searching look.

"All right," he says when he's done.

I feel squirmy under his gaze, and it takes everything in my power to keep from shifting in my seat. I sit tall instead, and tap my pen on my open notebook.

This time, I came prepared.

Because I feel like I have something to prove. To Gabe. To myself.

I'm nervous, but it's not the same kind of nervousness. Back then, I'd approached my interviews with a certain arrogance, a confidence that I could make something out of whatever I received.

Sometimes I look back on my twenty-six-year-old self and am amazed at the boldness with which she approached the world. Sometimes I look back and wince at her unfounded confidence.

Right now, I'm wincing.

"Your career has taken some interesting twists and turns since we last spoke," I say.

"That's a generous way of saying I drunkenly embarrassed myself in front of the entire world and got fired from a role no one thought I deserved in the first place," Gabe says. "And that was just the beginning."

"You still don't think you deserved to be Bond?" I ask, even though the answer is obvious.

When it was discovered that he had been partially correct—that the producers and Ryan Ulrich had lied about him being the first choice, when the real reason they'd chosen him over Oliver had been revealed, I'd thought about that. How it made sense that someone who had gotten the role of a lifetime could be as miserable about it as Gabe had been.

It's why I wasn't that surprised when his tenure as Bond ended the way it did.

He stares at his hands, palms down on the table.

"Who really feels that they deserve the good things they get?" he asks.

I don't have a response for him, and already this interview is more philosophical and unguarded than our last one.

Back then, Gabe seemed like he'd rather chew off his right arm than speak freely about anything. Now, he seems hell-bent on exposing himself—warts and all.

I don't know whether or not to take it personally.

"Let's talk about sobriety," I say.

Even though he's done numerous interviews about it, I know it's still the thing most people want to read about. I know *Broad Sheets* wants a quote or two.

"Let's," Gabe says.

"How long have you been sober for?"

"Coming up on two years," he says. "Tried a few times before, but this is my longest stretch so far."

I wondered how much Gabe remembers from all those years ago. If he even knows who he spoke to the night before he went to rehab that first time.

Like the question of Jacinda, I'm torn between wanting to know and wanting to willfully ignore the elephant in the corner.

"How does that feel?" I ask instead. Even if I want to know the truth, this isn't the time. "Maintaining your sobriety for that long?"

He leans back. "Honestly?"

"Of course," I say.

"It's the accomplishment I'm proudest of," he says. "Bond is nothing in comparison."

He looks up at me.

"What are you most proud of, Chani?"

What a question.

"This isn't about me," I say, annoyed that he's trying to turn this interview back at me. Again.

He shrugs.

"Is it a struggle to maintain your sobriety now that you're working again?" I ask.

"Sometimes," he says. "But I have a great sponsor and therapist, and I lean on them when I feel the urge to drink. I've had to reframe my impulses—training myself to go for the phone instead of the bottle. Or to a meeting, but that's a little harder when you're not really able to be anonymous."

It's sort of a joke, but I don't smile. Because even though I didn't give Gabe an answer to his question, I'm still thinking about it.

And I realize, in a way, *that* article is the one I'm proudest of.

It's not because it's the one that went viral, and got me an agent and a book deal. It's because it was special. Because I made it special.

Nothing since then has come close to feeling as satisfying or triumphant. And even so, that pride I feel at the work has been tempered by the reality of how it's been received. How *I've* been received.

There's no denying that my career is intrinsically linked to Gabe's. To Gabe.

No matter what I do—no matter what I write—that will always be a footnote in my career, if not *the* footnote.

It makes it hard to know if my pride in that piece is well-earned, or if it just went viral because of its content.

Our drinks arrive and we both stare at my beer.

"It's okay, really," he says. "I don't spend a lot of time at clubs or bars anymore, but I can handle someone having a drink at lunch."

I take the world's tiniest sip.

"How has sobriety changed your life?" I ask.

There had been rumors of Gabe's drinking problem during the filming of *Murder on Wheels*—his second Bond film—six or seven years ago, but his management had denied and distracted until they couldn't anymore.

"How hasn't it?" he asks. "Sobriety—like addiction—informs almost everything I do. When I was deep into my addiction, all I thought about was getting drunk."

"What did drinking give you?"

"Distance," he says.

"Distance."

"It was a way to avoid the things I didn't want to confront," he says. "Drinking was a way to pretend that they weren't happening. A way to escape what I was feeling. My insecurities. My fears. My shame. My inadequacies as an actor. As a person."

I notice then how still Gabe is. How he's sitting there, across from me, and not fidgeting, not restlessly moving.

"Sobriety gives me strength," he says. "The strength to face the things I wanted to hide from."

"Like your marriage?" I ask.

"Success" was what I'd meant to say. Not marriage. And I definitely hadn't meant to ask it in that bitter, angry tone.

I didn't really want to talk about him and Jacinda.

This interview already feels dangerously personal, with Gabe being as vulnerable and open as he is. It makes it hard to be angry at him. But that anger is what's protecting me. I need it.

"Chani," Gabe says, and his eyes are so very sad.

But before he can say any more, our food arrives.

He watches me put my fries on my burger and after I've taken a bite, swallowed, and glanced back at my notebook looking for another question, he picks up right where we left off.

"I fucked up a lot," he says. "And my marriage . . ."

He pauses.

"It was complicated. But I don't regret it."

It's a bit like a boot to the chest, those words.

"Why would you?" I ask, going for breezy. " 'Jacinda Lockwood is the most beautiful woman in the world.' "

That had been the headline they gave her when she landed on the cover of *Vogue* this last spring.

"She was a good friend to me," Gabe says. "*Is* a good friend."

"Mmhmm," I say, looking down at my notebook, looking for questions that will get us away from this topic.

"What about you?" he asks.

"*I* didn't marry Jacinda Lockwood," I say.

"You did marry the Novelist," he says.

"Jeremy," I say.

" 'The man with his finger on the pulse of modern literature,' " Gabe says.

It was a pull quote from *The New York Times'* review of Jeremy's first book.

The day he'd heard had been a good day.

It had been a struggle for him to write the book. When I moved to New York, the release date had been pushed out twice and he still barely had a manuscript. This time *he* had been the one struggling with focus. By that point, I was working consistently and managed to convince Jeremy to stick to a rigid writing schedule in order to get the book done.

He'd resisted at first, but it was successful in the end.

When we heard the news, we'd both been working nonstop—him gearing up for his book's release and me with an avalanche of projects that I had been happy to have but happier to be done with. We'd taken a day to enjoy the city, spending the morning at the Met and then walking across the Brooklyn Bridge, getting ice cream on the other side. The whole outing, really, had been an attempt to distract from the news that would be coming from Jeremy's publisher. And it had been there, at the base of the bridge, ice cream melting down my wrist, that Jeremy had learned that *The New York Times* had loved his book.

We'd shared a kiss that was sticky and jubilant and then, with a smear of my pistachio on his cheek, Jeremy had gotten down on one knee.

"You inspire me," he'd said. "Every day we're together, you inspire me. Please, Chani Horowitz, will you be my wife and my muse for the rest of our lives?"

There had been a crowd and when I'd said yes, everyone had applauded. I'd ducked my hot, happy face into Jeremy's neck while he beamed at Manhattan. We took a cab to Grand Central to eat oysters because it had felt so New York and so glamorous, and we'd walked home, Jeremy telling me that he loved me over and over and over again.

That memory combined with this current moment is like emotional whiplash. Gabe mistakes the look on my face for something else.

"You were always surprised when I was prepared," he says.

I refocus, and try to forget the melted-ice-cream kind of love that is now gone. That sometimes feels like it never really existed.

"Always?" I ask. "This is only the second time we've ever done this."

Gabe raises an eyebrow.

I feel like I'm on unsteady ground. Because I don't know how to think about that weekend. In some ways it seems so long ago; in other ways, it feels like I've been haunted by those days—the nights—we spent together.

"You moved back to Montana for a while," I say.

He nods. "My family wanted me to be close by," he says. "And Hollywood isn't great for people in recovery. Even if I was ready to start working again—even if anyone was interested in hiring me—the whole culture around movies, all the parties and events, it involves a lot of alcohol. And other stuff."

I remember how I had assumed there would be cocaine at his house party.

"You moved to New York," he says.

"It's what writers do."

He probably thought that, after I read about him marrying Jacinda Lockwood in Vegas right after my article about him was published, I ran back to Jeremy, moved to New York with him, and tried to out-happily-ever-after Gabe.

"You hate New York," he says.

I shrug. I don't want to talk about our exes.

It was almost a year after Gabe's marriage to Jacinda that I went to New York. Just for a visit. For work.

Jeremy and I had kept in touch, and he had invited me out to dinner.

He'd changed. I'd changed.

Dinner became late night drinks at his place and then brunch the next morning. The weekend became a week and then I was heading back to L.A. to pack my things. We were engaged a year later.

I didn't think about Gabe *at all*.

"You're back now," Gabe says.

I shrug again.

"I like the newsletter," Gabe says.

"Thank you," I say, because it seems rude not to.

I'd switched from blogging to a monthly newsletter about three years ago. I'd be lying if I said I didn't wonder if he kept reading my blog after that weekend. And I'd also be lying if I said I didn't occasionally check the emails of people who subscribed to my newsletter to see if he had subscribed.

I'd never seen his name, but then again, I wouldn't have been surprised if he had a private email account that he used.

We both eat our burgers, and when I've finished my fries, I push the remainder of them toward him. He finishes them without a word.

"So," I say, wiping my fingers. "*The Philadelphia Story*."

"Yeah," he says. "Someone once told me it was a movie that needed an update."

I know what he's doing. I know he's hoping I'll make some cute, flattered comment like "Oh, did they?" and he'll have an opening and we'll laugh and things will be friendly and casual.

I can't do that again.

That girl—that brave, brash, bold, stupid girl—has to protect herself. This interview has to stay professional. From start to finish.

"This is your third movie with Oliver Matthias," I say.

"With Ollie, yeah," Gabe says.

"No hard feelings it seems," I say.

"He's more forgiving than he should be," Gabe says. "I don't know if I'd do the same thing in his shoes."

"Yes, you would," I say.

He smiles.

I almost cave—his smile is just *that* good, *that* familiar—but I remind myself how I felt when I heard about him and Jacinda. I remind myself how it felt seeing him in New York.

I pay for lunch and I already know that *Broad Sheets* is going to be disappointed with the interview I turn in. It will be fine—it will be competently written and flattering to Gabe—but it won't be anywhere near the article that I wrote ten years ago.

Because we're not the same people we were ten years ago.

That's just going to have to be good enough for *Broad Sheets*. For the world.

We step outside the restaurant and I hold out my hand, wanting to end this on a professional note. As if a handshake will give me the kind of closure I was hoping for.

"Wait," Gabe says.

I don't want to. I've been looking at the door for the past hour, imagining myself bolting from the restaurant. Getting away from it. Getting away from him.

I put my hand away.

"Chani," he says.

He still says it perfectly. It still gives me a chill.

I hate it. I'm a grown-ass divorcee who lived in New York for fuck's sake, not a twenty-six-year-old fangirl with a boner for the future James Bond.

"Did you get what you needed?" Gabe asks.

"I got enough," I say.

He runs his hand across the back of his neck. His baseball cap is tucked into his back pocket, his sunglasses folded and hanging from the front of his shirt. It pulls the fabric low enough that I can see his chest hair.

I look away.

"I'd like to show you something," he says.

"I don't think that's a good idea," I say.

"Probably not," he agrees. "But what do you have to lose?"

THE RUMOR MILL

PACKING ON THOSE POST-BOND POUNDS

IT'S OUR FIRST SPOTTING OF THE FORMER BOND ACTOR since his fall from grace. Even in these grainy photos, it's clear to see that Parker has gained a significant amount of weight since he was officially fired from the Bond franchise.

Rumors of his drinking problem have plagued the actor for years, but he's been spotted out at clubs and bars on multiple nights, and there were several instances where paparazzi caught him puking out of the side of his car before being driven away.

The drinking has also put a strain on Parker's relationship with Jacinda Lockwood. Rumors of a potential split were fueled by her decision to remain in London when Parker made his Broadway debut in *A Raisin in the Sun,* and the two haven't been photographed together in months. Sources close to the couple insist they'll be divorced before the end of the year.

There had been whispers of Parker's bad behavior dating all the way back to *The Hildebrand Rarity*. While *Murder on Wheels,* his second Bond film, was in production, Dan Mitchell claimed that Parker had him fired. The up-and-coming star—who later landed the lead in the hilarious *Ivan the Not Too Terrible*—told *Entertainment Weekly* that Parker was jealous of him being younger and more fit, and personally ordered him removed from the project.

But it was a drunken incident on the third Bond set that seemed to be the final straw for Parker, who had been labeled as "difficult" and "combative." The film had already been delayed once due to Parker's behavior, but it seemed that his time away did nothing to fix the tensions on set. A video of the moment when Parker confronted the director, Ryan

Ulrich, went viral. Although most of the footage is out of focus and the conversation at times is hard to make out, several sources have confirmed that things had been tense between Parker and Ulrich since the very first Bond movie they did together.

After he was fired, Parker's team released a statement that read, in part, "Gabe is proud of the work he's done as the first American Bond, and looks forward to seeing who will be the next to step into the legendary icon's shoes."

The day after, he checked into rehab.

Chapter 10

THERE'S NO REASON I SHOULD BE FOLLOWING GABE IN HIS CAR right now. The interview is over. I should be heading home to get dinner with Katie and type up my notes. But, because I've learned literally nothing from the last time I did this, I'm driving in the opposite direction of where I need to go.

It takes me a while to realize that I recognize the windy road we're going up. Like the restaurant, things are different, but it's a subtle difference. Different landscaping on some of the houses, a few new structures and some unexpected paint jobs.

His house, however, hasn't changed.

He pulls into the driveway and gestures for me to do the same. I nose carefully into the space, leaving a wide berth between my Honda Civic and his top-of-the-line Tesla.

Just another reminder of how different our lives are. How different they've always been.

I'm angry. It's an anger I don't fully understand, but I know it's hiding something else. At least, that's what my therapist thinks.

"You go to rage first," she's told me. "It's your safe place when emotions are high."

If that's true then it makes sense. Because it's not as simple as being mad at Gabe for lying to me about Jacinda ten years ago. I'm full of a thousand nameless, conflicting emotions right now. If I'm being fair to myself, I've been churning with them since I got the assignment.

And anger is easier.

It's easier to be angry at Gabe for what happened ten years ago. Not just the embarrassment I felt in realizing that I'd been sucked into his magnetic pull and spit out. But I can also fault him for the way I can never tell if the success I have is due to my own skills or because of him. I heap all that blame on him. I lean hard into those feelings—those safe, powerful, angry feelings.

"You're still renting the same place?" I ask.

The words are only slightly bitter.

"I bought it," Gabe says. "You were right. I didn't need something big and grand."

We're standing in his front yard, like two neighbors. Like I might have stopped by for a cup of sugar or tea and we're catching up.

I realize, once we're in the house, that I'm looking for something.

Or rather, I'm looking for someone.

Gabe's dog.

She had been a puppy—just a dozen weeks old when we met ten years ago. A literal lifetime in dog years. It seems entirely possible that she's gone now.

I follow Gabe through the house, heading to the same place we'd gone that first time I'd been here: the kitchen. On the way, I don't see anything that indicates a dog lives here. There's no dog dish, no leash hanging by the door, no dog bed in the living room.

I look out into the yard but it's empty as well.

It makes me unbearably sad, the passage of time hitting me like a load of bricks. Ten years. Ten years have passed.

So much has happened. Madison at the restaurant has a ten-year-old kid. Gabe's divorced, sober, and planning a comeback. I'm divorced, desperately wishing I wasn't sober at the moment, and too scared to write anything outside the familiar brand I've created for myself.

And now Gabe's dog is dead too.

I want to cry.

"Water?" Gabe asks.

"Sure," I say, my voice embarrassingly thick.

I clear my throat before I speak again.

"I can't stay," I remind him.

It's probably the fifth time I've said that. At this point, I don't know if I'm telling him or telling myself. The addict's version of "just one more."

The truth is I don't know what I'm doing. I don't know what this is.

I take the water Gabe offers me and the two of us drink, standing in his kitchen, memories of our last time here closing in on me until I feel like I can't breathe.

"I'm sorry," he says.

For what? I think. *For feeding into the intense, unrealistic fangirl fantasy that I'd built up in my head? For being too good to be true and also human and fallible, which only made it harder to dislike you? For the seemingly unending ripple effects that our interview has had on my life—both professionally and personally? For all the moments I've replayed in my brain hundreds of times and all the things I'm unable to forget?*

For all the things I don't want to forget?

For my stupid, traitorous heart that hasn't learned a single goddamn lesson in ten goddamn years?

"For what?" I ask.

Gabe blinks, as if he wasn't expecting the question.

"For . . ." He pauses.

He thinks.

I wait.

"For lying," he finally says. "I should have told you about Jacinda."

"Yes," I say. "You should have."

I've seen her in person three times. Once at the premiere. Once in New York. And then once in a restaurant about twenty miles from where we are right now.

I'd been living in New York, but I would still come to L.A. for the occasional profile, always using the excuse to stay for the weekend and see my family.

We'd been out to dinner, the whole Horowitz clan, ordering everything on the menu at our favorite Taiwanese place in Mar Vista, when I spotted her across the room.

She was leaving, and even though it was a small restaurant in a neighborhood that saw its fair share of celebrities trying to have a quiet meal, people still stared. Most beautiful woman alive, indeed.

She had leaned over the bar, clearly familiar with the bartender, and the two of them exchanged cheek kisses. When she pulled back, her gaze found mine. Because I was staring along with the rest of them. For the same reasons and a different one as well.

We looked at each other, and then she tossed her head the way a famous international model who knows how to find her best angle might do.

"Was that . . . ?" my sister had asked.

"Uh-huh," I said.

"Wow," my sister said. "She is gorgeous."

"Uh-huh," I said.

There had been a pause when she saw me. A pause, and a wrinkle—a beautiful one—had appeared between her eyes. I'm certain the expression on my face had been the same one that everyone else in the room had been wearing—one of shock and awe—the result of being caught in the sights of a truly spectacular being. But she might have recognized me. Might have recognized that beneath that shock and awe was something else. Something she might have seen backstage at a New York theatre not long ago.

Both times, I'd been the first one to look away.

Gabe runs his hand through his hair.

"It wasn't fair," he says.

"To her," I say.

"To you," he corrects. "To both of you."

I shrug, even though his response hurts. I don't know what I want from him right now, but I'm pretty sure it isn't that.

It just reminds me how stupid I felt when I found out about the marriage. When it confirmed all the rumors about them. The rumors I had been intent on ignoring.

And how foolish I'd felt—all over again—when I went to see him in New York. I hadn't learned my lesson then, but I was doing my best to not make that mistake a third time.

"I should have known" is what I say.

I adjust my purse—the damn strap is always sliding down, reminding me that I need to stand up straight.

"You should have known?" Gabe asks. "What does that mean?"

I look him in the eye. "I should have known that something was going on between the two of you. That you lied through your teeth when you told me that you were just friends."

He flinches.

"It was complicated," he says.

"Oh, I'm sure it was," I say. "It's always complicated when you're planning to run off to Vegas with your secret girlfriend/co-star, but the girl they send to do a profile on you is dumb, adoring, and easy."

"You weren't dumb," Gabe says. "You're not dumb."

"Just adoring and easy."

"Those are your words," he says.

I am about one more stupid comment away from reaching over and throttling him.

He runs a hand over his face. It's annoying how nice his hands are. Strong and sturdy. There are some scars on his fingers. I don't remember those scars from before.

"Jacinda and me . . ." He pauses. "It was an arrangement, of sorts."

I cross my arms over my chest.

"I should have told you," he says.

"Told me what, exactly?" I ask. "About your 'arrangement'? Is that Hollywoodspeak for an open marriage? I've heard of the concept, you know. It's not exclusive to you horny celebrities—some people even do it ethically."

Gabe looks tired and part of me thinks that I should go easy on him, but another part of me thinks that I've spent way too much time in my life going easy on men.

I know that Gabe isn't Jeremy. That their failures aren't the same, the hurt they caused is different, but right now I really don't care. I want to be mad at a man, and this one will do just fine.

"It isn't what you think," he says. "It wasn't some big, grand plan. My management, my family, they were all just as surprised as you were."

"Don't flatter yourself," I say.

That seems to upset him.

"I was young and impulsive and stupid," Gabe says. "We *were* sleeping together—a friends-with-benefits kind of thing. Casual."

"I'm sure," I say.

If he thinks this is making things better, he's very, *very* wrong.

"I thought it would solve a lot of different problems," he says. "Because at the time, we both wanted the same thing."

"Well, I hope you got it," I say.

Gabe keeps rubbing the back of his neck. I imagine it's like a river stone back there, all that worrying making it smooth and hairless. I'd put my fingers there once before, though I can't remember what it felt like.

That isn't true—not exactly. I can't remember the specific feel of that specific part of Gabe's body but I do remember that I liked everything that I touched. And I do remember how much I liked it.

"People do it, you know," he says.

"Get married for stupid reasons?" I ask. "Yeah, I know."

"Was that . . ." He gestures.

It's vague—more like he's skipping stones than actually indicating anything specific—but I get what he's trying to say.

"No," I say. "I actually liked Jeremy."

Only partly a lie. I liked him sometimes. I even loved him sometimes.

"The Novelist," he says.

"Jeremy."

Gabe nods.

"I actually liked Jacinda too," he says. "I still do, in fact."

"Great," I say. "Should I expect to see a blind item about two former lovers rekindling their romance by renewing their vows in Vegas next week?"

"No," Gabe says. "I wouldn't do that to you."

"I don't care," I say.

"Of course," Gabe says.

I hate that he knows I'm lying.

This time I'm the one making the skipping-stone gesture, because I just want him to hurry and finish his dumb-ass apology so I can leave and go home and cry about his dead dog. Because I definitely don't want to cry about some stupid misguided sense of lost time and missed chances.

"I'm sure you read all the things they were writing about her around that time," Gabe says. "About the married directors. About the one who named her in his divorce proceedings."

"Sure," I said.

I'm steeling myself, because I really don't want to feel sympathetic or understanding about whatever arrangement Gabe and Jacinda had, but the truth is that I do remember what the tabloids said about her.

"She didn't. Sleep with them, that is," he says. "It was all one-sided. They propositioned her, but she turned them down."

I nod.

"It didn't really seem to matter, though," Gabe says. "No one believed her. As far as the tabloids were concerned, she was single and beautiful and therefore somehow responsible."

I'd been asked to interview her. Years ago—when there had been rumors that Gabe and her were on the rocks—someone had pitched it to *Broad Sheets*. They'd begged me to do it, knowing that it would certainly go viral.

I'd bowed to the pressure, but then, the night before I was supposed to meet Jacinda Lockwood in the hotel lobby of the St. Regis, I'd chickened out and called it off. Someone else had done the interview instead. It turned out just okay.

"Oliver is the one who introduced us," Gabe says. "We all thought it would be a mutually beneficial thing, but . . ."

He pauses.

"I didn't expect you," he says.

I freeze.

"I didn't expect you to show up at my house with your very big eyes and your bad questions and your smart mouth and . . ."

I'm clutching the counter behind me like it's the edge of a pool in the deep end and I'm a brand-new swimmer who isn't sure she's not going to sink straight to the bottom if she lets go.

Gabe looks up at me, and I hold on tighter.

"You surprised me," he says.

He smiles, that devastating grin of his—the one that launched a thousand memes.

"They weren't bad questions," I say.

"They were."

We stare at each other for ages.

"What is this?" I finally ask.

Gabe glances down at his glass.

"Water?"

I glare at him.

"What is *this*?" I ask again, gesturing emphatically between us. "What do you want from me?"

He seems speechless at the question, and I wait for what feels like an eternity for him to answer.

"I wanted to see you," he finally says.

I throw out my hands, knocking my own glass off the counter, getting water and glass everywhere.

"Shit," I say.

"Don't worry about it," Gabe says.

He doesn't move.

We stand there, water and glass at our feet, saying nothing.

"I'd like to take you somewhere," Gabe says.

"Somewhere *else*?" I ask.

He nods.

"Montana," he says.

I stare at him.

"You want to take me to Montana?" I ask.

"Yes," he says.

"You're nuts," I say.

He smiles at that. "Yeah, probably," he says.

"I can't go with you to Montana," I say.

"I'll take care of everything," he says.

"That's not why and you know it," I say.

"I know," he says.

We stare at each other for a long time.

"I can't go," I say.

He nods.

"I can't," I say again.

We both know that I'm lying.

ENTERTAINMENT WEEKLY

MATTHIAS AND PARKER: *Dynamic Duo*

[EXCERPT]

BY ROBIN ROMANOFF

I HAD BEEN WARNED THAT TRYING TO INTERVIEW PARKER and Matthias at the same time was a feat in and of itself. The two friends have known each other for so long and are so enamored of each other's company that it isn't long before the interview devolves into the two of them swapping inside jokes and speaking in the kind of shorthand only available to two people as close as they are. It's clear that their much-lauded friendship is the real deal.

"Well, Gabe is the only person I ever considered for the part of Dex," Matthias tells me.

"Only because you decided you weren't going to star in it yourself," Parker interjects. "We both know you do a much better Cary Grant than I do."

"That's the point," Matthias says. "I didn't want the movie to be a straight remake of the original. It had to be different."

The difference is something that's been long discussed.

"We wanted to update a few things," Matthias says. "And Gabe brought a lot to the table—especially when it came to the story line between Tracy and her father."

"It's horribly sexist and gross," Parker says. "He blames *her* for the affair and *she* apologizes in the end? We thought we could do better."

I'm not sure fans of the original will agree with such an assessment, but it's surprising to hear Parker speak so passionately and thoughtfully about the sexism woven throughout the original film.

It's clear this movie isn't going to be what audiences expect.

—

Saturday

BROAD SHEETS

GABE PARKER:

Shaken, Not Stirred—Part Two

BY CHANI HOROWITZ

THE WORLD IS DIFFERENT ON THE OTHER SIDE OF THE velvet rope. Us normals don't like to hear that, of course. We crave confirmation that stars, well, they're just like us.

I'm sorry to say but they are not.

Not even close.

You see, when I get ready for a fancy night out, if I'm lucky, I have a friend that can lend me an outfit, help me with my makeup, or even do my hair for me just to make me look like a slightly polished version of my actual self.

When someone like Jacinda Lockwood leaves her million-dollar home to go to the *gym,* she has a whole team of stylists to make sure that she looks like someone who doesn't have to go to the gym.

You've all seen the pictures by now. Of me standing with Gabe Parker's arm around my waist, smiling gamely at the crowd in a sparkly blue dress. Go Fug Yourself thinks that I might have chosen the gown to match Gabe's suit, but that presumes that I knew what Gabe was going to wear (I didn't) or that I have a closet full of fancy-party dresses to choose from (I don't).

The matching was just luck.

The whole evening, really, was just luck.

Because, dear readers, you and I both know that I shouldn't have been there.

Even in those pictures, I look out of place. Gabe's grin is ratcheted up to eleven, while I'm just trying to seem normal while the flashing bulbs of hundreds of cameras burn my retinas and a crowd of strangers yells at us to "look over here and smile." That hand I have on his arm? That's me holding on for dear life, unsure if I'll be able to see where I'm going when we have to move down the line and very unsure I won't just fall on my ass after wobbling forward in my uncomfortable heels.

I don't belong but I don't care. For one evening, I'm traveling amongst the beautiful people.

And Gabe, beautiful person that he is, is my gallant and charming tour guide.

He introduces me to everyone.

Most important, he introduces me to the man of the evening, the incomparable Oliver Matthias.

Much speculation has been made over *The Hildebrand Rarity*'s decision to cast Gabe, when his *Tommy Jacks* co-star seems a much more natural fit. And even further gossip about how the casting choice has driven a wedge between the two co-stars.

The opposite is true.

I experience firsthand the lack of animosity and competition between them. Gabe is thrilled to be attending the *Shared Hearts* premiere to support his friend, speaking at length about how talented Oliver is.

Like me, Gabe has been watching him on the BBC for years, as Oliver all but grew up in front of us. And this new film is just further evidence of how his talent has evolved. It's a delight for the senses—a glass of champagne in movie form.

"He's a legend," Gabe tells me. "Watching him on-screen

can be an out-of-body experience, but acting next to him? That's the education of a lifetime."

As a longtime fangirl of Matthias's Darcy (yeah, I'd choose him over Firth or Macfadyen—fight me), it takes everything in my power not to swoon at his feet when Gabe introduces us.

"It's a good thing he's playing Bond," Oliver says. "He'll finally be able to show the world that he's more than just a pretty face."

"I'm only pretty when I'm not standing next to you," Gabe makes sure to add.

I feel like Melissa Williams must have on the set of *Tommy Jacks,* with two of the hottest men in Hollywood, each playing the other's wingman.

While the two of them catch up—it's been almost six months since they've seen each other last, doing press for *Tommy Jacks*—I just stand there, trying not to hyperventilate at the absurd, wonderful comedy my life has become.

I don't catch the slightest whiff of jealousy. They're genuinely happy to see each other, and when Oliver's responsibilities at the premiere are finished, he invites Gabe—and by proxy, me—to join him at the after-party.

We're swept away to a nearby restaurant, where the entire place has been reserved for us. For Oliver.

He holds court, charming us all, and I drink one too many of the bespoke cocktails that are circulating—drinks that each have an orchid or a real silk umbrella or a Swarovski crystal–encrusted swizzle stick.

The whole evening is delightful and luxurious and Gabe is the ultimate platonic date.

"How crazy is this?" he asks me at one point, as if this is new to him as well. As if it still dazzles him.

It's hard not to be enamored with the future Bond.

I'm aware, the whole time, that I'm breathing rarified air.

That I'm beyond lucky to be spending my evening listening to Oliver Matthias and Gabe Parker talk about their favorite movies and actors they idolize. That they are wearing designer suits and my dress is safety-pinned to my bra. We're not even the same species, but tonight, they're letting me pretend that we are.

—

Then

Chapter 11

"HE'S GOING TO TRY AND FUCK YOU," JO SAID, PUTTING THE finishing touches on my face. "Though, I wouldn't take it personally."

That was Jo in a nutshell. If good or exciting things happened to me, I shouldn't take it personally. It wasn't me—it was circumstance. The job at *Broad Sheets*? They were just doing my old professor a favor. My relationship with Jeremy? Being with me was easier than trying to date in L.A. The Gabe Parker assignment? Everyone else was probably busy and it would be impossible for me to screw it up.

Jo and I weren't really friends.

We were roommates who gossiped viciously and used each other for favors.

It wasn't healthy, but I didn't have anyone else besides Jeremy.

My friends from high school had either lost touch or moved away and my friends from undergrad had gone home or stayed in New York. I hadn't been close to anyone in grad school besides Jeremy. I saw my family, but that wasn't the type of relationship I needed the most. I was alone in L.A., unsure of how to be an adult in the city I'd grown up in.

Jo was jealous and demanding. She didn't like Jeremy at all.

"He wears his jeans too tight," she'd say. "That means he's insecure about his dick size."

She would try to get me to confirm or deny those statements and called me prudish when I declined to discuss the size of my boyfriend's penis with her.

But she could do a smoky eye better than anyone I knew and I needed to look amazing tonight.

"You'll have to tell me all the details," she said. "I bet he's a total freak in bed. Celebrities always are. I heard one story about that former child actor, Don What's-his-name, who has his bodyguard pick up women at clubs and take them back to a hotel suite. When they get there, they have to sign an NDA, then they have to shave off all their body hair before they can even go into the bedroom, where he's lying on the bed wearing headphones. They can't say anything, they just have to hop on and fuck him while facing away. When he's done, they leave. No talking at all."

I would have dismissed that story as another one of Jo's bullshit "secrets of Hollywood" except I'd heard exactly the same thing from someone who didn't even know Jo.

"I don't think there will be any story to tell," I said. "I'm not his type."

She rolled her eyes. "Guys like that aren't having sex with you because they're *attracted* to you," she said. "They do it because they can. Because they know *you* want it. And that's what gets them off. Their type is anyone who can stroke their ego. And they care way more about *that* getting stroked than their dick."

I knew that if I said "Gabe's not like that," she would have laughed me out of the apartment. Because though I did believe it, I also knew it was ridiculous. Even after spending several hours together, I didn't *know* Gabe. He was an assignment. And a performer. There was no way I could truly trust anything he said to me.

"Is he picking you up?" Jo asked.

"*Someone* is picking me up," I said.

When I'd texted Gabe last night, I'd tried to be cool and casual about it.

If the offer stands, I'd love to see Oliver's new movie, I'd written.

He'd texted me back almost immediately saying he'd make it happen. Then I was put in contact with someone named Debbie at his agent's office, who had told me that a car would be coming to my house to get me at six.

"Hmm," Jo said, her face contorted into an exaggerated frown.

"What?"

"Maybe this is just for the interview," she said. "Maybe it's not a date."

I hadn't thought it was a date—he was Gabe Parker, after all—but I also hadn't thought of it as a continuation of the interview.

"Or, you might not even see him," Jo said. "Maybe he thought you'd write something nice if he got you tickets to the premiere."

I felt a slow sinking in my stomach, the same sensation I'd gotten when I discovered that everyone knew that Jeremy had been cheating on me back at Iowa. That realization that you're the last to know and feeling like a complete and total fool.

Jo could be right.

This whole thing could just be a way for Gabe to butter me up so I'd put together a complimentary piece. The thought rankled me, because I had already planned on writing a flattering article. I didn't need to be bribed to do that.

"He'll probably say hello," Jo said. "But I bet you won't be sitting with him during the movie and you definitely won't walk the red carpet with him." She looked at me in the mirror. "You weren't thinking you would, were you?"

"No," I said.

I might have been.

"You'll probably be home by ten," she said. "I'll wait up."

I didn't say anything, just sat there, wallowing in my own foolish feelings. Of course, I wasn't going to walk the red carpet. Of course, Gabe wasn't going to spend the evening of his friend's premiere hanging out with me.

"What are you wearing?" Jo asked, using a wide, fluffy brush to apply bronzer.

"The polka dot dress that I wore to Greg's wedding last year," I said.

Jo gagged.

"That thing?" she asked. "Please don't. It's hideous. They won't let you on the red carpet wearing it."

That "thing" was one of my favorite dresses, but now I knew I wouldn't be able to wear it without thinking of Jo hacking dramatically into her palm.

And apparently, I *would* be allowed on the red carpet?

"People will be wearing gowns, Chani." Jo tapped my forehead with the handle of her brush. "You can't wear some Forever 21 sack."

I wanted to push her hand away but she wasn't done with my lips. Instead I sat there, listening to her list all the dresses in my closet that she hated.

As much as I disliked her messaging, she was right about the dress code. People *would* be wearing gowns. I read Go Fug Yourself. I knew how actresses dressed to attend events like this—especially when the event was centered around a lush, romantic period film. The looks would be dramatic, to say the least.

I had a blue dress. A vintage dress that could be from the 1940s or the 1980s, with wide, theatrical shoulders and a slim skirt that flared just a little at the knee. The fabric was velvet, dotted with tiny crystal beads that glittered under the light.

It wouldn't compare to the designer gowns that most of the actresses would be wearing, but it was dramatic and eye-catching. I could brush my hair to the side à la Veronica Lake, and wear the silver pumps that pinched my toes but looked amazing.

But when I put the dress on, just as I was zipping it up, thinking that it looked pretty good, I heard a damning ripping sound.

"Fuck." I turned to the side and found the source.

A tear right along the zipper, exposing my bra.

I stood there for a moment, wondering if I could just shove my purse under my arm and not breathe too deeply for the rest of the night.

No. That wouldn't do.

But neither would any of the other dresses in my closet.

I was supposed to meet Gabe in forty minutes. I had to leave in ten.

This was my only option. I had to make it work.

Twisting uncomfortably, I managed to pinch the fabric together. Pulling a safety pin out of my desk drawer, and contorting enough that I was starting to sweat, I was able to pin the torn fabric to my bra. If anyone looked closely, it was a mess, but if I kept my arm down, kept my purse tucked against it, and prayed for dim lighting, I could probably make it through the evening without tearing the dress further and exposing the world's most boring black bra.

Jo was watching TV on the couch. My toes were already hurting by the time I reached the bottom of the stairs, but the shoes suited the dress so perfectly that I decided to ignore the pain.

"Wow," Jo said. "You look absolutely incredible."

For all her sharp comments and condescending compliments, when Jo really liked something, she could be effusive with praise. It was what kept me from completely despising her.

"He's totally going to fuck you," she said.

"Thank you?" I said.

"Use protection. He's probably filthy."

I shook my head, both flattered and disgusted.

My phone rang. It was the car service.

"I have to go," I said. "Thanks for doing my makeup."

"Remember everything," she said. "I'll want to hear every detail. Shaved body hair and all."

GO FUG YOURSELF

THE FASHION AT THE *SHARED HEARTS* PREMIERE

Oliver Matthias Checks the Box

DELICIOUS, DEBONAIR OLIVER MATTHIAS ONCE AGAIN delighted the senses with a green checked suit perfectly befitting his leading man status. *This* is how you show up to *your* movie when everyone has been talking about the part you didn't get. You put on an attention-getting suit, have your hair styled to perfection, and bring one of the most beautiful women on the planet—Isabella Barris—as your date.

Even better if that date can't seem to take her hands off you, while wearing a stunning vintage Versace gown.

Jacinda Lockwood Is Pretty Galore

JACINDA LOCKWOOD CAME TO BE SEEN. THE NEWEST BOND girl stepped onto the red carpet in a neon teal reproduction of a classic Gucci dress—practically daring you to stare directly at her. I couldn't—it was like looking into the sun. Though, I did see enough to suggest that the strapless number—in December!—might have benefited from a bit of a hoick.

Chapter 12

GABE WAS WAITING FOR ME AT THE END OF THE RED CARPET. He looked incredible, and when he gave me a hug—which I tried desperately not to sink into—I could smell his cologne. It was probably very expensive and smelled very, very nice. Like the world's most exclusive cedar tree.

There was also a hint of whisky on his breath.

"You made it," he said, as if there was some universe in which I might not show. "You look gorgeous."

I twisted on my heels a little, flustered not just at the compliment but at the way he was looking at me. He leaned back as he did it, as if he was trying to see all of me at once, and then ran his hand over his mouth.

My legs started trembling.

"You look gorgeous too," I said.

He laughed.

"Come on," he said, taking my hand and tucking it into the crook of his elbow.

So.

Jo was wrong.

The one thing I couldn't quite discern was whether or not Gabe considered this a continuation of our interview. If he was planning to show me his world just so I could write about it, or if this was something else. Something more.

It seemed very unlikely that it was, but still.

I needed to know.

But the moment we were led down the red carpet, I was hit with a wall of noise and lights so intense and abrupt that I stumbled, and almost fell.

Gabe's arm went around my waist, pulling me up against him.

"Gabe! Gabe!" people were shouting.

Flashbulbs were going off around us, and that's all I could see, an unending strobe of bright, white pops of light. I tried to smile, even though I felt like I was baring my teeth more than making any sort of attractive expression. It was as if I'd forgotten how to grin normally.

"We'll just give them a few shots," Gabe said, leaning his head toward mine, his cheek almost grazing my forehead. "Take a deep breath, and smile."

I nodded, following his instructions, as the crowd threw questions at us.

"Who's your date?"

"Are you excited about Bond?"

"When do you start filming?"

"Who's your date?"

"Who are you wearing?"

"Does Oliver know you're coming tonight?"

"Who's your date?"

Gabe didn't answer any of them, just kept his arm around my waist, lifting his other hand to wave. I'd noticed, though, that his posture had changed as we stepped in front of the cameras. He was standing straighter, his chest facing the photographers, his chin angled a different way.

He was posing. Subtly, but he knew what he was doing.

I tried to do the same as I held on to him.

"Come on," Gabe said after what seemed like a lifetime.

The red carpet was long, but we walked the rest of it at a fast clip, ignoring the other photographers and camera crews that were set up, assistants trying to wave us over while their bosses stretched out their microphones. Gabe's arm was firm around my waist, and I could feel his biceps flexing as he propelled me toward the theater. It was a miracle I didn't trip over my own feet.

"I'm just here to support Oliver" was the only sound bite Gabe would give.

It wasn't until we got inside and the doors shut behind us, cutting off the overwhelming cacophony, that Gabe released me.

"Wow," I said, suddenly exhausted.

"Yeah," Gabe said.

The smile and the pose had disappeared. He ran a hand across the back of his neck.

"It's a lot," he said.

"It's not so bad," I said.

He raised an eyebrow.

"Okay," I said. "It's a lot. How do you cope?"

"Practice," he said. "And this helps . . ."

He unbuttoned his jacket, opening it to reveal a slim silver flask tucked into his inside pocket. He took it out and unscrewed the top.

"Want some?"

It explained the whisky on his breath.

"Sure," I said.

He passed it over and I took a sip. I liked whisky and it was good stuff. It burned, in the best possible way, warmth wrapping around my throat and rib cage.

I gave it back and he took a long swig.

"I have to ask you something," I said.

"Anything," he said.

I was certain he didn't really mean that. And a little worried if he did.

"Is this . . ." I paused. "Is this still part of the interview?"

He had lifted the flask again but froze for a second before putting it to his lips and taking another drink.

"Do you want it to be?" he asked.

I didn't know.

We stared at each other for a moment. Then Gabe seemed to finish off what was left in his flask.

"Fuck it," he said. "Write what you want."

He sounded a little angry and a lot resigned.

"I—"

"Gabe!"

I turned toward the familiar voice and found a familiar face.

A face I'd grown up with, but always with the glass of the TV between us.

Oliver Matthias.

"Ollie," Gabe said, his expression going from tight and shuttered to warm and cheerful.

The two of them exchanged hugs—not the bro-y backslapping kind of hugs that most men usually engaged in as if they were afraid any display of actual affection was an affront to masculinity, but a close, arms-tight-around-the-shoulders, cheek-to-cheek kind of hug.

"I'm glad you came," Oliver said.

"Wouldn't miss it for anything," Gabe said.

I stood there, my hands clasped, not sure what to do, when Oliver's gaze swung over to me.

"Hello," he said.

"This is Chani," Gabe said. "She's interviewing me for *Broad Sheets*."

"I thought that interview was yesterday," Oliver said.

Interesting. Gabe and Oliver were close enough that they had spoken about the interview, and Oliver remembered that it was yesterday.

If there was any animosity between the two of them over the Bond role—or any truth to the rumors that Gabe had stolen Jacinda from Oliver—I couldn't sense it. Then again, they were both actors.

"We're extending the interview," Gabe said.

"I can see that," Oliver said.

The look he gave me was one that I'd given numerous times. It was the kind of look you gave the dirtbag guys your high school friends were dating when you'd heard rumors that they were cheaters.

It was a "watch yourself" kind of look.

Was *I* the dirtbag in this situation? Did Oliver think he needed to protect Gabe from me?

Maybe he did. Just like waitress Madison had tried yesterday. I was, after all, here because I was chasing a story. But I didn't like the feeling that I was someone to be wary of.

Especially when it was Oliver Matthias—child star, leading man, teenage crush—essentially telling me that he had his eyes on me.

The lights in the lobby blinked.

"Time for the show," Oliver said. "I hope you enjoy."

"Thank you," I said.

He gave me a nod but then turned back to Gabe.

"You'll come to the after-party?"

"Will there be beer?"

Oliver rolled his eyes.

"Of course I'll be there," Gabe said.

"You can come too," Oliver said to me, politely but with no real warmth.

"Oh, okay," I said.

The lobby lights flashed again.

"We'll see you after," Gabe said.

We.

I practically floated into the theater alongside Gabe.

As we walked to our seats, people turned and stared.

It wasn't something I was used to. Especially the confusion and disappointment I could see on their faces when they looked from Gabe to me. It was almost comical how shocked they were. "He's with *her*?"

Part of me wanted to correct them—to assure them that no, we weren't together, that they should believe that the rules of the universe that keep everyday and beautiful people apart were still very much in place—but the other part of me wanted to take his arm and snuggle close to him. Just to fuck with them.

As we sat, I felt more and more out of place, especially when several people turned to do the classic "stretch and stare" move. They weren't fooling anyone, especially when I saw one of them do a double take. It was half hilarious, half insulting.

I hunched my shoulders, wishing I was shorter.

"I don't belong here," I said under my breath.

"Don't be ridiculous," Gabe said.

Apparently, I hadn't been quiet enough.

"You're impressive," he said.

I blinked.

"Me?"

"Yeah, you," he said. "You write all these articles and you have your blog and you're also doing lots of other stuff too. You're smart and creative. That's impressive."

I wanted to argue with him. Wanted to tell him that among my peers I wasn't impressive at all. I didn't have a book contract, I didn't have a readership. I had to scramble and hustle for every single interview I got, had to prove myself each and every time.

But the expression on his face was so genuine, so earnest, that I held my tongue and let his words sink in. And when I did, I realized, with a certain pleasant surprise, that to someone like Gabe, I might actually seem impressive. Because I made my living off my writing. It wasn't a good living by anyone's standards but I was surviving. I didn't have to work a day job. My writing was supporting me just enough that I didn't need to do anything else.

I didn't know what to say.

"Thank you" is what I finally settled on, just as the lights went down.

Film Fans

BREAKING OUR *SHARED HEARTS*

[EXCERPT]

By Evan Arnold

THERE'S SOMETHING THAT ALL US CYNICAL, STONE-HEARTED reviewers seem to agree on when it comes to the latest Oliver Matthias film: Bring tissues. The movie is a tearjerker to the highest degree and it earns each and every one of those sniffles it pulls out of you.

If you saw him in *Tommy Jacks* and thought, *Wow, this is acting,* well, viewers, you haven't seen nothing yet.

Shared Hearts is a lush romantic film with an astonishingly talented cast, but Matthias stands out. He always stands out.

He will break your heart as Jonathan Hale, a down-on-his-luck salesman in postwar Britain, who stumbles into an ill-fated romance with Barbara Glory, who may or may not be a former spy.

Matthias is making a point with this movie. He's telling the audience—which presumably contains the very same people that made the world's worst casting choice—"*This* could have been your Bond."

One can only imagine the regret they're feeling right now.

Chapter 13

THE MOVIE WAS *AMAZING*.

"You liked it?" Gabe asked as we were pulled into the crowd of people leaving the theater.

My hand was against my throat—had been there for the last thirty minutes. By sheer force of will and a lifetime of learning how to suppress the embarrassment of public tears, I'd kept from crying, but I still felt raw after the experience.

"It was . . ." I swallowed. "It was very good."

I looked over at Gabe, expecting to see jealousy, but there was none.

"He's a legend," he said. "If you think watching him is an experience, try acting next to him. It's a master class in technique."

I managed a nod.

"Wanna head to the after-party?" he asked.

I remembered Oliver's face when he'd extended an invitation to me. Polite, but not really interested. He'd included me because of Gabe, but he didn't trust me.

"I don't know . . ." I said.

"Come on," Gabe said. "It'll be fun. And we can tell Ollie how you almost cried. He'll love that."

It was hard to say no to Gabe. And the truth was I didn't want to. I was having a good time.

And why wouldn't I? One of the most beautiful men in the

world—my personal celebrity crush—was treating me like I belonged. It was an intoxicating feeling.

"Okay," I said.

I also took the article into consideration, even though I was torn. Gabe had given me permission to write about this, but I knew that he had been drinking and maybe it wasn't quite ethical to take him up on his carelessly offered, ill-thought-out concession.

I also knew that I was getting access that any writer in my shoes would kill for.

Gabe was a big boy, I told myself. He knew what he was doing, and if he didn't, it wasn't my fault if I took his offer at face value.

I just had to keep telling myself that.

The after-party was at the restaurant in the hotel next to the theater. It was a big, beautiful, expensive old building that I was certain had hosted many events like this. No doubt the restaurant staff had seen things over the years.

Oliver was already there when we arrived.

"He never watches the whole movie," Gabe said. "First ten minutes and then he's out."

"Does he not like to watch himself on the big screen?" I asked.

Gabe shrugged as if to say "You'd have to ask him."

There were gorgeous, lavish flower arrangements at the center of each table and black-suited waiters carrying trays with tiny, delicate snacks and impressive-looking drinks. The room oozed money and glamour.

I tucked my bag tighter under my arm, painfully aware of the rip in the side of my dress.

"I'm going to get a drink," Gabe said. "You want something?"

"Sure," I said.

He flagged down one of the waiters so I could grab a pink ombre drink with half a pineapple stuck into the rim.

"Do you think you could snag me a whisky on the rocks?" Gabe asked the waiter.

"Of course," the waiter said.

Gabe handed him some money.

"Ask them to keep them coming, okay?"

It must have been a lot of money because the straight-faced waiter's eyes widened for a brief moment.

"Of course, Mr. Parker," he said.

Gabe put his hand on the small of my back and with a gentle push, guided me toward a round booth at the edge of the room. It had a little placard on it that read RESERVED.

I maneuvered myself and my drink into the booth, the leather squeaking as I did. I held my breath, waiting for the sound of velvet ripping, but luckily the dress held as I settled against the seat.

It wasn't until the waiter appeared with Gabe's drink that I realized how odd it was for complete strangers to know your name and how to find you in a crowd.

"Cheers," Gabe said.

We clinked our drinks together and both took a sip. The minute I tasted mine, I knew I was in trouble. It was exactly the kind of sweet, drinkable cocktail that could sneak up on you if you weren't careful.

And I wasn't feeling very careful at all.

"Are you having fun?" Gabe asked.

He had downed almost half of his drink already.

"I am," I said.

He nodded and leaned back.

"The first time is fun," he said.

"But not the second or the third or the fourth?"

I had my tape recorder in my purse but I was pretty sure Gabe would clam up the minute he saw it. I probably couldn't quote him on anything he said right now, but maybe I could still use some of it.

Gabe knocked back the rest of his drink.

"It's more fun when it's not your premiere," he said.

He was staring out across the room, and I followed his gaze to find that Jacinda Lockwood—impossible to miss in a neon teal gown, her locs swept back in a majestic updo—had just entered the restaurant.

I could tell when she saw him—when she saw me—because she paused, just for a moment. Then she turned her gorgeous, smooth shoulder toward us and gave the rest of the room the kind of smile that people paid thousands in dental bills to get.

"Are you going to say hi?" I asked, unable to help myself.

"Maybe," Gabe said.

Another drink had appeared in front of him—I'd been so busy watching Jacinda that I hadn't even noticed—and when I glanced back at her, she had faded into the dim light and crowd. I caught a glimpse or two of her un-ignorable dress, but she seemed to be keeping her distance.

"I guess you two will be spending a lot more time together on the Bond set," I said.

"Yep," he said.

"You leave in a few weeks?"

"Yep," he said.

The room itself was noisy and overwhelming, but over in our little corner booth, it was quiet. If I focused on Gabe, on my drink, the flower arrangement, and the candles burning at the center, it was a bit like being in our own world. So much so that whenever I did look up, it took a moment for my eyes to adjust and for the dark, moving blobs to become people.

"Your life is going to change," I said.

I surprised him with that.

"Yes," he finally said.

"You won't just be Gabe Parker." I spread my hands wide. "You'll be Gabe. Parker."

"That's what they tell me."

He was looking down at his glass, the ice clinking as he swirled the remaining whisky. I was certain a refill would be arriving momentarily. Somehow, I'd finished my own drink, and was nibbling on the pineapple, feeling loose and warm.

"I know all the reasons people think I shouldn't play Bond," Gabe said.

A role he didn't deserve—or so he'd said to me yesterday.

He held up his hand, ticking off each reason by lifting a finger.

"I'm not a big enough star. I kissed a man in a play in college. I'm

American. I'm not Oliver Matthias." He looked at his hand, and raised a fifth finger. "I'm too dumb."

"Too dumb?" I echoed, even though I knew exactly what he was talking about.

"You know," he said, attention still focused on his extended fingers. "I'm only good at playing hunky, dim-witted characters that get killed off in the first thirty minutes."

I didn't say anything. I'd read the article.

As expected, another glass of whisky had appeared on the table, delivered from the shadowy place beyond our cozy circle of light. They'd brought me another drink as well.

I knew I shouldn't, but I drank anyways.

"I don't think you're dumb," I said finally.

Gabe looked at me over the rim of his glass, eyebrow raised.

"I barely made it out of high school," he said. "Went to community college on a football scholarship." He knocked his knuckles against his temple. "Probably lost whatever few brain cells I still had on the field before I got injured. Never read them big authors like Hemingway or Fitzgerald or Salinger." His voice got real low and slow. "I cain't even pronounce the name of the guy who wrote *Lolita*."

"Nabokov," I said without thinking.

Gabe gestured toward me as if I'd just proven his point.

"There are different kinds of intelligence," I said, not exactly sure why I was stroking his ego right now.

"Oh, really?" Gabe asked, that suspicious eyebrow now permanently arched. "I'm pretty sure you're either smart or you're not."

I shook my head.

"Emotional intelligence," I said. "That's a thing."

"That's like telling someone they have a good personality when they ask if they're attractive."

"I'm sure you have experience with that," I countered. Sarcastically.

We looked at each other. He was annoyed. I was annoyed.

"The movie will prove them wrong," I said, as if I knew anything.

I didn't.

The truth was I wanted to believe I knew him. Because if I did, this little moment—this evening—was more than just the article. I could convince myself that something was happening between us. That the way he looked at me in my dress, the way he'd put his hand against my back, the way we were here in our dark little corner were all indications of something more.

Jacinda had appeared out of the crowd again, but this time she and Gabe were doing their level best to avoid eye contact. And I was doing *my* level best to pretend I didn't see them ignoring each other.

I realized I was a little drunk.

It wasn't unexpected—I'd had two enormous, boozy pineapple drinks and only two tiny, delicate, delicious crab cakes since we'd arrived at the after-party.

"I watched *The Philadelphia Story*," Gabe said.

I sat up.

"And?" I asked. "What did you think?"

Gabe sighed.

"Oh," I said.

Maybe *this* would be the thing that actually chipped away at my crush on him.

"It was amazing," he said.

"Oh," I said.

"The timing, the dialogue, the chemistry." Gabe threw up his hands. "How can any other comedy even begin to compare?"

I grinned, leaning forward.

"It is good, isn't it?"

"Good?" Gabe shook his head. "It's perfection."

"Best comedy ever made," I said, lifting my third pink pineapple drink.

I couldn't remember when it had appeared.

My lips were buzzing, which was a telltale sign that I'd already had enough to drink, but I was thirsty and the cocktail was *so* good.

"I saw a list of the hundred best comedies and *The Philadelphia Story* was number thirty-eight! Thirty! Eight!" I said, pressing my finger on the table for emphasis.

"Ridiculous," Gabe said. "It should at least be in the top three."

I shook my head. It felt very, very heavy.

"It should be number one." I made a wide, swooping gesture with my finger.

I was definitely drunk.

"It should be," Gabe said, but I could tell he was placating me a bit. Teasing me.

I didn't mind.

The heavy slope of his eyes indicated that he was getting toasted too, but he seemed to be a quiet, introspective drunk, while I was an exuberant, loudmouthed one.

"You know what the worst part about that list was?" I asked.

He smiled.

"I don't," he said. "But I hope you'll tell me."

"I will!" I said, finger still extended. "The worst part of that list was that it was full of not-funny movies made by not-funny people. *Pulp Fiction* is not a comedy! And don't even get me started on *Annie Hall*."

Interest sparked in Gabe's eyes. He leaned forward, elbows on the table, arms crossed. If *I* leaned forward, our noses could touch.

"Why?" he asked. "What's wrong with *Annie Hall*?"

I knew I should stop talking. Instead, I took another long gulp of my drink and just kept right on going.

"Well, okay, I've never seen it—"

"You've never seen *Annie Hall*?" Gabe asked.

"Woody Allen sucks," I said. "I won't watch his movies."

"Wow," Gabe said. "What did he ever do to you?"

"Woody Allen is a creep," I said, warming up to my own indignation. "He hates women. Obviously has some fucked-up obsession with girls, given that he routinely casts himself—a grown-ass man—opposite teenagers and, oh yeah, married his girlfriend's daughter! And even if you ignored all of that—which you shouldn't—his movies are bad and boring. They're the same thing over and over, gross wish fulfillment where he gets to monologue about how weird and awkward he is while young blond girls fall in love with him for literally no reason at all. Plus, he *hates* Jewish women. He uses his movies to promote *him* and make himself the arbiter of Jewish humor and talent while perpetuating hateful stereotypes about how Jewish women are shrill and controlling. He's not clever, he's not interesting, and he's not talented."

There I went again. Gabe was just trying to talk about movies and I had to go off on some feminist rant about how much I hated Woody Allen (which I did).

Before I could apologize, Oliver appeared at the end of our table. His tie was loose, his top button undone, and he'd lost his vest someplace between the premiere and the after-party. He still looked devastatingly handsome.

"What are you two talking about?" he asked.

"Why Woody Allen is a piece of shit," Gabe said.

I barely resisted putting my face in my hands. Who knew what Oliver thought about the director? Maybe he had worked with him or wanted to work with him in the future. Maybe he knew him. Or admired him. Most people loved him—or at least, they loved his work and ignored all the other stuff.

"Oh," Oliver said.

There was a long, long pause.

"He *is* a piece of shit, isn't he?"

I stared at him. It seemed I'd gone from dangerous dirtbag to trash-talking confidante with dizzying speed. Not that I was complaining.

"Shove over," he said to Gabe, who did as requested.

After all, this was Oliver's night.

We shifted to make room, Oliver sliding into the booth until he was directly across from me, Gabe's knee pushing up against mine. I resisted the urge to wrap my leg around his like a vine.

"What did it for you?" Oliver asked. "His overrated movies or the faux timidity he calls a personality?"

"Both?"

Oliver laughed, slapping a hand down on the table.

When people turned to stare, he leaned forward, putting a finger to his lips as if *I* had been the one making the noise.

We all leaned forward, closer to the candle, as if we were conducting a secret meeting. If someone had told my teen self that the thing that would endear me to Oliver Matthias, the Darcy of my dreams, would be how much I hated Woody Allen, I would have thought they were insane.

As it was, I still wasn't sure this whole thing wasn't a drawn-out fever dream brought on by staring at shirtless pictures of Gabe before going to bed each night.

"We should keep that on the down low, though," Oliver said, looking around conspiratorially. "You never know when the Woody fans will attack with their battle cry of 'separate the art from the artist.'" He looked a bit sour at that. "Of course, people only care about defending terrible people making terrible art."

"Chani thinks *Angels in America* is a great play," Gabe interjected.

It seemed like a complete non sequitur, but Oliver responded with a raised eyebrow.

"Oh?"

"And she thinks people who have an issue with the fact that I kissed a man onstage in college have bigger personal problems to deal with."

The two of them were having another conversation, completely independent of our other discussion.

"I see," Oliver said.

"Yep." Gabe took a sip of his drink and leaned back against the booth.

Oliver turned his attention to me, and smiled. A real smile.

"He told me you were smart," he said.

"I am," I said, the alcohol making me bold and flushed.

Or maybe the flush came from knowing that Gabe had spoken to Oliver about me. That I had been the topic of conversation between two of the hottest, most-sought-after men in Hollywood.

And the conversation had been flattering.

I actually pinched myself. Just to double-check that all this was truly happening. I pinched hard enough to give myself a bruise.

"We like smart women," Oliver said, giving Gabe a knowing look.

I nearly choked on my drink.

Had I completely imagined the suggestive nature of that comment? Or was this one step away from revealing the kind of unexpected, secret sexual proclivities that Jo had warned me about?

I was full-on staring at Gabe and Oliver now, trying to figure out if part of their covert conversation had been sussing out whether or not I'd be down for a threesome.

While I was trying to figure out if I *would* be down for a threesome.

"Speaking of smart women . . ." Gabe glanced around. "Where's your date?"

Or a foursome.

After all, Isabella Barris was stunningly beautiful. Agreeing to be in a foursome with someone like me would be akin to charity work for her.

Oliver waved a hand. "I sent her home," he said. "She did her part and she is now released from her responsibilities."

It was subtle, but Oliver's demeanor had changed. Like the missing vest and the undone tie, I sensed that something was loosening. Relaxing.

Considering I'd thought him completely at ease when he arrived at our table, I found myself even more impressed by his acting skills.

"Where's your drink?" Gabe asked, gesturing into the dark before Oliver could respond.

"I should stop," I said, but another cocktail was in front of me before I could resist too much.

"To *Shared Hearts,*" Gabe said.

We all raised our glasses.

"Did you like it?" Oliver asked after everyone had taken a sip.

"Like it?" Gabe put a hand on his chest. "Mate, you're an icon. They should bronze you and install you in front of Grauman's."

"The accent is coming along nicely," Oliver said. "Cheers."

"Say the word," Gabe said.

"Stop it." Oliver waved his hand.

I was confused.

Even in the dim light of the restaurant, I could see that Oliver looked tired. Not physically tired, but a deeper, more emotional exhaustion seemed to be at play. With every minute he sat with us, I could see the vestiges of his performance begin to fade.

Gabe reached over and clasped him on the shoulder.

"The movie is great," he said.

"I know." Oliver closed his eyes.

Gabe gave Oliver a squeeze, an affectionate form of the Vulcan sleeper-hold.

"It made Chani cry."

"That's nice," Oliver said.

His head had gone back, resting against the wall.

"Okay." Gabe slapped his hands together.

I jumped, but Oliver just opened one eye.

"We're getting out of here," Gabe said.

"We are?" Oliver asked, opening the other eye.

"Fuck yeah," he said. "Your movie is fucking great and we're going to celebrate."

Oliver sat up.

"I thought that's what we were doing," he said, gesturing toward the rest of the room.

"I know this isn't how you want to celebrate," Gabe said. "Not at some spendy event where everyone is kissing your ass and trying to make deals."

There was a playful gleam in his eyes, and Oliver seemed to perk up.

"No?"

"No," Gabe said. "Come on. You know you want it."

"Of course, I do," Oliver said. "But do *you* want it?"

I had absolutely no idea what was going on, but my heart did skip a beat when both of them turned to look at me as if they had just remembered I was still there.

"What about her?" Oliver asked sotto voce, inclining his head toward me.

Gabe lifted a shoulder. "It's up to you."

"Can we trust her?"

I was ninety-five percent sure that this wasn't sexual. That five percent, though . . .

"I don't know."

Gabe turned to me.

My throat went dry. Oliver was gorgeous but if I had the choice, I'd choose to be with Gabe. Alone.

"Can we trust you?" Gabe asked me.

Ninety-five percent.

"Yes," I said.

THE_JAM_DOT_COM .BLOGSPOT.COM

FAILING AT FRIENDSHIP

IF THERE'S ONE SIN THAT I'D LIKE HOLLYWOOD TO ATONE for, it isn't bolstering the belief in love at first sight or having one true soulmate. It's in convincing me that the kinds of friendships I saw on the screen were possible in real life.

You know the types of friendships I'm talking about.

The secret-handshake kind of friendship. The watching-movies-snuggled-under-a-blanket, shared-pint-of-ice-cream kind of friendship. The talk-on-the-phone-for-hours-after-already-spending-the-day-together kind of friendship.

The unconditional-love, endless-well-of-support, mutual-kinship kind of friendship.

I'm pretty sure those types of friendships are completely manufactured by Hollywood.

Because if those friendships really exist, I've never been part of one.

xoChani

Chapter 14

IT TOOK ME TEN MINUTES TO FIGURE OUT WHERE WE WERE.

"Is this . . . are we in a gay club?" I asked.

I blamed the alcohol because it was very obviously a gay club.

We'd bypassed the front of the building, coming in through a side entrance where we were taken immediately to a velvet-roped VIP area just off the main dance floor. The music should have tipped me off—they never played the good pop music at regular clubs.

And then there were all the half-naked men making out around me. The men who weren't otherwise engaged were eying both my dates equally, but it seemed that only one was eying them back.

I wasn't sure I could blame the alcohol for my being oblivious to the fact that Oliver was gay. Isabella Barris had clearly been used as a very beautiful red herring tonight, and I'd bought it—hook, line, and sinker.

"We are in a gay club," Gabe confirmed.

Both he and Oliver had left their jackets somewhere. I imagined that one of the perks of being a celebrity was being able to abandon articles of clothing and knowing they'd be fine. Or just not caring.

The music was so loud that the floor was vibrating.

I didn't know what to do with the knowledge that I was at a gay club with Gabe Parker and Oliver Matthias. And that both of them knew I was writing an article on Gabe.

"Are you . . . ?" I asked.

"No," Oliver answered for him. "He's just a very, very good friend."

He was leaning over Gabe's lap, so "very, very good friend" could have had a lot of meanings. Oliver registered my raised eyebrows and quickly clarified.

"He comes here to support me," he said.

"It's not a big deal," Gabe said. "I like the music too."

Both Oliver and I gave him a look.

He shrugged.

"Do you want Jell-O shots?" he asked. "I think we need some Jell-O shots."

Unfolding his lanky frame, he got up from the couch and headed to the bar.

"He's going to get swarmed," Oliver said.

He wasn't wrong. Everywhere heads were turning as people noticed who Gabe was. There were quite a few looky-loos slowing down as they reached our section as well.

I felt a twinge of concern. It seemed impossible that news wouldn't get out.

"Is that a problem?" I asked. "For either of you?"

Oliver looked at me.

"I don't know," he said evenly. "Are you going to make it a problem?"

This wasn't a story. This was *the* story.

Gabe Parker and Oliver Matthias spending an evening out at a gay club? It would be *everywhere*.

Right now, I barely had an article. After our interview yesterday, I'd spent an hour in front of my computer trying to find my angle. Trying to find the heart of the story. In the end, all I had was proof that Gabe was exactly as handsome and charming as everyone wanted him to be. It would be great for his career—another fawning, adoring puff piece—and exactly the kind of article that everyone would forget in a couple of days.

I'd written those kinds of pieces before. I was tired of writing them. Tired of seeing my name next to headlines—headlines I never wrote, of course—that read like the same thing over and over and over again.

Jeremy had always said I lacked voice. I knew that he was trying to be helpful. That his comments—his criticisms—truly came from a place of care and concern. After all, *he* had voice. All our teachers had said so.

"Your writing is ordinary," he would say. "It doesn't have personality."

The worst part was that I knew he was right.

I just didn't know what to do about it.

I wanted more. I wanted to work more. I wanted to write more. To be honest and real in my words. To put something out there that I was proud of. That felt like *me*.

It had been a long time since I'd written anything close to that, and even then, it hadn't impressed anyone.

This was my chance.

But.

"Can we trust you?" Gabe had asked.

I realized that I couldn't do it. I didn't have the stomach for it.

I didn't want Oliver to hate me. I didn't want Gabe to hate me. Maybe I was being naïve, thinking that I was here because of some genuine connection between us, but even if there wasn't, I didn't want them to think I was the kind of person who would do anything for a story.

I didn't want to be that kind of person. Not even if it meant I'd be a better writer.

"It's not a problem," I said to Oliver.

He relaxed.

"I'm not hiding," he said. "I just want to control the narrative."

"But won't someone here tell?" I asked.

"I'm a regular," Oliver said. "Have you ever heard about it?"

I shook my head.

"And Gabe's not . . ."

"No," Oliver said. "But I think you know that."

As if he could hear us—an impossibility given the volume of the music and the size of the room and all the people in between—Gabe turned to look back at us from the bar. Both Oliver and I lifted a hand. Gabe grinned, but didn't look away.

Instead, he did the same thing he'd done when he saw me on the red carpet—a long, agonizingly slow look—from the top of my head to the tips of my aching toes.

In any other circumstance, I knew what that look meant.

But he was Gabe Parker. And I was me.

I'd seen the way heads had turned when we walked into the after-party. I'd seen the way people had stared when we'd been at the restaurant yesterday. The way people on the red carpet had screamed and reached for him. The way club goers were looking at us now. Hell, I'd even seen the way the real estate agent had all but promised him a different form of commission if he put me back in my car and let her show him the hot tub on the roof.

He was a hunk. A bona fide, certified hunk. He could have anyone he wanted.

I was a tall, flat-chested writer with cute little cellulite dimples on her cute little butt. I plucked a hair off my chin the other day. I still broke out all across my shoulders. I didn't wax.

We were from different worlds.

And yet, he was staring at me.

"Did you get your story?" Oliver asked.

"Huh?"

Gabe was walking back toward us with a tray.

"Here," he said.

"Cheers," Oliver said, and this time, we clinked Jell-O shots.

Even though I'd already had three and a half cocktails, and a swig of flask whisky, I swallowed the Jell-O shot—cherry—and immediately felt like I was in college again.

Gabe leaned back against the velvet couch, his arm stretched out across the back of it. He nodded his head toward the space between us. Moving there would mean sitting close to him, snuggling up against his long, hard body, his arm already in position so he could pull me even closer. He could put his hand in my hair if he wanted. If I wanted.

I wanted.

I really, really did.

I took another shot, but didn't move. My lips felt bee-stung.

"Now that you're done with your research, let's have some fun," Oliver said.

He passed me another shot. I took it. Downed it.

I felt *good*.

Oliver smiled. "Come on." He pulled me up, and I eagerly followed.

Gabe stayed where he was, only shifting to move his long, long legs so we could pass.

"He never leaves the couch when we go out," Oliver said.

He swung me around as if we were ballroom dancing instead of in the middle of a gay nightclub where everyone was half-naked, sweaty, and about one Jell-O shot away from retreating to a corner to fuck.

"Oliver—"

"Ollie."

"Ollie." I'd just connected a few things that I hoped weren't connected at all. "Does Bond know about this?"

I gestured to the room, to him. Remembering that I was here because of a job was stabilizing. Necessary.

He went still for just a moment. Enough to know that I was right. Then he began swaying along with the music.

"They wanted me to sign a morality clause," he said.

"A morality clause?"

"It was all very vague and lawyer-y, but the gist was that if I did something that they could say was 'morally objectionable,' I would be fired immediately," Ollie said. "It was pretty clear that they didn't want me coming out."

I wrinkled my nose, not sure what to say. It seemed ridiculous that anyone would care, but I knew they did. And the way that articles kept bringing up Gabe's role in *Angels in America,* from when he was in *college,* made it abundantly clear that there were plenty of people who cared a lot.

"*He* didn't know," Ollie said.

I tilted my head.

"Gabe." Ollie jerked his chin in his direction.

He was still on the couch, his long fingers drumming along his knee.

"He knew about me being gay. But he didn't know that they reached out to me first. About Bond," Ollie said. "When he found out, he threatened to quit."

We spun around, the glittered mirror ball throwing light across our faces.

"I thought about it," Ollie said. "I told myself that I wasn't ready to come out yet so why not just stay in the closet for a while longer?"

He tilted his head back.

"But signing something called a 'morality clause'? Allowing them to equate my sexuality with an issue of morality?" He looked back down at me. "No. I couldn't do that."

I nodded, but I was lost in thought.

Ollie stopped spinning, stopped both of us moving.

"Please," he said.

I knew what he was asking. This time, I didn't hesitate.

"I won't," I said.

He nodded, but I could tell he wasn't completely sure if he could trust me.

"My story is about Gabe," I said. "We went to see your movie and it was great. He's a fan of your work—you support him. You're friends. Good friends. There's no competition between the two of you—in fact, you insisted that he's the right person for the job."

Ollie let out a breath.

"Thank you," he said.

We danced, practically cheek to cheek, him holding my hand between us like an old-fashioned movie couple. Nothing about it should have felt normal, but somehow it did.

Of course, I was slow dancing in a gay club with Oliver Matthias. Of course.

"My manager thinks it will ruin my career," he said. "I'm afraid he's right."

I couldn't promise him otherwise.

"Or maybe it will just make you even more famous and fabulously unattainable," I said.

He laughed.

"I don't want to be brave for coming out. I don't want to be a hero or an icon or anything. I just want to be an actor. Maybe a director someday. A famous one. A famous, handsome, rich one. I don't want to be the famous, handsome, rich, *gay* one."

"I get it," I said. "I'm used to being the token Jewish friend."

"You're from L.A.," he said.

I nodded. "Still."

He let out a low whistle, barely audible over the music.

"A kid in middle school asked me where my horns were," I said.

He laughed, a dark humor kind of laugh.

"Everyone would want to know when I first 'knew,'" he said.

"They want to know what I think about Santa Claus."

"They'd want to know who the catcher is."

I cringed.

"I'd make a joke about circumcision," I said. "But I'd rather cut this conversation short."

Ollie laughed. And laughed. And laughed.

It wasn't that great of a joke, but we were both well on our way to being very drunk and maybe becoming friends and things that were usually horrible could seem funny and fun when you felt like that.

I wasn't sure what I'd done to deserve this—Ollie's apparent trust and friendship—but I'd take it.

"I like you," he said.

It was hard to separate Ollie the person from Oliver the movie star and I couldn't deny the rush of endorphins I got knowing that Oliver the movie star—the person I'd been watching since I was a preteen—liked me.

"And I think he likes you too," he said.

He spun me around so I got a quick look at Gabe, still sitting on the couch. He was watching us.

"He's jealous," Ollie said, and put his hand on my hip.

"He is not," I said. "He's Gabe Parker."

"You think he doesn't have feelings?" Ollie asked. "He's an actor. He has all of them."

"Did you just quote *The First Wives Club* at me?"

"Did you just know that I quoted *The First Wives Club* at you?"

We grinned at each other.

"I knew it," he said. "I have impeccable taste in people."

"I'll accept that," I said.

He swung me under his arm just as the music began to cross fade into a new song. A song I knew very well. It jolted through me the same moment that I realized exactly how drunk I was.

"I love this song!" I shouted over the music.

"Me too!"

It was one of those classic, pure pop songs, a song that made you sing along while leaping into the air, hands waving wildly. There was no way to avoid it. The music became part of you. It *became* you. When a song like that came on, you were nothing more than a vessel for its splendor.

I was drunk enough and daring enough that as I shook my hips, I swiveled in the direction of the VIP area. Of Gabe. He was still sitting there, his long fingers stroking the velvet back of the couch, as if to tell me that there was still a place for me there. That if I came back and sat down next to him, that hand could be on my arm. Along my neck. Against my jaw.

Instead, I gave my shoulders a little shimmy and stretched my hands out toward him. Beckoning him.

"He never dances," Ollie said, wrapping his arms around me, the two of us forming a two-headed, four-armed creature, both of us reaching out to Gabe. "He won't come."

"His loss," I said, and turned around in Ollie's arms. "We're having a great time."

I focused my attention on dancing, but Ollie was distracted.

"Bloody. Hell," he said.

I turned and there he was. Gabe. On the dance floor. In front of me.

"Hey," he said.

At least, that's what I thought he said. It was so loud that I couldn't be sure, but he'd said *something*, his lips curved in a smile after mouthing something that probably wasn't any more complicated than "hey."

But it felt like he'd said a lot more. Just in standing there. In being on the dance floor with me and Ollie.

Ollie who was practically losing his shit over Gabe being there.

"You did it," he said, hands on my shoulders, giving me a shake. "You saucy Jewish siren—you got him on his feet."

Gabe rolled his eyes at Ollie and then gave me a look. One that said that he'd maybe prefer being on his knees. In front of me.

No. I was being ridiculous. Even though I was drunk, and he was drunk, I was still somewhat tethered to reality. Gabe was a flirt. It wasn't personal. It was an instinct. A reflex.

Still, my own knees went weak, and the combination of the intense sexual tension suddenly crackling between us and the shots, which had made me brave enough to summon him, had me jerking forward in a way that was neither sexy nor seductive.

It did make Gabe reach for me.

A smarter girl would have planned it exactly that way. She probably would have made it more charming and seamless, a slight swoon right into Gabe's arms.

As it was, I jerked and flopped like a dying fish, into his arms and then right back out.

He gave me a strange look—who could blame him—and then shrugged.

The music was blaring—how was this song still going on?—so I let that and the alcohol take over. My shoulders took the lead, swaying as the music flowed through me. No one in my life could ever accuse me of being a good dancer, but I was enthusiastic and I loved it. *Loved* to dance.

Ollie was a good dancer, giving himself completely to the music, head thrown back, arms up, hips hitting each bass note like they were playing the drums themselves. I could sense that Gabe was still there, but I couldn't look at him. If he was a dorky dancer—like most straight men—I wasn't ready for my fantasy of him to dissolve completely.

The music shifted and switched over. It was another great song—whoever was in charge of the music tonight must have just plugged the speaker directly into my memories. It was the perfect nostalgia overload—all my favorite pop songs from college. From a time when I actually went out on a regular basis—when I could drink vodka–Red Bulls and still go to class the next day. I knew that I'd be hurting tomorrow, but the music was so good and I felt so good that I didn't want to stop.

I didn't have moves, but I had a lot of hair, so I swung it around, loving the way it felt against the low-cut back of my dress. A little intimacy that I could share with myself. I was having fun.

I swung my arms out at a key moment and hit something hard.

Gabe's stomach.

I'd done my best to avoid touching him. It was unprofessional.

But I wanted to. Wanted *him*.

Wanted him with such an intensity that it scared me a bit.

I pulled my hand back, but he'd already caught me. With a move that was impossibly smooth, he gave my wrist a gentle yank and spun me into his arms.

All the touching I'd tried to avoid was happening now. From chest to knees. We were pressed up against each other, my hand trapped between us, his palm flat against my lower back. He felt good. He felt incredibly good.

I stared at his throat. There was a little sweat there and I could smell whatever extremely expensive cologne he was wearing mixed with something more primal. More like him.

I was too drunk. Not just on alcohol, but on the intoxication of being close to someone I'd lusted after for a long, long time. Someone who'd felt untouchable. Unattainable.

Someone who was definitely getting hard.

I could feel the unmistakable press of him against my stomach. Slowly, I looked away from the collar of Gabe's shirt and upward toward his face.

He was watching me. His gaze was intense, unwavering, and I could *feel* him take a breath—could feel how unsteady it was.

My heart was pounding so hard it was almost painful.

The music felt like a thick steam, surrounding us, capturing us, isolating us.

The dance floor was dark—not that dark—but dark enough. I didn't know where Ollie was. He could have been right behind me, he could have been across the room. I couldn't focus on anything but Gabe's face. On his eyes, staring, fixed, unblinking.

I'd practically memorized his face on-screen. Thought I knew it. But this was something new. Something different.

He still wasn't quite real, even though I could feel him—*all* of him—against me. It felt like a fantasy. A really, *really* great fantasy, but a fantasy nonetheless.

There was a voice in the back of my head that kept trying to break through the surreal haze that had settled around me. Reminding me that I was a reporter and Gabe was my subject and there were a whole bunch of questionable power dynamics at play here.

I'd been so worried that he'd think *I'd* do anything to get a good story that I hadn't stopped to consider that he might not have any reservations about doing it himself.

Then his hips pressed harder against mine. For a moment, I thought I might be falling, might be losing my balance, but then I realized he was moving in time with the music, his hips swaying forward, back, side to side.

He was a *good* dancer.

He wasn't flashy or enthusiastic or even that demonstrative. He was subtle. I doubted that anyone but me could tell that he was even moving to the music. But he was. Perfectly. Seductively.

One hand moved to my hip, the other pressed in the curve of my spine, just above my ass. Keeping me close. Not that I was going anywhere. In fact, I just melted further into his arms, my own hands moving to his biceps. Shit, they were hard.

He was hard. *So* hard.

I didn't want to think about all the ways this was professionally problematic. I didn't want to think about how this might be Gabe's way of buttering me up, making sure I'd write a good article about him. I didn't want to think about how completely insane all of this was.

What I wanted was to be closer to him. To touch him.

The hand on my hip moved upward, stroking my side, my arm, and then coming to rest against my chest. Not my chest-chest, but my sternum. His thumb stroked my clavicle and I sighed. It wasn't loud enough that he would have heard, but he definitely felt it.

I could tell, because he smiled.

A slow, wicked smile.

Then, with his other arm wrapped fully around my waist, he gave my chest a gentle push.

Somehow, I knew exactly what he was doing, and this time, I did swoon back. I let my body go limp and collapse over his arm.

He should have stumbled. Should have lost his balance.

But he was Gabe Parker and he knew *exactly* what he was doing.

His grip on me was ironclad, and before I knew it, I'd been swung back up into his arms.

What is this Dirty Dancing *shit?* I thought as I was pulled upright.

My mouth was hanging open. It felt like a scene out of a movie. The whole thing was bizarre and surreal and unbearably sexy.

Gabe was looking down at me, smiling a very smug smile. The competitive side of me couldn't let that stand. I did a move of my own, circling my hips against his, arching my back so my breasts—as modest and inoffensive as they were—pressed up against his chest and his hand slid back to touch my ass.

The smugness vanished into surprise—as if he hadn't been expecting that. Hadn't been expecting any of it. Especially how he felt. Because I could feel *exactly* how he felt. And it felt good. Felt intoxicating. Felt powerful.

Here was one of the hottest guys on the planet—according to *People* magazine—and he was turned on and pressed up against me.

I licked my lips. He watched.

Something was going to happen.

Except, it didn't.

Because at that exact moment, Ollie resurfaced, dancing right into us. We broke apart, Gabe adjusted his pants, and I did my best not to stare. I didn't succeed much, and when Gabe caught me, he gave me the same naughty, wonderful grin as before. The kind of grin that told me that if I wanted to get out of there with him, very, very wicked things might be in my immediate future.

"Come on," Ollie said, either not noticing what was happening between me and Gabe, or saving me from it.

He gave my hand a tug, and I heard a rip. I didn't have to look to know that my dress had torn—I could feel the slight breeze against my side.

Ollie pulled me away, deeper into the throng of bodies on the dance floor. I caught a glimpse of Gabe standing there on the edge of it all. He lifted a hand and then he was gone.

Film Fans

THE HILDEBRAND RARITY REVIEW

By Nicole Schatz

WITH EVERY NEW BOND COMES A CHORUS OF DISAPPROVAL. Consumers are fickle—they crave something new, but not *that* kind of new. They want to be challenged but comforted at the same time. They desire fresh takes, but only in a form that's familiar to them.

That's to say, audiences will accept something different as long as it feels the same.

No one wanted Gabe Parker to play Bond. The cards were stacked against him from the moment he was announced—especially when it was believed he was chosen over his *Tommy Jacks* co-star, Oliver Matthias.

At first it was an insult due to the fact that Matthias is British and Parker is decidedly not. Future audiences had already begun cringing at the thought of Parker, whose image was one of sweet, bro-y boyishness, acting suave while attempting to do a British accent.

Then when his audition tape was leaked and it was clear that the accent wasn't going to be a problem—nor the boyishness, which he folded into his Bond-ness in a particularly charming, unique manner—critics had to find another reason why Parker was ill-suited for the role.

That reason came in the form of the unsubtle homophobic backlash at the reminder that Parker had dared to play a gay man dying of AIDS in his college production of *Angels in America*.

How, Middle America cried, *how could Bond be played by someone who had kissed another man onstage?*

The answer, we now know, is very, *very* well.

Parker's Bond is a revelation.

And Chani Horowitz warned us that it would be. If you were one of the millions who read her profile of the star, you'll know that she did everything possible to prime the pump, as it were.

It's clear that the producers knew the film had only a few moments to convince the audience that they'd cast the right man and they use those minutes perfectly. Parker's entrance is reminiscent of other great character introductions—where the acting, the editing, the directing, the music, all coalesce to make something truly unforgettable.

Think Hugh Grant's entrance in *Bridget Jones's Diary*. Rex Manning's introduction in *Empire Records*. Darcy in any decent *Pride and Prejudice* adaptation.

That's Gabe Parker as Bond.

Iconic.

We don't even see him at first. It's a sea of men in dark suits and dark hair at a gala, the occasional beautiful woman sprinkled throughout. All are powerful, confident men. Except one.

He's shot from behind, but his body language doesn't beg attention. It's the opposite. Bond is hiding in a corner, shoulders bent, eyes—behind Clark Kent–esque glasses—focused forward, sipping on his signature drink.

He's watching someone. He's not the only one. The whole room is watching the latest Bond girl, Jacinda Lockwood, resplendent in a wine-red gown that floats on her skin as lovingly and intimate as a nightgown. She's dancing with someone twice her age.

Bond watches from afar, but we see his eyes up close. They're full of longing.

Lockwood looks up from her partner's shoulder and sees him. The dance ends and she walks off the dance floor, away from Bond.

He deposits his drink on a passing tray, and then the

transformation begins. Parker walks toward her, his shoulders straightening, his hand smoothing back his hair, his glasses deposited into his pocket.

By the time he reaches her, he's another person.

He pulls Lockwood into his arms and they drift to the dance floor. They dance closely, the whole room watching as Bond wraps his arm around her waist. His other hand traces her collarbone, and with a not-too-gentle push, she swoons backward and he dips her, long and slow, drawing a half circle with her body.

When she's pulled back upright, she—and the rest of the room—has fallen in love with Gabe Parker's Bond.

It's no wonder Jacinda Lockwood married him less than a week into filming.

Now

Chapter 15

I'M MAKING A TERRIBLE MISTAKE.

"I should cancel," I say.

"Should you?" Katie asks.

She's doing that thing that I hate.

"I should," I say.

Katie shrugs. She's sitting on my couch, her hair in that haphazard bun of hers—the one that always seems so effortless on her but looks like a hairy cinnamon roll whenever I attempt it. She's reading a magazine and seems unconcerned with my dilemma. I'm fairly certain she's waiting for me to leave so she can sage my entire apartment. According to her the vibes in here are very destructive to my well-being.

I'm pretty sure the only thing in my apartment that's destructive to my well-being is me.

"I'm going to buy you a plant while you're gone," she says, still looking at her magazine. "Maybe two."

"I'm just going to kill it," I say. "Don't make it a double homicide."

"I'll get you an un-killable plant." She flips a page. "You need it."

When we left New York, Katie packed up her entire—already overstuffed—apartment and had her life shipped across the continent. I shoved four boxes of books into the corner of her moving truck, filled two suitcases with clothes, and left everything else behind.

It took Katie three days to re-create her cozy, colorful bohemian home. I've been in my place a year and I still haven't bought a bed frame. The couch is from the "As Is" section of Ikea, the table from my parents' attic, and the dresser from the last person who lived here.

I could have taken half of what I'd had in New York, but I hadn't wanted any of it.

"This place looks like a depressed college student lives here," my sister had said the last time she visited.

I used to love nesting. I'd search for art and vintage furniture and weird ceramics to fill my home. Right now, the only decoration in the whole apartment is a half-finished puzzle on my dining table.

My therapist thinks I'm afraid to put down roots again.

I don't think she's wrong, but knowing that doesn't mean I've been able to do anything about it.

If I leave for the weekend, I'm certain Katie will do more than just buy a couple of plants for me.

"I can't go to Montana with Gabe Parker," I say.

"With Gabe," she corrects. "He's just Gabe."

I glare at her.

"You're supposed to be the voice of reason."

She laughs. It is, of course, a complete lie. No one has ever accused Katie of being the voice of reason in any situation.

"You know that's not why I'm here," she says.

She's the kind of person you call when you need to rob a bank and you want someone to give you permission to rob that bank.

My bag is by the door. The car will be here any minute.

"If you really want, when your ride gets here, I can go outside and tell them that you've changed your mind," Katie says.

I gnaw on the corner of my lip.

"*Is* that what you want?" Katie asks.

"This is a bad idea," I say.

She pats the sofa cushion next to her. I sit.

"You know what I'm going to say."

"Maybe," I say.

I still want to hear it. Because Katie is the only person who knows the actual truth about what happened between me and Gabe. She knows because after the Brooklyn party, after everything Jeremy said, after I showed up on her doorstep, soaked to the skin, throat sore from crying, I told her *everything*.

Katie believes in the power of the universe and karma and purpose. I know, as far as she's concerned, the reason that Gabe is back in my life is some sort of sign. And it's my responsibility to follow such a sign.

"He's not Jeremy," Katie says.

I let out a breath.

She's right, but that's not the only reason I'm hesitating.

I can't escape Gabe, and it feels almost pointless to try.

After my first book came out, I was invited to appear on *Good Morning Today*. My first TV appearance, and I'd been excited and nervous. Jeremy hadn't been able to come, but Katie had been my plus-one in the greenroom and she'd helped calm me down before I went on. I'd worn a blue-patterned dress that another writer friend assured me would look good on TV. I'd had someone do my hair and makeup.

It was going to be a short segment—a chance for me to talk about the collection—and my agent was excited for the exposure.

I hadn't been prepared for how bright and alienating the set had felt. I was grateful that I hadn't had to walk out on camera, that I was seated during their commercial break and mic'ed up. It had felt as if Carol Champion—the host—and I were on a little, isolated island in the middle of blinding lights.

All I could see was Carol, and I focused on her like she was the life raft I was swimming toward.

It started out fine. Carol asked about the book and I was able to string together several coherent sentences. I'd even made her laugh. Then, with a conspiratorial smile, she had leaned toward me.

"We obviously have to talk about *the* article," she'd said.

It had felt like my own smile was bolted to my face.

"Obviously," I'd said.

I'd been prepared for it. I was always prepared for it.

What I wasn't prepared for was the way Carol sat back and looked directly over my shoulder at the camera.

"You all know the article I'm talking about," she'd said before giving a big, broad wink. "The one that made Gabe Parker a household name."

"Well, I'm sure he didn't need my help with—"

"Have you seen him since the article?" Carol asked.

My hands had gone cold.

"No."

"Really?" Carol's face had been a contortion of faux surprise. "You haven't kept in touch?"

"It was just one interview." I'd tried to redirect the conversation. "There are several others in the book—"

"What would you say to him if you saw him?" Carol asked. "If he walked out onto this stage right now?"

I don't even remember what I said. I just know that my brain panicked, like it had been dropped into quicksand and was flailing and only sinking deeper. The thought of Gabe coming out—of the two of us meeting again this way—had caused every part of me to shut off, like a computer booting down.

But Gabe hadn't been there, and I think Carol apologized for the "harmless prank," as she called it afterward. Katie said that I had pulled it off fine, but I was pretty sure my impression of a deer in headlights had just added further fuel to the ever-burning rumors that something salacious had happened that weekend and I was just being coy.

Ten years ago, at lunch, I'd thought about fame. About how I wanted it.

I'd been so stupid then. I hadn't realized that wishing for fame was the ultimate monkey paw of wishes. You'd never see the cost until it had already been paid. Until it couldn't be undone.

It wasn't as if I was *famous,* but I was known.

And it was clear very early on that the only reason for that was because people wanted to know about that evening. They didn't want to know about my writing, or my ideas, or literally anything else about me. They wanted to know if I had fucked Gabe Parker at his house one night in December.

My *parents* had even asked.

"Should we expect him for Shabbat dinner?" had been my mother's way of inquiring.

"Does he even know what Shabbat is?" was my father's.

I had laughed it off the way I laughed off all the other questions. I waited for people to stop caring. I had done my best to rise above it and now I was letting myself get sucked right back in.

I should have said no.

I should say no now.

"I can send him away," Katie says. "I'd be happy to—hell, I'd even put it on my résumé." She spreads her hands wide. "Los Angeles–area woman sends Gabe Parker—alone—to Montana without a care."

"It's unprofessional," I say.

"That's not really what you're worried about," she says.

I hate how she's always right.

"This whole thing is ridiculous," I say. "What am I hoping will happen? I'm not a starstruck twenty-six-year-old kid anymore."

"That's true," Katie says. "You've both changed. You've both grown up."

That seems debatable.

"I don't know what he wants from me," I whisper.

"I think you do," she says. "I even think that you might want the same thing."

I shake my head because I'm too scared to admit that it's the truth. Because it feels like my second monkey-paw wish. Hope for one thing and get something completely different.

"Go to Montana," Katie says.

My phone buzzes. The car is here.

"You don't have to decide anything else," Katie says. "Take all the time you need. It's been ten years. There's no rush."

It's permission to rob the bank. Slowly. Thoughtfully.

I take it.

Because no matter what, I need to know how this story ends.

I lug my overnight bag outside and hand it to the driver. He opens the door and I find Gabe in the backseat.

"Oh," I say, sliding in next to him.

"Do you mind?" he asks. "I figured it would make things a little easier."

"No," I say. "I don't mind."

I do. I thought I would have a little more time to brace myself for what was coming next. Thought I'd have the car ride to LAX to prepare.

Still, I remind myself, there's no rush.

"I told you I'd get you out to Montana," Gabe says.

"Don't get cocky," I say.

His smile droops, but just a little.

It's uncomfortable here in the backseat. The driver has the radio on, but whatever is playing seems to be drowned out by the incredibly awkward tension between me and Gabe.

"I'm not sure this is a good idea," I finally say.

He shifts, turning toward me.

"I'm not sure either," he says. "But what's the worst that could happen?"

It's not exactly a statement that inspires confidence in me. I don't like not knowing. The last time I did something this impulsive, I ended up living in New York for almost eight years.

"I think you'll like Montana," Gabe says. "We have seasons."

"Never heard of them," I say.

He grins, and I can't help but do the same. I really like the gray in his hair—some of it sprinkled throughout his beard as well. I like the lines bracketing the corners of his eyes.

"I heard they had those in New York," he says. "Seasons."

My smile drops away.

"Yes, well," I say.

"Is he still there?" he asks as if he doesn't know the answer. "The Novelist?"

"Jeremy," I say. "He loves it."

"You didn't."

Since he knows about my newsletter, he can probably gauge how I felt about living in New York.

"I didn't think you would," he says.

"You don't know me that well," I say.

He shrugs. "You said you didn't like the city," he reminds me.

I hate that he remembers our conversations. It makes all of this so much harder. Makes it harder to be angry at him. And I *want* to be angry at him.

It's easier than being angry at myself. It's easier than being scared.

"I didn't know what I was talking about back then," I say. "I'd never lived there before."

"But you knew you didn't like it."

"What did I know?" I ask. "I was twenty-six. You don't know anything at twenty-six. I'm astonished by my own arrogance. Of thinking I knew anything."

"Isn't that always the case?" he asks. "Don't you think you'll say the same thing ten years from now?"

"Yes," I say, my hackles up.

"You're awfully hard on yourself."

"My past self deserves it. She was foolish and naïve and stupid. She believed things she should have known better than to believe."

He doesn't say anything. We both know what I'm talking about. We both know that I'm talking about him. He's the mistake. The thing I had believed in.

"My past self was pretty stupid too," he finally says. "Didn't know a good thing when he had it."

"You didn't have me," I snap. "You barely knew me."

"I was talking about my career," he says.

My face gets hot, and I turn away. I feel guilty and like a fool. I want to go back to my sad, empty apartment. I want to write the fastest, laziest version of this article and send it off to my editor. I want to completely, permanently sever my connection to Gabe Parker. I want to be over it. Over him.

"But not just my career," he adds. Quietly.

It doesn't help.

Then, as if things couldn't possibly get worse, the radio starts playing *the* song. The song that Gabe and I danced to that weekend. The one where we'd been smushed together, from our chests to our knees, and Gabe had wrapped his arms around me before dipping me low.

Back then, I'd thought it was the sexiest, most romantic thing that had ever happened to me.

Then Gabe married Jacinda Lockwood almost immediately after the article was released and I had to watch him dip her in the *exact same way* on the big screen in the opening sequence for his first Bond movie.

The tension in the car has gone wire taut, and I know that Gabe remembers this song. I know he's thinking about what happened at the club.

"About that night," he says.

I cross my arms.

"That whole weekend," he amends. "I'm sorry."

"You already apologized," I say.

I don't want him to be sorry. Sorry is confirmation that he'd been faking it the whole time. From getting my phone number to bringing me to the premiere and then inviting me to his party.

"It's fine," I say. "We were both young and stupid. I should have known better."

There's a long pause.

"What about now?" he asks.

"I should know better now too, but . . ." I gesture at the car, at him. "I guess I haven't learned anything."

I lean my head back against the seat and look out the window. It's then that I realize we're not going to LAX.

Since I'm fairly certain Gabe isn't kidnapping me, I don't say anything until we arrive at a small private airport in the Valley. When we drive onto the tarmac to where a plane is waiting, that's when I turn to Gabe, incredulous.

"A private jet?" I ask.

Gabe, at least, has the good sense to look sheepish.

"It's not my plane," he says. "And it wasn't my idea."

I give him a look, but he raises his hands.

"This is ridiculous," I say, trying to be as annoyed as possible, but the truth is I'm a little impressed.

And annoyed at myself for being impressed.

I'm supposed to be above all this. Supposed to be immune to his charms. Immune to the siren call of Hollywood stars and all the fancy trappings that come with them.

It's disappointing to discover I'm just as easily taken as Jeremy always thought I was.

"You love celebrity," he used to say. "You *want* to be famous."

He'd say it as if it was the most disgusting thing a person could want. As if wanting it meant that I deserved what happened. That I deserved people assuming that my success was a direct result of fucking a celebrity.

Not that Jeremy was exempt from wanting that kind of attention. He refused to admit it out loud, but I knew the truth. He wanted people to talk about him. Wanted people to know him.

He'd get down on his knees for a private jet.

I'm pretty sure, at least.

At least I know I'm not willing to do *that*. Not for a private jet.

I also know that I'm still mad about the whole dance thing, which I know technically isn't really Gabe's fault and when it comes down to it, I'm really angrier at myself than anything, but right now it's easier to be annoyed about a private jet.

"It's not mine," Gabe says again as we get out of the car. "And he insisted."

I'm confused until a familiar face appears at the top of the ramp. He strikes a pose.

"Darling!" Ollie says, arms akimbo. "It's been ages."

I can't help it, I'm thrilled to see him. And grateful that I don't have to spend an entire private plane ride to Montana with just Gabe. The car ride was tense enough.

Gabe helps the driver unload our bags as Ollie skips down the stairs and pulls me into a hug that lifts me off my feet.

"When I heard that you two crazy kids were re-creating your famous interview, I begged Gabe to let me crash," Ollie says, once I'm back on the ground.

"I refused," Gabe says.

"He refused," Ollie confirms.

His hands are on my arms and he's leaning back, looking at me like a proud parent whose daughter just returned from her first year at college.

"He wanted you all to himself," Ollie says sotto voce.

"I did," Gabe says, walking past us with our bags.

Even though I'm still a little irritated at him, I flush. It's hard not to feel overwhelmed and befuddled by all this attention.

"A private jet, huh?" I ask, looking up at the beautiful, shining plane.

"It's ridiculous, I know," Ollie says. "Terrible for the environment. Very, very extravagant." He gives me a wink. "But I told you I'd do it."

It's true. He did tell me. I feel a strange rush of pride on his behalf. He really has accomplished exactly what he hoped to accomplish. But with that pride, there's some jealousy too. I swallow it down.

"I'm happy for you," I say.

He wraps an arm around me and squeezes.

"Let's get you two crazy kids to Montana."

THE JAM—NEWSLETTER

THE ZEN OF PUZZLING

I'VE BEEN PUZZLING FOR A LONG TIME.

It allows me a distraction from my own brain. To help me deal with occasional bouts of depression, of loneliness, isolation.

It gives me something to do that doesn't require my full attention.

My perfect puzzling situation is this: Put on a movie after dinner, pop an edible, and puzzle until it kicks in. That usually happens when I can't figure out what's happening in the movie anymore and I'm staring at the puzzle board with my empty hand hovering above the pieces.

I like to start with the edges.

I want to create boundaries—context—for whatever I'm making. I want to know where it will end. This is not the most fun way to start a puzzle—or a project—and sometimes the edges can be a nightmare, but it's the only way I know.

You never know if a puzzle is going to be good until you get into it.

The fun part starts when I know my limits. When I know what I'm working with. That's when I begin sorting through my pieces, grouping them in order of color or pattern. I don't put them down on the board—not yet—but I build piles of them outside the edges. Not quite ready to piece them together.

Until I am.

There's no logic to it. There's no reasoning. It's instinct.

And there's something deeply satisfying about finishing a

puzzle. About placing that last piece, that satisfyingly soft snap of it fitting together perfectly.

That's not my favorite part, though.

My favorite part is after I spread my hands over the smooth, assembled surface, marveling in the work I've completed, I then undo it all.

xoChani

Chapter 16

"YOU KNOW"—OLLIE LEANS BACK IN HIS SEAT, ONE FINGER against his chin—"divorce suits you."

"Jesus," Gabe says.

"What?" Ollie elbows him before turning back to me. "It does. Your skin is glowing, your hair is luxurious. Everything about you is lighter, almost as if you got a five-foot-nine growth removed from your side."

"Ollie," Gabe says.

"He wasn't five foot nine," I say.

Ollie glances over at Gabe, and mouths, *Yes, he was*.

Gabe rolls his eyes.

"I'm just saying you look great," Ollie says.

"Thank you?" I say.

"She always looks great," Gabe says.

"*She* is right here," I say.

"Ollie insults your ex-husband and you're annoyed at *me*?" he asks, with more amusement than anything.

I shrug. I don't know if I'm annoyed at him. I don't know *how* I am.

"I didn't like him," Ollie says, determined not to be left out of this conversation.

"You met him once," I say. "For five minutes."

"It was enough," he says.

Unlike with Gabe, who I'd only seen that one time in New York, I'd crossed paths with Ollie on several occasions over the past ten years. In addition to the highly publicized interview I'd done with him, we'd occasionally run into each other when I was in town.

The last time, three years ago, had been a fluke. The rare occasion where Jeremy had come with me to L.A. I'd had an interview scheduled at Little Dom's in Los Feliz, so Jeremy had busied himself at the nearby indie bookstore, charming the booksellers and signing stock. When I was done, I texted him, but as I walked toward the door, a hand had emerged from one of the booths and gave my arm a friendly tug.

Ollie and his husband, Paul, had been drinking mimosas and sharing a plate of silver dollar pancakes.

There was a girl at the bar not-so-discreetly trying to get a shot of Ollie. When he waved at her, she'd squeaked and dropped her phone. He'd beckoned her over, taken a picture with her, and signed her napkin. She was leaving just as Jeremy walked in.

I made introductions; everyone shook hands. We talked for a few minutes, but it was enough time for Jeremy to offer to go back to the bookstore to get a copy of his book for Ollie.

"I'll grab one on my way out," Ollie had said.

"Do you think he will?" Jeremy had asked maybe five more times that day.

"I'm sure he will," I'd said, even though I knew he wouldn't.

I'd both hated and loved how superior the interaction had made me feel. Jeremy was the one who had all the clout in our community in New York. He was the well-respected novelist, I was his puff-piece-writing wife.

In L.A., however, I was the one chatting with celebrities who I knew had no interest in Jeremy's work.

That memory did serve to prove his point, though. I didn't love fame, but once I had a taste of it—no matter how bitter the aftertaste—I wasn't willing to give it up.

If I was, I would tell my agent that I didn't want to do another collection of essays. I would tell her and my editor what I really want to write. I would take a fucking risk.

"How's Paul?" I ask Ollie, thirty thousand feet over New Mexico.

"Dying to get to know you better," he says. "Now that you're back in L.A., you'll have to come have dinner with us. He's a fan."

"Of me?"

"Yes, you," Ollie says. "He loves your writing."

"Oh, that's very nice of him," I say.

"Not nice," Ollie says. "Honest. Paul has absolutely exquisite taste. It's why he married me."

Gabe snorts.

Ollie ignores him. "He loved the *Vanity Fair* piece."

When Ollie had decided to come out, he'd contacted me to write about it. I'd been proud of the article, even more proud that Ollie had trusted me with his story.

"I never thanked you for the flowers," I say. "They were lovely."

"Well-earned," Ollie says. "It made my mum cry, you know."

"Mine too," Gabe says.

"Did she cry at the *Broad Sheets* one too?" I ask.

It's sort of a joke, but there's a long, terrible pause, and my stomach gives a lurch.

"She liked it," Gabe says, not looking at me.

I realize immediately what that means.

"But you didn't," I say.

For a moment, I think I'm going to be sick.

"It was well-written," Gabe says.

"Gabe," Ollie says, voice quiet.

"Wow," I say. "Wow. You *hated* it, didn't you?"

He doesn't respond, but he doesn't have to.

I'm stunned.

Despite my conflicting feelings about what it had done for my career, I knew it was a good article. No. It was a fucking amazing article. It had been flattering and fawning and had made Gabe look like he was the only possible choice to play James Bond. It had shifted the narrative around his casting and though it hadn't quieted all of the haters, it had certainly shut enough of them up. I wasn't the sole reason that *The Hildebrand Rarity* had been a hit, but I had helped pave the way.

That wasn't just my ego speaking. That was what numerous reviews had said. They'd pointed to my interview with Gabe as the reason they had gone into the film with an open mind.

And Gabe had *hated* it.

What the fuck was I even doing here?

"This was a mistake," I say, getting up from my seat, wishing I could just drop myself out a window.

"Chani," Gabe says, but I wave it off.

It hurts. It hurts more than it should.

The plane is small but there's still enough space that I can escape to another quartet of seats in the back. I throw myself into the chair, arms wrapped tightly around my torso as if I can contain all the horrible, angry feelings roiling inside of me.

I lean my head against the window, watching snowy states fly by beneath us.

I'm furious and tender.

I hadn't known it at the time, but the article was a trade-off. Attention and career stability in exchange for a certain kind of notoriety. A *reputation*. It had always seemed foolish—and pointless—to wonder if it had been worth it, when at the very least I had been pleased with the work. Even when everyone seemed to focus on the content of the article, I'd been proud of the writing itself.

But now, knowing that Gabe hadn't even liked the article made the trade all the more difficult to stomach.

Just the latest in a long line of unexpected consequences.

After Gabe's article, my agent had gotten a glut of requests from the people who represented the most promising up-and-coming stars. A few actresses, but mostly people wanted me to interview young, handsome actors. The implication was clear, and there was always an underlying quid pro quo to those interviews, but no one came right out and said it to my face.

Until Dan Mitchell.

The latest addition to the second Bond film, he'd greeted me with a lingering hug and kept trying to get me drunk throughout the interview, which he had insisted take place at the Chateau Marmont, where he was staying. I declined the drinks he offered and the conversation was awkward and stilted. It was clear that he was frustrated, and that frustration boiled over when I declined to go with him up to his hotel room to see "something cool."

"Look," he'd said. "Why don't we cut to the chase? Let's just go upstairs, and you can blow me. Okay?"

He'd had the temerity to wink when I stared at him in shock.

"It'll make for a great story, and I can guarantee you that my dick is way bigger than Parker's."

I had left immediately, and shed no tears when he was released from the movie a week later due to "scheduling conflicts." A diplomatic way to say he'd been fired.

At the other end of the plane, I can hear Gabe and Ollie talking. Their voices are low and slightly muffled by the deep, underlying humming of the engines and the wind. They're talking about work—the upcoming press junket for *The Philadelphia Story* and something called MOTC.

"Are you going to be all right?" Ollie asks.

"Me? Oh, sure. When am I not all right?"

There's a long pause.

"You don't have to worry about me, Ollie."

I can practically hear Ollie rolling his eyes.

"I'm okay," Gabe says.

"Are you?"

"I am. Look at me, I'm in a private jet."

The last time I had flown, I was leaving New York. Leaving Jeremy.

Katie and I had spent the first half of the flight watching the feminist masterpiece *Magic Mike XXL* on the plane until she fell asleep. I did what I was doing now—staring out the window, looking for the meaning of life in the fast-passing clouds.

I hadn't found it then and I didn't think I was going to find it now.

Moving to New York to be with Jeremy had been a mistake. I was fairly certain that going to Montana with Gabe was also a mistake. A different kind of mistake, but a mistake.

If I was smart, I'd never leave California.

Even though I've never once in my life been able to fall asleep on an airplane, the private jet manages to lull me into sleep and I don't wake until I hear the pilot say we're beginning our initial descent into Cooper, Montana.

The first thing I see once we pass through the clouds is the cathedral. It's a proper one with a tall, reaching spire and a wide spread.

Cooper is small. The airport is at one end of the town and from this distance the whole place—Gabe's hometown, the keeper of his childhood adventures—feels like it could fit in my palm.

Whenever I would fly back to L.A. to visit my family, I always felt this relief that I hadn't known I had been missing. As if I'd become accustomed to breathing out of one lung.

It feels like that now. Like I'd been operating on half-oxygen for who knows how long.

I take a deep breath.

Below me, everything is covered in snow.

I'm glad I borrowed a huge, extremely puffy coat from Katie that I had to strong-arm into my suitcase along with a pair of snow boots she insisted I buy. The world looks brisk and vast and unknown. I shiver, but it's not just from the imagined cold.

It's almost like I'm coming home. Not to a place, necessarily, but to a feeling. To a possibility of more.

And that completely and utterly terrifies me.

VANITY FAIR

OLIVER MATTHIAS:
He Is What He Is

[EXCERPT]

BY CHANI HOROWITZ

We're sitting in Oliver Matthias's backyard and he's telling me about the first time he fell in love. It's the perfect setting to hear a love story. It's fall and the air has just the right amount of crisp in it. We're sitting on lawn chairs, covered in Pendleton blankets ("a gift from a friend"), drinking hot apple cider.

Halloween is just around the corner. Halloween is when Oliver first fell in love.

"It's always been my favorite holiday," he tells me. "There's a freedom to it—where everyone gets dressed up and pretends to be someone else and it's not because you're hiding or you're deceiving, it's because on that day we all seem to acknowledge that it's good to put on a mask once in a while."

He takes a long drink of his apple cider. I'm content to let it warm my hands for now, though the rich smell of apples and butter and cinnamon is just as intoxicating as the splash of whisky we added to our mugs before we came outside.

"Fortification," Oliver told me.

We both know why I'm here, but I'm not about to rush him, because if I know anything about Oliver Matthias, it's that he knows how to tell a story.

"I'd bet a lot of actors have an affinity for Halloween," he says. "Though, we do it a little differently in Britain."

I nod as if I know—I don't. I've lived in the United States my entire life. My only trip abroad was to Amsterdam to visit Anne Frank's house with my temple youth group.

Oliver has been all over the world, but has recently settled in Los Angeles, buying a house in Brentwood, up in the hills.

"It's a good neighborhood for trick-or-treating," he says. "Or so I've been told."

This will be his first Halloween here.

"Every year I would go all in," he says. "And that year, I wanted to go as Xena."

He smiles, remembering.

"My mum had always made my costumes and she went all out that year. I'm one of four boys, you see, and the whole thing about a mother wanting a daughter was quite applicable."

"Are you still close with your mother?"

He nods. "There I am, in full Xena regalia, marching down Piccadilly with my brothers, who were, of course, dressed as soldiers. They were always dressed as soldiers."

"Technically," I interject, "you were a soldier too."

Oliver laughs. "Not quite," he says. "I was a warrior."

I stand corrected.

"There I am, full warrior mode, strutting my little heart out when—bam—I walk right into someone else. Another Xena."

It's easy to picture this. A young, adorable Oliver Matthias, his blue eyes glinting, his chin lifted high, too high for him to realize that he's about to collide with someone else dressed exactly like him.

"I'm furious, of course," Oliver says. "How dare this other Xena—this imposter—ruin my walk?"

"Of course."

"I look up—because this person is much taller than me—and I see that this Xena is also a boy. Well, a man, really. He looks down at me, smiles, and gives me a wink. And then he's gone."

Oliver puts his hand to his chest.

"And I was in love."

It was a love that brought heartbreak—not then, not even when he came out to his family and friends—but years later when he told the director and producers of an upcoming film that he was gay.

And they told him, in no uncertain terms, that they'd never cast him to play James Bond.

Chapter 17

WE GO TO DINNER—A STEAKHOUSE WITH RED LEATHER booths and dim lighting and stone walls. It feels like I'm inside a classy hunting lodge, which I'm certain is the point. I'm just grateful that the mounted animal heads on the wall are at a minimum. The restaurant is mostly empty and the waiter seats us in a back room that's set aside from the rest of the place, so we have far more privacy than we need.

It seems rude not to order meat.

I'm feeling surly and also get a whisky on the rocks.

At lunch yesterday, Gabe insisted that he was fine watching other people drink, and Ollie also orders a drink—an old-fashioned—but I'm still at risk of being disrespectful.

I know I need to be an adult about this whole situation. That I need to deal with my hurt pride, and get through this weekend without bruising any other tender emotions.

Instead, I mainline the whisky on an empty stomach and turn to Ollie.

"I should probably get a quote or two from you about the movie," I say. "Since you're here."

"Of course," Ollie says.

I look over at Gabe. "If that's okay with you," I say. "I wouldn't want to write another extremely flattering profile that you inexplicably hate."

So much for being an adult.

"I didn't hate the article," Gabe says, but I wave a hand at him.

"I'm talking to Ollie now," I say.

I've moved from being passive-aggressive to just plain aggressive and I know it. I can't help myself. The anger I feel is raw and covering a whole host of other emotions that I'm not ready to deal with.

"Why *The Philadelphia Story*?" I ask Ollie once I've taken my phone out and started recording.

"I'd been told it was a movie that could use an update," he says.

It's almost exactly what Gabe said to me. Apparently, it's going to be one of their go-to press junket sound bites.

"Cute," I say, giving Gabe a look.

He shrugs, not taking the bait.

"It's a great play," Ollie says, clearly trying to defuse the ever-growing tension. "It was always on my list of potential material, but Gabe was the one who thought we should do it as a modern remake."

"You started out in the theatre," I say to Ollie. "Any plans to go back?"

He exchanges a look with Gabe.

"Actually," he says. "That's one of the reasons I'm here in Cooper."

I'd been so distracted by the private plane and the subsequent revelation about the *Broad Sheets* article that I hadn't even stopped to think about *why* Ollie was chartering us to Montana.

"Better clarify that this is off the record," Gabe says.

I don't like his tone, nor his implication.

Still, I make a point of putting my phone away. Ollie is looking between us, clearly not sure how to proceed.

"I don't know if you remember," Ollie says. "But Gabe did a show on Broadway a few years ago."

The tension at the table suddenly ratchets up to eight.

"Oh, I remember," I say.

I'd known that this conversation was inevitable, just like I know I'm going to have to ask Gabe about *the* phone call. I just hadn't expected Ollie to be the one to shine a flashlight on this particular elephant in the corner.

"She saw it," Gabe says.

"I saw it," I confirm. "I saw the who-ole thing."

The whisky has made my tone a little loopy.

Ollie's eyes are ping-ponging back and forth between the two of us.

"I see," he says.

He doesn't. He has no idea what we're talking about.

"She came on opening night," Gabe says.

Recognition dawns, and Ollie looks down at his phone.

"Oh look," he says. "An important call."

"Your phone didn't even ring," I say.

"I must take this," he says, getting up from the table.

"You're not that good of an actor," Gabe says as Ollie walks away, his un-rung phone against his ear.

Gabe looks at me. I look back.

"So," he says.

I hadn't planned on going. When I saw that Gabe had signed on to play Karl Lindner in *A Raisin in the Sun* during his Bond hiatus, I had planned to completely avoid Times Square for the duration of the limited run.

Then I was sent a ticket. To opening night.

I hadn't told Jeremy. He'd been working nonstop on his second novel and things had been strained between us for months.

Gabe was still married, but the gossip columns had made a big deal about the fact that Jacinda was not relocating to New York with him and was staying in London. According to everyone, they were either separated or days away from getting a divorce.

I told myself that the invitation meant nothing. That it was business. That maybe someone on his team thought I'd write something about it. That maybe Gabe didn't even know I was coming.

But I'd worn my nicest dress and gotten my hair blown out. I wore lipstick. Heels.

Jeremy didn't even notice when I left the apartment.

It would be nice to see Gabe after all these years, I'd told myself on the subway. Like old friends. I took my seat at the theatre, feeling nervous and jittery, as if I was going to be the one onstage.

And when I saw him . . .

It was as if the entire theatre disappeared around me. As if the rest of the cast vanished. All I saw was Gabe.

Seeing him that close after all those years was like a drug.

And then, during intermission, one of the ushers came to my seat.

"Mr. Parker would like you to come to his dressing room," she told me. "I'll escort you back after the show."

I spent the rest of the play in some sort of fugue state, barely registering what was happening onstage. All I could think about was what would happen when I saw him backstage. What would I say? How would I greet him? A handshake? A hug? A cheek kiss?

By the time the curtain went down, my entire body was vibrating with nervous energy. My fingers were ice-cold, my throat burning hot.

After the theatre had emptied out a bit, the same usher came to find me, and I followed her backstage, the narrow corridors overflowing with flowers and people.

"Here it is," the usher said, leaving me in front of a closed door with Gabe's name on it.

She left. I knocked, overeagerly turning the knob as I did.

That was my mistake.

I'd opened the door and found Gabe. With Jacinda in his arms.

As I'd backed away from the scene, stumbling in my heels, I realized that I had lied to myself about why I'd come. The way I always lied to myself when it came to Gabe.

In my attempt to flee, I made a wrong turn and ended up onstage. The curtains were closed and the whole space felt far smaller than it had appeared from the audience.

"You can't be out here," a stagehand said to me.

"She's with me," Gabe said.

He had been in his costume. Still wearing his stage makeup, but I was pretty sure that smear of lipstick on his cheek wasn't from the show.

"Chani," he'd said.

It was like someone dragging a finger down the length of my spine. I'd shivered.

"You're here," he said.

"Thank you for the ticket," I said. "But I should go."

I'd turned to walk away, but the other side of the stage was blocked by set pieces and sandbags. If I wanted to leave, I'd have to go through him. So I screwed my courage to the sticking place and faced him, if only so I could get away.

"Gabe, I should—"

"I was hoping—"

"The show was good." I'd been grateful for the truth and used it as a shield. "You were good."

He'd ducked his head. "Thank you."

We'd both stood there for a moment. My feet had been aching. My pride too.

"You look nice," he'd said.

"You have lipstick on your cheek," I'd told him.

He swore and rubbed at it with the base of his palm.

Out, damned spot, I'd thought.

"Jacinda is—" he'd started.

"Waiting for you in your dressing room, I imagine."

Gabe glanced back toward it.

"It's not like that," he'd said. "She surprised me."

"Likewise."

"My mom is here too," he'd said.

As if that made things better.

"Wow," I'd said. "That's not—I mean, really?"

He'd let out a breath, his frustration evident, its recipient unclear.

"Can we . . ." He'd gestured toward the couch on the center of the stage.

I'd lifted an eyebrow. He wanted to sit? *Here?* Like we were overdue for a cozy chat?

The worst part was that I'd wanted to do it.

"Won't you be missed?" I'd asked.

Gabe had rubbed the back of his neck. I hadn't known what to expect when I came to the show—when I came backstage—but this hadn't been it. If anything, I'd imagined something so far out of the realm of reality that it had been a hard, vicious comedown.

"There's an after-party," he'd said. "You could go with—"

"You and your wife?" I'd asked. "What fun."

"I could introduce you," he'd offered. "She knows your work."

"You've got to be joking," I'd said.

A wrinkle had appeared between Gabe's eyes as he frowned at me. I'd seen the wheels turning in his head, and wondered what he had hoped to accomplish.

"Yeah," he'd said. "Sorry."

"Well," I'd said. "I should go."

"It's good to see you," he'd said.

The sincerity in his words was like a punch in the chest.

"It's good to see you too." I'd been clutching my purse like it was a lifeline. The truth, again.

He'd nodded, his eyes sweeping over me, stopping at my hand.

I followed his gaze and found that he was staring at my wedding band, which suddenly felt like it weighed a thousand pounds. He nodded, and I felt a wave of shame. Because for a moment, I'd forgotten.

"Give my regards to the Novelist," he'd said. Pointedly.

"Jeremy," I'd said. "And tell Jacinda I loved her last movie."

Gabe had given me a curt nod.

"Thanks for coming," he'd said.

"Anytime," I'd said, and headed for the exit.

As I passed him, I had been able to smell his cologne. Expensive cedar tree. I'd almost stumbled, but didn't.

When I'd left the theatre, it was dark and cold, but people were waiting by the stage door, hoping to catch a glimpse of James Bond. I'd walked home, feeling the same way I'd felt when I heard that he'd married Jacinda. Like a deflated balloon on the bottom of someone's shoe. Like I'd been played for a fool.

It's a feeling I should do well to remember right now.

Ollie is still somewhere in the restaurant, pretending to be on his phone. Gabe is looking down at his water, rotating the wet glass between his palms like he's ineffectively trying to start a fire.

"I didn't know she'd be there that night," Gabe says. "I thought she was in London and then when I got offstage, she was in my dressing room."

He looks up at me.

"Is that supposed to make it better?" I ask.

"I don't know," he says. "I just know how it looked and it wasn't supposed to be like that."

"How was it supposed to be?" I ask.

"I don't know!" He's angry. Frustrated. The feeling is mutual. "I don't know. I thought—I mean, you hadn't written about *him*—"

"The Novelist."

Gabe blinks at me.

"Jeremy," I self-correct.

Gabe pauses like he's counting to ten in his head.

"You hadn't written about him in a while, and Jacinda and I were never really, you know—" He gestures. "It wasn't real."

"Did Jacinda know that?" I ask. "Because she certainly seemed surprised to see me too."

"It might have been my impulse to get married," Gabe says. "But our initial arrangement was *her* idea."

"She didn't care that you and I . . ." I trail off, not exactly sure what I'm laying claim to.

Gabe looks down at the table. "She didn't know," he says. "About that weekend."

I cross my arms—feeling vindicated and also like shit.

"I told her about it," Gabe says. "But later."

"Nice of you," I say.

"Stupid." Gabe points at himself. "Young."

I nod, not disagreeing.

"She *does* know your work," he says. "And she likes it."

"That makes one of you," I say.

"Chani," he says.

I'm thinking about the interview I was supposed to do with her. How I'd chickened out.

"I was *so* glad to see you," Gabe says. "You have no idea."

"You were still married," I say.

"I know!" He runs a hand through his hair. "But don't forget, so were you."

I open my mouth. Close it. He's right, and it all suddenly feels absurd. We're both angry at the other for the exact same reason. Both angry at each other for something neither of us really has a right to be angry about.

It takes all the air out of my rage.

"I was glad to see you too," I say.

Gabe releases his glass of water and reaches a hand out toward me. I take it without a second thought.

"Why did you invite me?" I ask.

"I couldn't not," he says. "It's not a good enough reason but it is the reason."

"I couldn't not go," I say.

"I—" he says.

"Well, it looks like neither of you have killed the other," Ollie says.

He sits down, oblivious to the moment he just interrupted. My hand has already returned to my lap. Gabe's is flat on the table.

"No," Gabe says.

"No murders committed," I say.

Neither of us is looking at the other.

"Great," Ollie says. "Glad I can trust the two of you with steak knives. Let's eat."

TIME OUT NEW YORK

Bond on Broadway

[EXCERPT]

By Nina Wood

THIS WEEKEND, GABE PARKER RETURNS TO HIS ROOTS.

"It's a bit like being back in college," he tells me. "And I'm just as nervous as I was then."

He's taking time in between the Saturday matinee and evening previews to talk about his Broadway debut as Karl Lindner in *A Raisin in the Sun*.

The part is not the one you'd expect a big-name star like Parker to take, but he says he's always loved the play and jumped at the chance to be involved, in any way possible.

"I'm not completely naïve," he says. "I know there will be plenty of people coming to see if I mess up my lines or get lost onstage or something like that. But you know, if it gets people to buy tickets and come to the theatre, they can cheer for my failure all they want."

He says it with a smile, likely knowing, as well as I do, that he seems to do his best work when he's considered the underdog.

"The lower the expectations the better," he jokes.

I ask about his family—if they're looking forward to his Broadway debut.

"My mom's my date for opening night," he says. "She's very excited."

And his wife, former model and Bond girl Jacinda Lockwood? Rumors are that she's still in London, unable to see her hubby's debut.

"She's always cheering me on, in spirit, if not in person," Parker says.

Chapter 18

"I'LL CHECK OUT THE SITE TOMORROW," GABE SAYS TO OLLIE AS we cross the parking lot.

"We could go right now," he says. "It's not too late."

Gabe looks at me. This trip has a distinct third-wheel vibe, but the truth is, I'm not entirely sure if I'm the third wheel or if Ollie is.

"I'm pretty tired," I say.

Gabe looks at Ollie. Something wordless passes between them and Ollie shrugs.

"Yeah," Gabe says. "It's been a long day."

To any casual observer, the rest of the meal probably looked like a subdued affair. But my entire body felt as if it was on high alert. I didn't know what Gabe was planning to say before Ollie returned, but things between us have shifted. I can still feel the rough press of his calloused fingers against mine. The heat has lingered, and there's a line of tension running between us, pulled so taut that I'm certain it's bound to snap.

I don't know what will happen when it does, but I'm both eager and terrified to find out. It's the reason I got another whisky on the rocks. The reason I'm feeling just a little bit tipsier than I'd like.

Ollie gives me a hug. If he's disappointed that he's lost the battle for Gabe's attention, he doesn't show it. If anything, he looks positively gleeful.

"Go gentle on him," he whispers. "He's delicate."

"*He's* delicate?" I ask. "What about me?"

He leans back and gives me a look.

"Sure," he says.

When he hugs Gabe goodbye, he looks over his shoulder at me and gives me a thumbs-up.

I worry that I'm going to disappoint him.

Gabe has a truck, and knowing nothing about cars, I can still tell it's an expensive one, even though it needs a wash. We sit there, in the parking lot, the heater blasting, my fingers pressed against the vents.

We'd been outside for less than ten minutes but it was enough. Even the winters in New York were never this cold—almost as if there's an absence of anything beyond the chill in the air. It's bracing.

"You have a choice," Gabe says. "I can get you a hotel room. A nice one. For Cooper, that is. Or you can stay with me. I have a guest room. Plenty of space."

"I don't know if that's a good idea," I say, practically on autopilot.

Gabe nods.

"Maybe not," he says. "But you're already here. What's one more bad decision?"

Describing Gabe's home as an apartment is a misnomer. It's a house on top of a bookshop.

I hear her before I see her. That wonderful, comforting, perfect sound of nails across a hardwood floor. I put my bag down in the entryway of Gabe's apartment and kneel as she comes around the corner.

"Hey, girl," I say.

Her muzzle has a lot of white on it, and she's tall now—so tall—the puppy weight long gone, replaced by a leanness that indicates her age. I can see the knots of her hip bones, but she's wagging and when she sees us, she barrels toward the door—ten weeks old again.

At first, I think she's going to fling herself against Gabe—her owner—but she throws her body into mine, knocking me off balance. I hit the floor with my butt, hard, but I don't care.

Gabe's dog is alive and licking my face.

I start to cry.

"She remembers you," Gabe says, not yet noticing my tears.

"Good girl," I say, burying my face in her side.

I know it's ridiculous and I'm definitely still a little buzzed from the whisky, but I inhale and convince myself that there's still the tiniest hint of puppy smell there.

"Hey, hey, hey." Gabe is kneeling down next to us. "Are you okay?"

I wipe my nose on my sleeve—it's wet and sloppy and extremely gross but I don't care.

"I'm fine," I say. "I'm just happy to see her."

"She's happy to see you too," Gabe says with the hushed, slightly questioning tone of someone who doesn't understand why another person is crying but doesn't want to do anything to set it off again.

"What's her name?" I ask.

The whole point of this weekend, I'm realizing, is to get answers to unanswered questions. I just never thought this would be one of them.

"Teddy," Gabe says.

I look at him.

"I never was a very creative adult," he says.

I wipe my nose again and give Teddy a scratch behind her ears. She leans hard against me and then slowly slides onto her back, showing me her stomach. We sit there in the entryway of Gabe's apartment for a long time, me rubbing her belly, her tail thumping on the hardwood floor.

"I'll take your bag to your room," Gabe says.

He gets up and leaves us alone.

I know the apartment is above the Cozy—the shop that Gabe bought for his mom and sister—but we came in from the back, so I didn't get to see the building.

I stand—much to Teddy's chagrin—and brush her hair off my legs.

There's a little table in the entryway where I'm standing and it's covered with framed photos.

Most of them are of Gabe's niece, Lena.

I smile at what must be the most recent one—a thirteen-year-old girl scowling at the camera in a typical thirteen-year-old-girl fashion. I can feel that scowl deep down in my soul.

There's a family photo on the end—Gabe, his mom, his sister, Lena, and a round-faced guy with Lena's eyes.

My smile fades.

I'd read about Gabe's brother-in-law. How he'd died in a car accident a few years ago.

We'd spoken about him, briefly, during that first interview. How they were going to go on a trip together—to Italy. How he—Spencer—had never left the country before. There'd been articles after his death, mostly as an excuse to show grainy photos of Gabe and Jacinda, combined with breathless reporting that they were as strong as ever.

There's another picture—the oldest one on the table—of Gabe and his sister when they were little. They're maybe two and three. They're each on a lap. Lauren is on her mom's. Gabe on his dad's.

I'd never seen pictures of Gabe's dad before but it's clear that he got a lot of his looks from him. The thing I appreciate the most, though, is the enormous bushy mustache turned upward above his smile.

I step into the living room, Teddy following me on her big, fluffy feet.

Gabe's apartment is huge. Two bedrooms, at least, a big, beautiful kitchen, and a living room with the largest TV I've ever seen. Still, despite the size of the place, it's cozy. The vintage-looking metal fireplace in the corner, painted a lovely rust red, makes the place look like a cabin from the sixties.

On the coffee table is a half-completed puzzle.

"You puzzle?" I ask as Gabe comes out of what I presume is the guest room.

"I do," he says. "It's become a part of my recovery."

I check out his choice in puzzles.

"Mammals of Yellowstone."

He's gotten about forty percent of it done.

"You start from the edges," I observe.

"Uh-huh," he says, folding his arms.

He leans up against the kitchen wall, looking gorgeous and comfortable. Teddy settles into her bed next to the couch. The whole thing veers in and out of normality. Am I really in Montana in Gabe Parker's apartment?

What is going on here?

In order to ignore the cognitive dissonance that keeps threatening to unmoor me, I lean over the puzzle board, searching for pieces.

"I thought we'd established that I read your work," Gabe says.

I straighten. I'd forgotten. Or, hadn't made the connection.

"You started puzzling because of me?" I ask.

"In a sense," he says, pushing away from the wall. "Tried a bunch of things, but this one stuck."

The look he gives me is so intense that I have to glance away. It makes me feel vulnerable. Exposed.

"Are you cold?" Gabe asks.

I realize I've wrapped my arms around myself.

"I'm always cold," I say.

He smiles a little at that, brushing past me, headed to the fireplace. It doesn't take long, but I enjoy watching him work. It's elemental, watching this big hunk of a man build a fire to keep me warm.

The fire does its part to add to the atmosphere, crackling merrily and casting the room in a golden-red glow. Teddy lifts her head, leaning her chin off the edge of her bed as warmth begins to spread through the apartment.

"Gabe," I say. "What am I doing here?"

He pushes out of a crouch, and comes toward me.

"Don't you know?" he asks.

My breath catches, and this thing that I think I remember as hope surfaces inside of me like a long-lost dinghy.

I shake my head.

He smiles a little. "Chani," he says.

"You never called," I say. "You could have called. After. Later."

My voice is steadier than I am. I'm waiting for him to say that he did. Waiting for him to mention the call.

He doesn't.

"You were still married," Gabe says. "Contrary to rumors, I'm not that kind of guy."

I give him a look.

He holds up his hands. "I was faithful the entire time I was married," he says. "That was one of our rules. We were supposed to insulate ourselves from outside gossip, not do anything that could provoke it. The drinking was bad enough. I wasn't going and *looking* for trouble with married women."

"Inviting me to your play doesn't count?" I ask.

He winces. "Touché."

We look at each other.

"And then?" I ask. "After I . . ."

I skip some invisible stones.

"I tried to learn from my mistakes," he says. "By not calling. By waiting. I wanted to give you some time."

I wasn't sure I understood.

"I've been divorced for over a year," I say.

His expression is pained and yet inscrutable.

"What?" I demand.

"You've been divorced for over a *year*?" he asks.

"Separated longer than that," I say. "It's been over for almost two years."

He puts his head in his hands. For a moment I don't know what's happening and then I hear him laughing. It isn't a "ha ha ha" type of laugh, more of a "what the fuck" kind of laugh.

"What?" I ask again. "What are you laughing at?"

He looks up at me, his eyes so green. There's this kind of hopeless humor to them.

"I only knew about your divorce because you wrote about it," he says. "A month ago."

"Oh," I say.

Of course.

How in the world could Gabe have known? If my newsletter was the way he kept up to date on my life, then of course he would have thought I had *just* gotten divorced.

"I was going to wait six months," he says, almost talking to himself. "Six months seemed fair."

I'm not sure if I'm hearing what I'm actually hearing.

"I was going to wait six months and then text you. Or call you. I hadn't decided which would be better. I thought the timing would be right. The movie would be out, either my career would be revived or permanently in the toilet. I'd be more than two years sober. I would have made some decisions."

"What happened?" I whisper as if this is a secret I'm not supposed to be hearing.

"My management. Your agent," Gabe says. He lets out a laugh. Short. Pained. "I don't know whose idea it was, but when it was pitched to me, I couldn't say no."

"No?"

"No," Gabe says. "I wanted to see you. Like that night in New York. That's what it was. That's why I invited you. Even though I knew it was a bad idea at the time, I couldn't help myself. I wanted to see you so badly. Wanted to see how you were doing."

He lets out a breath.

"And now . . ."

"I'm doing good," I say.

It's the dumbest thing to say, but Gabe grins.

"Yeah, I can see that," he says.

Everything shifts.

"You're two years sober?" I ask.

He nods.

"I'm divorced," I say. "*Happily* divorced."

"Are you?" he asks. "Happy?"

I lift a shoulder. "I could be happier, I guess. Couldn't we all?"

He reaches a hand out, his fingers sliding through my hair, thumb brushing against my temple. I shiver. Not from the cold.

"I could make you happy," he says.

I swallow. Hard.

"Yeah?" I ask.

"Yeah," he says.

"Show me," I say.

THE RUMOR MILL

JACINDA LOCKWOOD BREAKS HER "BONDS"

THE ONLY SURPRISING PART ABOUT JACINDA LOCKWOOD announcing her divorce from shamed former Bond Gabe Parker is that it took this long for her to do it.

Reports about them being on the outs have circulated since he was fired from his third Bond movie, and when he checked into rehab (again), the countdown to the divorce announcement began in earnest.

The last time we saw the two together was at the funeral of Parker's brother-in-law, who was tragically killed in a car accident. Grainy photos of the two of them in Montana circulated and gave Gabcinda fans a glimmer of hope that their marriage would survive his continuous fall from grace.

But it's clear that whatever spark had them rushing off to Vegas all those years ago has finally gone out.

Sunday

BROAD SHEETS

GABE PARKER:
Shaken, Not Stirred—Part Three

BY CHANI HOROWITZ

REMEMBER WHAT I SAID EARLIER ABOUT BEING A LIGHTweight? Well, I wake up on Sunday morning with a pounding headache and the reminder that while they are beautiful and delicious, pink ombre drinks are not my friend.

The reason I'm awake, though, is almost enough to cure my hangover.

Because it's a text from Gabe checking in on me.

Yes, the future Bond, James Bond, texted me the morning after a premiere—and after-party—that I basically weaseled my way into and drank too much at. Texted to check up on me and give me his cure for a hangover.

Eat a big breakfast, he tells me. *No caffeine. Lots of water.*

It's very sweet.

Somehow, I'm able to roll myself out of bed and sit upright at my computer. My intention, of course, is to write this article.

Before I can—there's another text from Gabe.

If you're free, I'm having a party tonight.

If I'm free.

I've never been more free in my life.

I spend the rest of the day hydrating and telling my reflection that we are not allowed any drinks. Of any kind.

Reader, I'm sure it won't surprise you to learn that these

pep talks amounted to bubkes in the face of a celebrity's house party and an open bar.

Let me set the scene for you.

There's the aforementioned open bar. There's a beautiful backyard with a pool and hot tub. It is filled with equally beautiful people. Yes, it's December, but it's also California and the pool is heated. I can see the steam floating off it from where I'm standing in the living room waiting for the next round of Running Pyramid to start.

That's right. Running Pyramid.

I'm not good at games.

I'm not good at running games. I'm not good at word games. I'm not good at games.

You will not be surprised to learn that Gabe is very, very good at Running Pyramid.

You may be surprised, however, to learn that this is usually how his house parties go. Not the booze-soaked, endless orgies of Hollywood lore. Nope, instead, we all take turns running from room to room, reading prompts off a list and trying to get our teammates to guess correctly with a few choice words.

I was assured that it would be easier with a drink under my belt.

That might be true for some, but I tried it, and trust me, it did not get any easier. I'd like to share with you stories of how actors like Oliver Matthias and designers like Margot Rivera killed at this game, but unfortunately, after only one drink on very little sleep, I completely passed out.

In Gabe's dog bed.

I don't remember much of the rest of the evening, but I do know that at some point, Gabe himself lifted me up and out of the dog bed, and carried me into his guest room. Where he tucked me in and left me to sleep off the second drunken night we'd spent together.

The evening didn't end there.

When I woke up—head aching, mouth dry—I had no idea where I was at first. I was in a strange, dark room. There was the soft, muffled sound of talking on the other side of the door. It sounded almost familiar. Somehow, I hoisted myself upright, and found my way out. It wasn't until I got to the living room that I remembered what had happened.

It helped that Gabe was sitting on the couch watching TV. He filled me in on some of the more unfamiliar details—like the fact that I'd uncovered a natural talent for Running Pyramid and was also a very sore loser. Apparently, I had ended up in the dog bed because I hadn't liked how the other team kept winning. I had been convinced they were cheating.

Gabe helped soothe my embarrassment by offering me popcorn. He has his own little machine that he set up on the counter of his kitchen. That way he can give the puppy some before he puts his own toppings on it.

His toppings of choice? Cinnamon and sugar.

The TV show he paired with it? *Star Trek: The Next Generation*.

That's right, my dears, Gabe Parker is a Trekkie.

I'm a Trekkie as well, but let's face it, that's not surprising at all.

Gabe's favorite character? Worf. Mine? Data. I'm certain a therapist could go to town with those revelations, but all Gabe and I did with it was watch several episodes of our favorite show before we went to bed.

Gabe in his room. Me in the guest room.

—

Then

Chapter 19

MY HEAD AND MOUTH FELT AS THOUGH I'D BEEN DRAGGED hair-first through a sandstorm, and considering I couldn't remember how I had gotten home last night, it wasn't completely out of the realm of possibility.

At least I'd managed to take off my shoes and dress before falling into bed, though I apparently hadn't taken anything else off. By touch alone, I discovered I was still wearing my bra and it still had a safety pin in it. The fact that it was closed seemed to be due more to dumb luck than any forethought on my end.

I kept hearing a rattling, buzzing noise, but it wasn't consistent. It would buzz once, stop, buzz twice, stop, and then buzz again.

It took me a good five minutes to realize that it was my phone shimmying across my bedside table.

Someone was texting me.

It felt like a personal affront, especially considering I couldn't peel my eyelids open far enough to read whatever was on the screen. Every time I tried, the bright light from the bedroom window made me recoil like a vampire. I might have even hissed during my first attempt.

Finally I managed to dislodge the sleep crumbs caking the corners of my eyes enough to blink and peer at the screen. It took ten seconds for anything to focus.

Then it took another ten seconds to believe what I was seeing.

Texts. Multiple ones.

From Gabe.

Get some chilaquiles, he'd texted. *Best hangover cure I know.*

No, wait, a burger. A big, greasy burger and fries. That had been the second text.

In total, Gabe sent me seven text messages with seven different suggestions of food I should eat. My heart was touched, but my stomach rebelled and I spent the next fifteen minutes remembering that in addition to the pink drinks from the after-party, I'd also had several red Jell-O shots at the club. My toilet looked like someone had been murdered in it and I never wanted to eat anything that tasted like pineapple or cherry again.

When I pulled myself off the floor and back to my bed, I found that Gabe had sent me several more text messages.

Ollie says no caffeine, he'd said. *But I finally found Preeti's chai recipe so here it is.*

He'd included a photo of a handwritten recipe on a piece of paper with Spider-Man on the top.

Lots of water, he'd also written. *A bathtub of water.*

That I could do.

I started in the shower, gulping down as much as I could while washing away the dried sweat and sticky remnants of spilled drinks. As I began to come back to life, the rest of the evening returned to me.

After Gabe had left, Ollie and I had danced for a couple more hours and then he'd gotten a car to take me home. By some sheer force of will, I hadn't fallen asleep or thrown up in the backseat of the car and had managed to operate my front door keys as well as maneuver the staircase leading up to my room before wrestling my dress off and passing out.

When I emerged from the shower—my bathroom completely steamed up—feeling like I'd scrubbed myself into a mild semblance of normality, I found that I had even *more* texts from Gabe.

Wrapped in my towel, I sat on the side of the bed, reading through messages that were surprisingly devoid of acronyms or texting slang. Apparently, Gabe Parker preferred a full-sentence text.

I'm having a party at my place tonight, he'd messaged. *There will be fun and games aplenty.*

Aplenty.

Gabe Parker used "aplenty" in his text messages.

I remembered then the moment on the dance floor. How it had felt. How *he* had felt.

My skin was soft and red from the hot shower, but the warmth I felt was from something else entirely.

Gabe had danced *aplenty* close to me last night. Gabe was—at the very least—physically attracted to me. Gabe was inviting me to a party at his house.

Suddenly the once-absurd possibility that something could actually happen between us didn't feel so absurd, after all.

My phone buzzed.

You can bring your tape recorder if you want.

The text was followed by a winky face.

That winky face threw a dash of cold water on my flickering hope.

Because I had completely forgotten about the article. The whole reason Gabe was speaking to me in the first place. Obviously, he wanted me to come over so he could dazzle me with another element of his glamorous life. Which I would then put in the *Broad Sheets* piece.

They had said I would be getting unprecedented access.

If he had wanted to make a move, he would have made it last night. He wouldn't have disappeared in a haze of smoke and Jell-O shots just when things were getting good.

Right?

I looked at my phone, weighing my options.

After last night, I had more than enough to use in my article. I couldn't talk about Ollie—about how homophobia had blocked him from getting Bond—but I could talk about his friendship with Gabe. About how there were no hard feelings. I could make it believable, and that would help Gabe. Would help his image.

It probably would be unprofessional to go to the party tonight.

But it had definitely been unprofessional to invite myself to a premiere and then go to a gay club where I ended up a hairsbreadth away from being blackout drunk.

What time? I asked Gabe.

Instead of working on my article—which was due that week—I spent the next several hours trying to get over my hangover while preparing for Gabe's party.

I didn't ask Jo for help.

I didn't know what to wear to a gathering at a Hollywood star's house. I didn't know what the vibe would be. I was pretty sure it was going to be intense—plenty of beautiful people, a bunch of famous actors, and, probably, lots of drugs.

Eventually, I settled on a pair of jeans that Jeremy had once said made my ass look incredible and a top that was maybe a touch tighter than I usually would have worn. I checked myself out in the mirror, while also practicing how to graciously turn down the cocaine I assumed I'd be offered.

"No thanks," I said to my reflection with a toss of my hair. "I'm already totally high."

Was that even the correct terminology?

"I'm good," I tried again. "I'm high on life."

I shook my head.

"You're ridiculous," I told myself. "No one is going to waste cocaine on you."

I hoped that was true.

When I arrived at Gabe's house, I expected to see people passed out on the front lawn or doing obscene things to his gate, but no one was outside. The house was brightly lit and I could see people inside, but so far it looked like every other party I'd ever been to.

My heart was thumping against my ribs as I walked toward the house. I could hear laughter and chatter as I approached. I felt so unbelievably awkward—not knowing if I should knock or just open the door. Was this something other people worried about or was I just extremely high-strung? In the end, I did a combination of both, I rapped my knuckles on the door as I pushed it open.

I expected no one to notice my arrival, or if they did, it would be nothing more than confused looks from beautiful people wondering why this normal person had been allowed to be in their presence. I expected to mostly be ignored.

Instead, a dozen heads swiveled in my direction and to my great surprise—and relief—I recognized one of them.

"You're here!" Ollie approached me with open arms, sweeping me into a hug.

"Hi," I said.

"Gabe said he invited you," he said, looping his arm through mine. "I'm glad you came."

"Thanks," I said.

"Let's get you a drink." He steered me into the kitchen, introducing me to people as we went. "Chani, this is Margot. She's a fabulous clothing designer, based in New York. And Jessica writes for one of my favorite fashion blogs. Chani is a writer too. She's doing a profile on our dear host."

He said it like I was someone important. People looked at me with new interest.

I was overwhelmed with all the faces—some of which were very beautiful, but also many who were beautiful in a normal kind of way. It made me feel a little less out of place.

"What would you like?" Ollie asked, gesturing toward the bar. "Gabe is well-stocked on beer, but the cocktail selection is pretty minimal. Davis here could probably make you a martini if you'd like." He indicated a tall, skinny guy leaning against the fridge.

"Or we could get you some of the stronger stuff," Davis said. "It's in the living room."

I panicked.

"No thanks, I don't do cocaine," I quickly said.

Davis and Ollie looked at each other and then at me.

"I was talking about whisky," Davis said. "Or tequila."

Ollie laughed. "I don't think Gabe has any cocaine," he said to me gently.

I'd never felt like such an embarrassing idiot. Both naïve and overly jaded at the same time.

Thankfully, Ollie didn't linger on my faux pas, and swept me through the rest of the house instead. I still hadn't seen Gabe.

"Gabe said something about fun and games?" I asked tentatively.

Ollie let out a groan. "Gabe and his damn games," he said.

I wondered belatedly if *that* was code for sex games. That I'd unwittingly accepted an invitation to a Hollywood orgy.

No. I was being ridiculous. If there wasn't cocaine, there probably wasn't any free love. Despite the house—with its raunchy seventies vibes—practically begging for it.

"What kind of games?" I asked.

"He'll explain it to you," Ollie said.

And then, like it was an actual movie, not just a living fantasy with a movie star, the crowd seemed to part and there he was.

Gabe.

He was holding court at one end of his living room, his still-unnamed puppy sitting at his feet. He was barefoot and every time the dog licked his toes, he'd give her something off the little round paper plate he was holding.

"You're spoiling her," Ollie said as we approached.

But Gabe wasn't paying attention—he was looking at me. Staring, in fact.

"It's you," he said.

"Hi," I said.

Ollie patted my shoulder.

"I'll leave you two to discuss Running Pyramid."

Then he was gone.

Even though the living room was full of people and there was music and talking and laughing, all of that seemed to mellow into a quiet kind of hush. The expression on Gabe's face wasn't much different from the one he'd worn when I met him on the red carpet.

Only I wasn't wearing a beautiful, glittering dress, I didn't have a full face of makeup, and my hair was wavy and frizzy and messy the way it usually was.

Still.

"Hi," he said.

"Hi," I said again.

The puppy let out a little, short bark. We both looked down at her, and she looked up innocently, as if she had no idea why we were suddenly paying attention to her.

"Ollie is right," Gabe told her. "I am spoiling you."

He handed me the plate and knelt down, hefting her up into his arms. She was little now, but it was easy to tell from her catcher's mitt paws that she was going to be a big dog. She licked his face.

"Feel free to spoil her too," Gabe said, nodding at the plate in my hand. "It's just cheese."

I fed her a few crumbles, which she ate eagerly, her soft tongue cleaning my fingers.

"She likes you," Gabe said.

"I think she likes anyone with food," I said.

"Just like her master." He nuzzled the dog with his nose and she sniffed his face. "Good girl."

"Good girl," I echoed.

Gabe grinned. "Let's get you a drink," he said.

THE RUMOR MILL

GABE PARKER: WITHOUT A FATHER FIGURE

[EXCERPT]

BY NOW, WE'VE ALL SEEN THE PICTURE—OF GABE PARKER, who drew the world's attention in the steamy, rustic drama *Cold Creek Mountain,* attending the movie premiere with his mother.

Not a budding starlet, not his gorgeous co-star, not anyone in the industry at all.

It was enough to make his new legion of female fans swoon.

What followed were numerous interviews about how close he is with not just his mother but his sister as well. He even calls her his best friend.

One has to wonder how Parker managed to maintain his undeniable masculinity while surrounded by so much femininity.

Especially since he refuses to discuss—or even mention—his father.

Speculation has run rampant and Parker's silence does nothing to quell the rumors. In fact, it only serves to amplify them.

If there isn't a story, then why won't Gabe talk about his father? Who *is* the patriarchal Parker?

But nothing stays hidden in Hollywood—and that includes details about Parker's family life.

The Rumor Mill has discovered the truth behind Gabe's silence, and it's tragic.

Thomas Parker was a contractor in Cooper, Montana,

where he was born and raised. He married Elizabeth Williams when they were both twenty-seven. They had their first child—Gabe's sister, Lauren—at twenty-nine, followed by Gabe the following year. Ten years later Thomas was gone. Dead from a brain tumor.

Chapter 20

I WAS *EXHAUSTED*. THE NIGHT BEFORE WAS CATCHING UP TO ME, it was way past my bedtime, and I was bored. Pretty much everyone around me was drunk and even though Oliver had insisted there was no cocaine available at this party, I was pretty sure that there were a few people over in the corner that had brought their own.

I kept a fair distance from them—I still wasn't sure of the cool way to refuse.

I felt ridiculous and Gabe was being weird. Or maybe that was just me.

He'd gotten me that drink—a pretty hefty pour of whisky into a red cup of Diet Coke. I'd taken one or two sips, been reminded of how I'd felt that morning, and left the cup on a table somewhere.

The minute I'd had that drink in my hand, though, Gabe was gone. He and the puppy disappeared into the crowd, leaving me alone by the bar in a house full of people I didn't know.

It was his party, so I tried not to be too disappointed. He had friends to talk to, people to entertain. I'd probably assumed too much about the invitation—he likely had included everyone he knew in L.A.

I thought about my purse—left in the massive pile of bags and jackets on the bed in the guest room—and the tape recorder stuffed into the bottom of it. Gabe had said to bring it but now I couldn't tell if that had been a joke. He didn't seem to want to be interviewed any further—he seemed to be fully avoiding me—and I didn't really know anyone else here besides Ollie, who was entertaining in the backyard.

I didn't want to interrupt.

I sat myself on a couch in front of a bowl of jelly beans, trying to ignore the twin feelings of embarrassment and awkwardness. I'd never been good at parties. That was one of the things that Jeremy and I had in common. We were both, for the most part, homebodies. We'd enjoyed nights in, watching movies or just reading on the couch with our feet tangled up together. We'd go to the occasional party—mostly book launches and smaller gatherings at friends' houses but nothing like this. For a brief, unexpected moment, I missed him.

I watched Gabe from across the room. He seemed completely at ease with all these people around him—with all the chaos and noise.

I felt a bit like a creep, the way my eyes would find him in the crowd, the way I began monitoring where he was and who he was with. I kept shifting my gaze to the door, wondering if Jacinda Lockwood would show up.

I continued eating jelly beans, and I could feel the sugar warring with my exhaustion. I shifted on the couch, and it squeaked loud enough that two people turned to look at me.

"It's the sofa," I said, waving a hand at it.

They both just frowned and turned away. It seemed possible that I looked completely insane—sitting by myself, shoving handfuls of candy into my mouth—but I kept telling myself that no one cared. No one noticed me.

The thought was both comforting and depressing.

I told myself I'd leave after I found one more sour-apple jelly bean.

When I did, I pulled myself to my feet, swaying a little as I reached my final altitude. I was buzzing from the sugar but I was still tired. My eyelids fought with gravity.

Gabe stepped to the center of the room.

I sat down again, the rapid movement taking most of the energy out of me.

"Okay," Gabe said. "It's time to play."

My head felt heavy and wobbly but I was determined to keep it upright. Even if I had to rest my hand at the base of my throat, using my palm to stabilize it like my neck was that slippery, unsteady column of birthday cake in *Sleeping Beauty*.

"How long do these games go for?" I asked the person next to me.

They looked at me with boozy, sleepy eyes and gave me a thumbs-up. It wasn't the answer I was looking for, but I returned the gesture anyway.

It was just another reminder of how out of my element I was. This was Gabe's life—all this endless partying—and two days in I was already exhausted. How could someone maintain this kind of lifestyle?

I looked around and could see that some of the veneer I'd admired when I first arrived—the same kind of polish I'd noticed at last night's premiere—had begun to rub off.

Tucked in among the younger, more fresh-faced guests were a few that looked like they had been partying since this house was new. There was a worn-out seediness to them, those deep lines around the eyes that said they'd been around this town far too long.

It felt like a warning.

To me. To everyone here.

Jelly beans sloshed around in my stomach, all alone.

"Come on," Gabe urged his guests, most of whom seemed to have a general idea of what was going on.

Some of the more wizened partygoers made their retreat, taking out packs of cigarettes as they migrated to the backyard. Whatever was about to happen, it was clear that it wasn't for them.

I had no clue what was going on, but I got back on my feet anyway.

Gabe was walking around the room, pointing at people and saying "one" or "two," like my PE teacher did in middle school when it was time to play dodgeball.

Gabe reached me—his finger mid-point. I should have been a one.

"Two," he said instead, and then pointed at himself. "Two."

He finished going around the room and then he was back in front of me.

"Come on," he said, taking my arm. "You're on my team."

The game was called Running Pyramid. All of us were instructed to write a list of ten things. We were to show them to no one.

"I don't know what to put on my list," I said to no one in particular.

"Anything you want, darling," Ollie said. "But don't get too complicated."

He had appeared next to me, though I couldn't say when. If he was drunk, he was hiding it well.

Gabe too. If not for the heavy hood of his eyes and the slight lean that only the most focused observer might note, I might have assumed he was sober.

"I don't even know what would be too complicated," I told Ollie.

Someone passed out paper and pencils. I was impressed by how well-organized this game was, but by the time the materials had reached me, I'd already forgotten what I was supposed to do with them.

"Ten things?" I asked Ollie.

He glanced over at me and gave me a sympathetic smile.

"Oh, love," he said. "You're just about tits up, aren't you?"

"I don't know what that means," I said. "But I do think my tits are tired."

He patted my hand.

"Here," he said. "I'll do your list and mine."

"Thank you." I handed over my paper, though I still had no idea what was happening.

"Is everyone ready to play?" Gabe asked. "Ollie, you ready to embarrass yourself?"

Ollie gave him the V sign.

"Ollie's ready," Gabe said. "Chani?"

I looked up at him, though I wasn't sure how I managed it since my head felt so dense.

"I'm sleepy," I said.

"She's drunk," Ollie clarified.

I shook my head. "Not drunk," I said. "I had too many jelly beans, though."

"Come on." Gabe hoisted me up out of my seat, gripping my arm. His hand was warm, his palm rough against the soft skin on the inside of my elbow.

"Team Two with me," Gabe said.

I followed him, though I didn't have much choice. He was still holding my arm.

"Cool party," I said.

It came out sarcastic.

"Not a fan of games?" Gabe asked.

I shook my head but lost control of the gesture halfway through and couldn't stop. I just had to let myself run out of momentum until my head was tilted to one side, looking up at Gabe. He was so tall.

"You *are* drunk," he said.

"I'm not good at games," I said.

"No?"

"No."

It came out the same way a child might respond if someone offered them vegetables, a long, drawn out whine.

Gabe didn't say anything but I could see him reassessing his opinion of me. I didn't like it.

"I'll try," I said.

He smiled.

"Good." He clapped me on the shoulder like we were football players and turned to the rest of the team. "Who wants to go first?"

It was then that I realized we had moved from the living room to his bedroom. Us and about a dozen other people.

Everyone else seemed to know exactly what they were doing. A slim licorice-haired girl in a sweater dress and a big colorful necklace waved her hand.

"I'll go first," she said, and then began doing long, exaggerated lunges.

I stared, horrified.

"Is that part of the game?" I asked.

Gabe laughed. "No," he said. "Adrienne is just warming up."

I didn't understand until Ollie's voice from the other room called out:

"Are both teams ready?"

"Ready!" echoed all around me.

"Okay, go!"

Adrienne raced out of the room. Within a few seconds, she was back.

"Okay." She was out of breath, but still managed to sing, " 'Thank you for being a friend . . .' "

"Golden Girls," a girl to my left shouted. She was wearing a pair of red clogs.

Adrienne pointed at her triumphantly and Red Clogs bolted out of the room.

Then she was back.

"Fred Astaire. Backward. Heels," she said.

"Ginger Rogers," someone shouted.

"Yes!" Red Clogs said, and the person who had answered correctly ran into the living room.

We did this seven more times until I heard the sound of cheering come from the other room. The puppy was barking too, clearly having aligned herself with the winning team.

"Dammit," Adrienne said.

"It's just the first round," Red Clogs said. "We'll get into the groove."

"Maybe if Gabe actually started playing," Adrienne said, tossing us a look that was both playful and threatening.

Gabe laughed. "I'm just teaching the newbie how to play," he said.

"Sure," Adrienne said, throwing her hair over her shoulder.

I stuck my tongue out at her and she laughed.

"Why is your tongue purple?" she asked.

"I told you," I said. "Too many jelly beans."

"Getting the hang of it?" Gabe asked.

He was standing very close to me. I felt the warmth of his whisky-laced breath against my temple.

"I think so." My voice was husky.

"Good," he said.

I wanted to lean back against him and it wasn't until gravity began its downward pull that I realized I'd started to do just that. Of course, I hadn't checked exactly how close he was, and for one horrible second, I was convinced I was about to fall on my ass.

Gabe, however, scooped me up under my armpits and hoisted me back to my feet before I could complete my London Bridge impression.

"All right here?" Adrienne asked.

"Just dandy," I said, feeling embarrassed and surly.

"You gonna give it a try this round?" Gabe asked.

The challenge in his tone sparked my mostly dormant competitive nature.

"Yeah," I said, lifting my chin.

"That's my girl," he said.

I blushed. Fiercely.

Even though I was certain Gabe had already seen it, I turned my face away, doing an over-the-top impression of someone who was watching the door.

Adrienne was stretching again. Her lunges were so deep that her knees touched the floor.

"You ready?" she asked me, V-ing her fingers and pointing to her eyes and then at me and back again.

"Oh yeah," I said.

I wasn't.

Team Two lost three more rounds.

"This is bullshit," said Red Clogs, whose name, I had learned, was Natasha. "Who picked these teams?"

Everyone pointed at Gabe. He shrugged, and took another drink of whatever was in his red Solo cup. From the smell, it was a delicate mix of whisky and whisky.

"At least I'm trying," he said.

Everyone looked at me.

"Jelly beans," I said.

"Okay." Gabe put his cup down and raised his arms over his head before bringing them down and extending his elbows out and away. His shirt had ridden up, exposing his flat, smooth stomach. I stared. I didn't even pretend not to. He stretched more, taking up space.

"I'll go next," he said.

Before he left, though, he put his hands on my shoulders and his face real close to mine.

"You can do this," he said.

I hated this party.

He jogged out of the room and I heard him give a whoop of glee. Then he was back in the doorway, one hand on the doorjamb, the other pointed at me.

"He's a piece of shit," he said.

"Woody Allen?"

"Yes!" he said.

I felt a rush of satisfaction. I'd gotten it right. Of course, I had completely forgotten what came next.

About five pairs of hands were on my back, shoving me forward, and I stumbled toward the door, barely managing to stay upright.

"Go! Go! Go!" my team was chanting.

Right. I had to run into the next room and get the next prompt.

As I passed Gabe, he gave me a friendly, sportsmanlike slap on the ass. I punched him in the arm.

"Ouch," he said.

"Baby," I said over my shoulder.

Somehow moving helped clear my head. I raced to Ollie, who was standing in the living room, a piece of paper in his hand. It seemed as if he was the referee. Or something. I still wasn't completely sure how the game worked. He showed me the next prompt.

Cary Grant.

I ran back to the bedroom, and before I was even through the doorway, I was shouting:

"C. K. Dexter Haaaaaven!"

"Cary Grant!" Gabe pushed past.

When he came back, his eyes were fixated on me.

"Charming, not sincere."

"Into the Woods!"

The rest of the round went like that, rapid-fire exchanges between me and Gabe until I ran back to Ollie and he waved the paper at me.

"You won," he said.

I whooped like I'd never whooped before. It was so loud that it startled the dog, who was sleeping in her dog bed near the TV.

"We won!" I told my team, who burst out in cheers as if we'd just won the Super Bowl or some other big, important sports thing.

Gabe swept me into a hug, lifting me off my feet as he spun me across the bedroom.

"Wow," Adrienne said, once he'd put me down. "You two really are the dream team, aren't you?"

THE_JAM_DOT_COM .BLOGSPOT.COM

THE PERFECT DAY

THE NOVELIST AND I USED TO PLAY A GAME CALLED THE Perfect Day. We'd usually play this game on the few evenings when we could afford to go out for a nice dinner.

The Novelist had a very detailed, very specific Perfect Day that required more luck than money. He loved the beach, especially ones with those old-fashioned boardwalks. His Perfect Day would be at one of those boardwalks on the East Coast. It would be summer, hot but not unbearably so. We'd get a hot dog and a frozen lemonade, then, by some wonderful chance, the moment we wanted to get out of the sun, we'd walk by a bookshop. We'd duck in to find that they were about to host one of the Novelist's favorite writers. One of the literary Jonathans, like Safran Foer or Franzen. It would be a small, intimate event that hadn't been advertised at all. In fact, we'd be the only ones there. And the literary Jonathan would look out into his audience of two and say, "What the hell, let's just go grab dinner together." And we would. A fancy seafood restaurant where we'd eat lobster in those plastic bibs. The Novelist would get a funny picture of the two of them. They'd talk about books and the literary Jonathan would say something like "that idea sounds incredible. Here's my personal email—send it to me when you're done. We'll get it published."

My Perfect Day was different in almost every way, except it also involved walking around and finding a bookstore. Fitting, I suppose, since that's where the Novelist and I met.

I didn't have a specific place where my Perfect Day would occur. I just knew it would be somewhere that it got cold. I wanted to be wearing a cozy sweater and warm jacket. It didn't need to be freezing, but I imagined the weather would be chilly enough to make my cheeks red. I'd be in a small town. The kind of town where people knew you. Where you'd walk past a store and the owner would pop their head out the door trying to lure you inside to see the latest jewelry they got in stock, or to try a new recipe they were testing. At some point, I'd get a hot chocolate with lots of marshmallows, using the heat from the cup to keep my hands warm. I'd walk down a street lined with twinkly lights and garlands draped between lampposts. Everyone I walked past would say hello. When it got just cold enough, that's when I'd walk past the bookshop. It would smell like cider inside and sure enough, there would be a little beverage cart near the door with cups and a cheery sign that would read HELP YOURSELF. I'd switch out my hot chocolate for a cider and wander around the store. It would be large but full of books and leather chairs and maybe even a cat lounging on some shelves. Every book I wanted to buy would be in stock and I'd find a few more that I hadn't even known I wanted. But the thing that made it the Perfect Day would be that when I went to check out, the salesperson would recognize me. *It's you,* they'd say, and then point to a shelf where my book was prominently displayed. *Would you mind signing some copies?* they'd ask. *We're big fans of your work.*

That, I think, would truly be the Perfect Day.

xoChani

Chapter 21

MY HEAD HURT AND MY TONGUE WAS FUZZY. I FELT QUEASY and I knew that if I tried to go back to bed, all I'd get was a few hours of weird, uneasy sleep and possibly bad dreams mixed in as well. I'd feel gross and tired and I knew that I was going to be spending the rest of this day lying in bed.

Then I realized I wasn't home. And it wasn't daytime.

It was dark, but there was light coming through the floor-length curtains—enough for me to get a decent view of where I was. A bedroom. A big bedroom. The bed was ridiculously large. I'd never been in a king-sized bed before but this seemed even more massive than that. Like I could start rolling to one side and it would be morning before I got to the edge. The sheets were really nice—soft and luxurious. They smelled good too.

It took a moment for me to realize exactly *what* they smelled like. An expensive, exclusive cedar tree.

I sat up fast, my head hating me.

I was in Gabe's house. In Gabe's *bed*.

Looking around, I confirmed that I was alone and—except for my shoes—I was fully clothed. I slumped back against the very nice pillows.

Shit.

I didn't know what was more embarrassing—that I'd passed out in Gabe's bed or that I was in Gabe's bed *alone*.

I could practically hear my roommate groaning.

"You were that close to fucking him and this is what happened?" she'd say to me.

I definitely needed new friends.

I tried to piece together the rest of the evening. I'd had a sip or two of whisky, followed up by a bucket of jelly beans. Then we'd been playing Running Pyramid, and I'd been very bad until I wasn't, probably around the time my jelly bean sugar high hit, and at some point, we had been celebrating winning. Gabe's dog had been jumping and barking and everyone had been laughing and after that I could remember lying down on the dog bed next to the puppy, who had been so tired and overwhelmed by the party that she'd put herself to bed, and I apparently had tried to do the same thing and now I could remember Gabe trying to get me off the dog bed, laughing as he did, while I kept trying to swat him away.

My stomach and heart both gave a lurch as the rest of my memory came back. Gabe had knelt down next to me—his face close to mine.

"Are you ready for bed?" he'd asked.

I must have nodded or snuggled in even closer to his puppy, who had let out a sigh of contentment, and I think I said that I would just stay there with her, but Gabe said that I couldn't sleep on the dog bed and then he had put his arms around me and lifted me up against his chest. I wasn't a small person—I was tall with lots of lanky limbs—and yet, he'd picked me up like I was the puppy herself and carried me into this room.

Into *his* room.

I vaguely remember some people clapping and hooting and hollering. Gabe had ignored them and put me on his bed. I'd crashed. Hard.

I'd flopped onto the mattress face-first, grabbing a pillow and holding it close. I could vaguely remember him taking my shoes off—I cringed at the thought of him coming into contact with feet that were probably very smelly—and then he'd left, closing the door behind him.

I had no idea what time it was. I didn't have my purse or my phone. They were probably exactly where I'd left them—with my coat, in the guest room.

Why Gabe hadn't put me there—with the coats—I didn't know.

I realized then that the house was quiet. Mostly quiet. There was some noise coming from far away, but it was a hushed nighttime kind of noise, not the kind of noise that you'd expect from a party that was still going on. It sounded like a conversation between people. Maybe Gabe and a friend.

Swinging my feet over the side of the massive bed, I found my shoes, neatly sitting side by side.

Even though the last thing my body wanted was to leave the comfort of an extremely soothing and cozy bed, I couldn't let Gabe give up his room—and I couldn't let myself stay any longer. I was light-years away from what was appropriate behavior and I wasn't sure how I was going to write this article without looking like a complete creep. If I'd hoped to dispel the stereotype of the female reporter getting her story via her feminine wiles, well, I was doing a shit job. Not that my feminine wiles had gotten me that far, but still. It was *so* unprofessional.

My tape recorder was still in my bag. If I wanted to talk about what had happened tonight—and I wasn't sure that I did since it was so embarrassing—I would have to re-create it from memory, and right now my brain seemed to shrivel up at the mere suggestion that I might have to do some deep thinking.

That was a problem for my de-sugared, hydrated mind to sort through. First, I had to get out of there. Had to get my shoes on, find my purse and my jacket. I needed to call the taxi company I'd used to get here. I needed to get home.

Shoes in hand, I opened the bedroom door.

The noise was coming from the other side of the house, but it became pretty clear pretty quickly that it wasn't Gabe. It was a woman and a man—but the man was British. Unless Gabe was practicing his Bond accent in the middle of the night with another guest, it seemed far more likely that he was watching TV.

That was confirmed when I crept toward the sound—which was also in the direction of the guest room—and found the distinct blue light of a TV illuminating the living room.

Part of me hoped that Gabe had fallen asleep, that I would be able to get out of there without him seeing me, but instead, the quiet dialogue stopped immediately, the image freezing on the screen.

"Hey," Gabe said.

He was sitting on the couch. Alone.

He was still wearing what he'd been wearing at the party—a pair of jeans and a T-shirt—but he looked a lot more rumpled. As if he might have been lying down on the couch.

"Hey," I said.

My head hurt and I was embarrassed beyond reason.

"How are you feeling?" he asked.

"I'm really sorry," I said as a response.

He grinned at me.

"You were pretty funny," he said, his face scrunched up in a teasing manner.

"You didn't have to put me in your room," I said.

"I couldn't leave you on the dog bed," he said.

He gestured toward it, the puppy still fast asleep.

"You could have put me in the guest room," I said.

"People would have been coming in and out of that for a while," he said. "Party only ended about an hour ago."

"What time is it?" I asked, feeling completely out of sorts.

"Only three," he said.

"Three?"

Only three.

"You shouldn't be sleeping on the couch," I said.

"I wasn't," he said. "I was going to go sleep in the guest room when I got tired."

"You shouldn't sleep in the guest room," I said.

He raised an eyebrow. "Is that an invitation?"

I didn't know what to say. Was he serious? And if he was, *was* it? An invitation, that is?

Could I actually take him up on it?

"You probably need some water," Gabe said, thankfully saving me from answering. "Sit."

He patted the couch as he got up and headed into the kitchen. I perched there, on the edge of one of the cushions, watching his dog sleep. She was very, very cute, her nose tucked under her tail. It was then that I finally directed my attention to what Gabe was watching on TV.

"It's true," he said when he returned with a large glass of water. "I'm a huge nerd."

"I love this episode," I said after I'd drunk most of it.

"Yeah?" Gabe asked.

"I mean, Data is probably my favorite character, followed by Worf, but the Picard-centric episodes are pretty spectacular."

Gabe looked at me.

"I'm also a huge nerd," I said, though I imagined it was less of a surprise to discover that *I* was a *Star Trek: The Next Generation* fan than to find out that Gabe Parker was one.

"Want to watch it with me?" he asked, holding up the remote.

"I should go," I said.

But I didn't move.

"I can call you a cab in the morning," he said. "Come on. Watch an episode with me."

We watched three. The one he was already watching, my favorite episode, and then his favorite. He had all of them on DVD.

Gabe made popcorn—a little bowl of plain for the dog, then sprinkling cinnamon and sugar on the one he made for us.

The whole thing felt weirdly nice. And normal.

More normal and nice than the entire weekend had been.

"Did you grow up watching *Star Trek*?" I asked.

"Yeah," Gabe said. "My dad loved it."

There was a long, weighted silence. Gabe looked at me.

As if he was giving me permission.

"Who was his favorite character?" I asked, carefully pushing the boat out.

"He loved Geordi," Gabe said. "I think because he was an engineer at heart. Liked to fix things."

"Were you close with your dad?" I asked, still bracing myself for the brush-off. For him to shut down, turn away, and tell me to fuck off.

But Gabe softened. Smiled.

"Yeah," he said. "The whole family was close but I was the only one who wanted to go to job sites with him. I could spend all day there, breathing in the sawdust, listening to his team hammer and cuss. Watching them watch my dad. He was great at his job—everyone admired him."

"You loved your dad," I said.

"I know what you're thinking," Gabe said.

The general assumption was that there was something dark and sordid about Gabe's relationship with his father. That Gabe's reluctance to talk about him was covering something up.

He leaned back into the couch, his feet up on the coffee table.

"What do you know?" he asked. "About him?"

I repeated everything I'd heard—just the facts—the kind of things that might be listed on his Wikipedia page.

"You weren't . . . estranged?" I asked.

I thought about my tape recorder in the other room. But I knew that Gabe wasn't telling me this because of the article.

"No," he said. "He died when I was ten and he was my hero—cheesy as that sounds—and to an extent, he still is. Losing him was the worst moment of my life."

He rubbed a hand over his face.

"My dad was thirty when he had me," he said. "My age."

I sensed that I was just supposed to listen.

"You've written a lot of articles on celebrities," Gabe said.

It wasn't a question so I didn't bother answering. Also, "a lot" was relative.

"I've read plenty of articles on celebrities. I know how it works when you have a story like this. It becomes part of the narrative, part of your DNA as an actor. As a public figure. My dad . . ." Gabe paused, hand swiping over his face again.

Every time he did that he seemed a little older, a little more tired.

"I've never liked talking about it—talking about him. When he died, people would ask about him, about how I was doing, and it always made me uncomfortable. Almost like there was this weird performative aspect to it."

He shook his head. "I know it doesn't really make sense, but it always made it hard to talk about him. That hasn't changed just because people want to know about my personal life. My dad is more than just a single line in my bio," Gabe said. "He's more than my tragic backstory. Can you understand that?"

I did. And I knew exactly what he was saying, because my own writerly, reporting brain was already building that narrative:

Gabe Parker: Haunted by Beloved Father's Loss

Gabe Parker: Becoming the Man His Father Never Got to See

Gabe Parker: What Loss Gave Me

"My father—his memory—is private," Gabe said. "I understand that part of my job is sharing myself with the public. Sharing stories and intimacies of my life. But I can't do that with my dad."

He shrugged.

"I know it's ridiculous—I know that refusing to talk about him has made him into a source of interest—but some things aren't for my fans."

"It's not ridiculous," I said.

I knew that if I included this in my article, it would be a huge boon for me. It would get me attention. It would get me work.

Because I would have gotten the story that no one else had.

Gabe studied my face with an intensity that made me want to curl back into myself like a startled pill bug, but I forced myself to stay still. I waited for him to ask if I was going to write about this.

Instead, he redirected the conversation back to a safer topic. Almost as if he didn't want to know the answer.

"How'd you get into *Star Trek*?" Gabe asked. "Your family?"

I shook my head. "My first semester of grad school was rough," I said. "I moved to Iowa without knowing anyone, and had a hard time making friends. I'd get DVDs from Netflix and watch them alone in my room."

Gabe looked thoughtful. "I can't imagine it," he said.

"Oh," I said. "I was very awkward."

"I can imagine *that,*" he said.

I made a face of mock outrage and he laughed.

"I guess I just thought that you'd be the same kind of awkward as the other grad students," he said. "All of you in sweaters with elbow patches, smoking pipes and debating the actual intention of the guy who wrote *Lolita*."

"Nabokov," I said.

Gabe gave me a knowing little smile and I realized I'd walked right into that one. Again.

"There were no pipes," I said.

"No?"

"Okay, maybe one or two," I admitted. "And a few sweaters with elbow patches—but I didn't have either."

"You and the Novelist aren't cut from the same cloth?" Gabe asked.

His tone was sardonic.

"Jeremy," I said. "And no."

"Hmm," Gabe said.

I could hear the judgment in that one simple sound.

"He's a good writer," I said.

"Hmm," Gabe said again.

Better than me, I thought. After all, Jeremy had an agent and a book deal. I was hustling to write puff pieces.

Gabe's attention had shifted back to the TV.

"This," he said.

He was watching a very young, extremely beautiful Famke Janssen explain to Patrick Stewart that she had been raised and bred to please her future partner. That she took pleasure from being what someone else wanted her to be.

"They are fulfilled by what I give to others," she said, in response to Picard asking about her wishes. Her needs.

"What about when there are no others. When you're alone?" he asked.

"I'm incomplete," she said.

I looked at Gabe. He kept his focus on the TV, the bright glow of it making him seem both younger and older at the same time—the light sinking into the lines around his eyes, while blurring other parts of him.

"This?" I asked.

"This is how it feels," he said. "Being an actor."

I didn't say anything.

"When I'm in front of the camera," he said, "I know who I am."

"And when the camera's gone?" I asked.

He shrugged.

"Pathetic, isn't it?" he asked. "That I'm more comfortable playing pretend than being myself."

"No," I said. "I don't think it's pathetic."

Gabe didn't respond.

My eyes wandered. The room was pretty clean considering that it had been full of people a few hours ago. There were some empty cups strewn around, but for the most part, the place was tidy.

Like Gabe's bedroom, there were piles of books and movies everywhere. A box set of the entirety of *Star Trek: The Next Generation* was sitting next to the TV alongside some leather-bound books. I would have bet this month's rent that *Lolita* was in a pile somewhere.

"What's that?" I said, pointing to his end table.

I knew what it was, of course. I had a stack of them on my bookshelf. I'd practically memorized the spine.

"Oh, this?" Gabe asked with a grin that indicated that he knew that I knew exactly what it was. "I told you that I did my research."

"You read it?"

He looked at me. "Yeah," he said. "Some of them big words were real tough, but I got through it."

I'd noticed he did that. Put on some slow, hick-like accent any time we circled around the idea of his intelligence.

"I don't think my *parents* have read it," I said.

"Oh," he said.

I picked up the literary magazine, stroking the front of it like I'd done with the first copy I got in the mail. There was a line on the spine that indicated it had been cracked open, the pages pulled into place. I let it fall open in my lap, balancing it next to the popcorn bowl.

"The Garden" by Chani Horowitz.

"I'm bad with titles," I said.

"I liked it," he said. "Wasn't expecting the dragons, though."

I flushed.

No one in my grad program had expected them either and considering that this was the only piece of fiction I'd ever managed to get published, I was pretty sure that my tendency to weave fantasy elements into my naturalistic fiction wasn't something that people were clamoring to read. The piece had been personal—not the way my blog was personal, where I just blurted out details about my private life—but intimate. It was about the way my mind worked—how I thought, how I felt—like sawing open my skull and letting people look inside.

While also writing about dragons.

It was a metaphor.

"I guess I don't really get it," Jeremy had said when he first read it.

"It was an experiment," I told Gabe. "I don't really write stuff like that anymore."

"That's too bad," he said.

"I'll probably just stick to nonfiction," I said.

"I like your nonfiction," Gabe said. "But I like dragons too."

I did as well, but they weren't serious. They weren't real literature. They weren't *good* writing.

At some point while watching *Star Trek,* we'd moved closer together. I hadn't noticed—not like I had at the club when I had been almost painfully aware of his proximity at all points. But now, I'd been distracted by talking about the short story, so when Gabe put his hand on my knee, I wasn't expecting it.

In fact, I was so surprised that I jumped—tossing the magazine and the bowl up off my lap and into the air, spraying popcorn everywhere.

"Oh my god." I clutched my chest, more out of embarrassment than anything.

"Wow," Gabe said. "I don't think I've ever gotten that reaction before."

"I'm so sorry." I got off the couch, gathering up the popcorn kernels I'd thrown across his floor.

"Hey." Gabe was next to me on his knees, stilling my hand. "Hey. I'm the one who should be sorry."

We sat back on the couch. My face was hot, and I knew it was probably an extremely unattractive splotchy shade of red. I put my hands against my cheeks.

"I'm so embarrassed," I said.

"Don't be," he said. "I should have . . . well, I guess I should have read the mood a little better."

I looked at him.

"The mood?"

Now he looked a little sheepish.

"I thought, you know . . ." He gestured between us.

"Oh," I said. "Oh!"

Gabe gave a little shrug. "Don't worry about it," he said. "I just thought—"

I kissed him. Before he could even finish his sentence, I flung myself at him and planted my lips on his. Aggressively.

It was a terrible, *terrible* kiss. My lips hit his teeth, making my eyes water.

Gently, Gabe put his hands on my shoulders and pushed me back.

"Oh my god," I said again. "I am really, really sorry."

I closed my eyes, wishing I could just disappear.

"Hey," he said.

I felt his hand on my chin. His thumb stroked the line of my jaw, sending chills through me. I opened my eyes.

His face was right there. His beautiful, perfect face.

"Hey," he said again.

I could smell the whisky on his breath, but I didn't mind. I was certain my own breath was probably still fragrant from jelly beans.

"Hey," I whispered.

Time inched forward as his lips moved toward mine. I thought dimly that if I could live in this moment, in this beautiful anticipation, I would be pretty damn happy. Then Gabe's mouth touched mine and I realized that this was far, far better than I had ever imagined it would be.

This time, his lips seemed to fit perfectly against mine. They were warm and firm and soft and his hand was still on my face and the combination of the two sensations was enough to turn my insides to Jell-O. I wobbled and sighed and leaned closer.

I was kissing Gabe Parker. Or rather, he was kissing *me* and I was kissing him back.

His hand slid back and upward, getting lost in my hair. That's when his lips parted and I slipped my tongue into his mouth. His fingers tightened against my scalp and I thought I felt his breath catch. As if I had caught him off guard. As if I had surprised him. I liked how that kept happening.

If he was surprised, he recovered quickly.

I pressed my palms against his chest and felt the rumble of a groan deep inside. Hot little sparks spread through me as he gave my hair a tug, opening the kiss, taking my tongue with his, his other hand sliding down to my hip to pull me closer.

I didn't need much encouragement to climb onto his lap, my legs on either side of his hips. My own hips moved forward, the seam of my jeans coming into direct contact with the zipper of his—and everything that was happening behind it.

I sighed. He smiled. My hands clutched his shoulders, his squeezed my ass.

I could taste the whisky on his tongue, but also something minty. Like very fancy toothpaste—the mint grown in the same forest as his exclusive cedar cologne.

It was all happening so fast. Heat rippled through my body, short-circuiting any rational thoughts I might have had. Because if my brain had a chance to catch up, it might have told me that what I was doing was a very bad thing. That Gabe was used to women throwing themselves at him. That if I did this, I would be just another star-struck fangirl who slept with her favorite movie star. That if I ever wanted to have a normal relationship with a normal person then I was setting myself up to be disappointed after this kind of experience.

Jeremy would probably never forgive me.

It was completely and utterly unprofessional.

But I wasn't thinking any of those things.

I was thinking that Gabe's hands and mouth and all the rest of him felt fucking amazing. I was thinking that I wanted desperately to tear off his clothes and lick him like a lollipop. I was thinking that it was very, very possible I could come apart just like this.

Gabe's arms were wrapped around my back, and I could feel them shaking. It was unbelievably hot knowing that he was just as affected as me. That he wanted me as much as I wanted him. Or if he didn't, he was an *incredible* actor.

He pressed his forehead against mine, both of us breathing heavily.

"This okay?" he asked.

"Uh, yeah," I said. "Very okay."

He leaned back far enough that I could see his grin. It was a little soft, a little droopy.

"Good," he said. "Great."

Then, before I could comment on his level of sobriety, and with great balance and dexterity, Gabe flipped us both so I was lying back on the couch, and he was on top of me.

"Still okay?" he asked.

"*Yes,*" I said.

His body settled on mine, his hips moving, his hand sliding up my shirt. He was going so fast but I didn't want him to stop. Instead, I shoved my palms beneath his shirt, bunching it up under his arms.

He leaned back as I did, just far enough for me to pull it over his head.

And there was his chest. His movie star chest—all mine for the touching. He was strong. Lean. I could feel the slight stubble on his chest as if he'd waxed or shaved it recently and it was just starting to grow back. It was a reminder of the work required to look the way he did. Work that I was *very* grateful for in the moment.

His skin was damp, his hair sticking to his forehead, which he pressed against mine as I raked my nails down his back.

"Do that again," he ordered, stretching in my arms like a bear rubbing up against a tree. "Oh yeah," he said, his voice a low rumble, his mouth hot against my throat.

He reached down, grabbing my leg and wrapping it up against his hip. My body opened up to him and he pressed himself against me. Right *there*. And then he began to move.

My head went back, eyes closed.

Oh. Holy. Wow.

We were still mostly dressed, but I was close. So incredibly close. Gabe was still kissing my neck, his body pressed against mine, so lost in his own rhythm that it seemed possible that he didn't know I'd almost just come from the sheer pleasure of us moving together.

"Fuck," he murmured. "I want . . ."

Whatever he wanted, I was completely willing to give him.

"You feel so good," he said. "You feel so good . . . *baby*."

It was the pause that slapped me out of my sexual haze. The hesitation between his sweet, hot praise and his whispered, unearned endearment.

He knew my name. I *knew* that he knew my name.

But something about the way he had paused, the way he'd said "baby," quiet and questioning, made me think that there was a very real possibility that in that moment Gabe had completely forgotten who I was.

It was the metaphorical cold shower I needed but didn't want.

Suddenly all the thoughts I hadn't allowed myself to have—all the very real reasons I should *not* sleep with him—came rushing back.

"Wait," I said.

I said it quietly, the word lost in the sound of his lips against my throat, the squeak of couch beneath us, and our shared heavy breathing. Because that metaphorical cold shower was already heating back up.

I was about five seconds away from losing myself in the pleasure again.

Gabe was moving against me, and I kept forgetting why I wanted to stop. It felt so good. *He* felt so good.

Baby.

It pinged across my brain.

"Wait," I said.

This time he heard me, and his arms, his hips froze, pressing hard against me. A body-length shudder rippled beneath my hands as he buried his face in my neck. His skin was damp, my hair still fisted in his hand.

He let out a groan of disappointment.

"Sorry," I said.

"Shit," he said.

What was *wrong* with me?

Neither of us moved for a long moment, and then slowly, Gabe raised his head.

He didn't look me in the eye as he untangled his fingers from my hair and lifted himself off me. My stomach dropped as he pulled back.

We sat next to each other on the couch, the silence awkward and overwhelming.

"I'm sorry," I said again. "I—"

Our words overlapped.

"Did you—" He started, paused, and tried again. "Do you—"

He was making some sort of gesture with his hand that I didn't quite understand but he also wasn't looking at me. His brow was furrowed as if he was trying to figure out how to get out of this situation.

"I should go," I said quickly.

"No," he said. "No, don't go."

"It's okay," I said.

He tapped his fingers on his knee.

"Really, it is," I said. "I can just get my stuff."

"Just, uh . . ." He looked away. "Just give me a moment, okay?"

"Um, yeah, of course," I said.

He got off the couch and left the living room.

I picked up a pillow and screamed into it. What was wrong with me? Why had I stopped something that had felt so good, and so right, because of one stupid word? Also because of journalistic integrity but that had been about a horse behind my own galloping libido.

So what if Gabe had forgotten my name in the heat of the moment? I was fooling myself if I thought that this meant something. He was a movie star. He had women flinging themselves at his feet, and he was here with me. Did I really think this was going to be anything more than what it was?

I'd had one chance with him and I'd blown it.

When Gabe came back into the living room, I was sitting up, hands on my knees, still trying to figure out how to salvage this moment.

"Look," he said. "We can still—I can still—if you—"

"It's late," I said.

"Yeah," he said.

I got to my feet. "I'll go."

"Don't be ridiculous," he said, putting a hand on my arm.

We both looked at it, and then he removed it, putting both hands first into his back pockets and then into his front ones.

"You can stay in the guest room and I'll call you a cab in the morning," he said.

I nodded.

"Thanks," I said.

"Yeah," he said, and turned to go.

"Gabe," I said.

He turned—and it was probably my imagination that made him seem eager.

"I'm sorry," I said.

"It wasn't your fault," he said.

I didn't really know how to respond to that. Were we just going to pretend that what had happened on the couch didn't actually happen?

"We can talk more in the morning," he said.

He gave me a smile—it seemed genuine but also tired.

"Okay," I said.

I went into the guest room and closed the door. I stood there.

"Come on, honey," I heard Gabe say, and then the *click click click* of his dog's nails across the wood floor.

At the other end of the house, I heard his bedroom door close.

Film Fans

RISICO REVIEW

[EXCERPT]

By Helen Price

IT'S THE MOVIE EVERYONE HAS BEEN TALKING ABOUT. NOT for good reasons. And it's the movie everyone wanted to see—but again, not for good reasons.

Everyone wanted to know if Gabe Parker's rapid decline, alcoholism, and weight gain had been captured on camera.

If that's the only reason you're planning to see this movie, I'm sorry to say, you'll be disappointed.

The movie is good. It's not great—not the way *The Hildebrand Rarity* was great—but it's not bad either. It's not the train wreck that everyone was expecting and (let's be honest) hoping for.

If the altercation between Parker and director Ryan Ulrich hadn't been recorded and then leaked online, then we, as a culture, would probably proclaim this film to be a fairly solid but unimpressive Bond film.

Instead, it's a memorandum of two things.

The first, of course, is Parker as Bond. Could he maintain the magic he'd initially brought to the franchise despite the obvious disagreements on set spilling outward?

Yes and no. Watching it with a critical eye, it's easy to see the rift, the dissonance between what the actor is willing to bring and what the director wants.

As for the ravages of Parker's alcoholism, whoever did the costumes and makeup deserves an Oscar. You would have never known that the Gabe Parker we saw months later, heavy and bearded, taking a walk on the grounds of his rehab facility, is the same Parker in the movie.

And then there's the fact that *Risico* is the first film released since Oliver Matthias's stunning admission that, contrary to what Ulrich and the Bond producers originally claimed, Parker was not their first choice. As we all know now, Matthias was offered the part, only to have it rescinded when he told the Bond team that he was gay and did not want to remain in the closet.

It's hard to watch Ulrich's Bond trilogy now without thinking of that. Without imagining what it would have been like if Matthias had actually gotten a chance to play Bond.

At least we all now know the context for Parker's once-cryptic, volatile parting shot, which was seen in the viral video from the set. Where he turned to Ulrich and practically spat, "You got the actor you deserved."

Now

Chapter 22

THERE'S A GLASS OF WATER ON THE BEDSIDE TABLE.

Embarrassment is a hot, prickly wash over my entire body as I remember what happened.

Gabe standing in front of me, his hand in my hair, eyes focused on mine.

"I could make you happy," he'd said.

I had wanted him to kiss me. To pull me into his arms, kiss me, and take me to bed.

Instead, just as I tilted my head back, eyes fluttering shut, preparing for his lips to meet mine, he'd withdrawn his hand and stepped back.

"You've been drinking," he'd said.

"It's okay," I'd whispered.

It was, of course, the absolute wrong thing to say. Because even though I hadn't been drunk, I definitely had been drinking. The whisky on my breath probably hadn't been the greatest turn-on for a recovering alcoholic.

Gabe had kindly, gently, shown me to my room and closed the door on his way out.

I'd fallen asleep, manifesting weird, vivid dreams born of unresolved sexual tension.

Those feelings are still burning inside of me now. I feel itchy with need.

I'm also thirsty. I gulp down the water, but it's not enough so I drink from the faucet in my private bathroom, wash my face and get dressed. My skin feels tight, like lust is a wild animal pacing beneath it.

I'm divorced. And so is Gabe.

I want him. He wants me.

I wonder what would happen if I just took off my clothes and crawled into bed with him.

Then I hear muffled whistling and realize that Gabe is already up.

Surely, he'll want to pick up where we left off last night.

Where we left off ten years ago.

I hesitate—my instincts going Jekyll and Hyde on me. Wanting him, but also wanting to run. Because I know now what I'd tried to ignore last night. That this isn't just about one weekend. This isn't about closure or unfinished business.

This isn't the end of something. It's the beginning.

And it terrifies me.

When I emerge from the guest room, I find Gabe fully dressed, drinking a cup of coffee and looking not like a man who wants to spend the entire day in bed, but rather like a man who has things to do.

I'm relieved and disappointed.

"Good morning," he says.

"Good morning."

"How's your head?" he asks.

I put a hand to it as if I'm checking if it's still there.

"It's fine," I say.

My heart on the other hand . . .

He comes toward me.

"I've got plans for us today," he says.

I'm fairly certain, from his tone, that they aren't the same plans I was making in my room. In fact, it seems possible that I completely blew it last night.

"I'm sorry," I say. "I had a little too much to drink."

"I know," he says.

Gabe cups my elbow, thumb rubbing on the inside of my arm. Heat licks through me, this endless fire that never really went out, but previously had almost always been under control—this smoldering ember that I did my best to ignore.

"I've done far stupider stuff when I was drunk," he says.

"I know," I say. "I've seen the video."

He laughs.

"Ulrich deserved it," he says.

I nod.

"Let's go," he says.

"I need shoes," I say.

"Take your time," Gabe says. "I'm not in any rush."

He's not talking about my shoes.

I exhale. Inhale. Exhale.

I sit on the couch as I pull on my boots.

There's a pile of magazines next to the puzzle on the coffee table. On top is an issue of *Broad Sheets*. *The* issue.

I'm holding it when Gabe comes into the room, my bootlaces loose and untied.

"Let me explain," he says.

"You hated it," I say.

I don't say it out of anger, but out of hurt. I need to understand. Need to know.

"Chani," he says.

"It was a good article," I say.

"It was," he says.

"But you didn't like it," I say.

"It's not that I didn't like it," Gabe says.

He pauses.

"What, then?" I ask. "Just tell me."

I'm bracing myself for the truth. Because Jeremy had been perfectly clear what *he* thought of it.

"I'm a good writer," I say.

My voice cracks.

Gabe frowns.

"You are," he says.

I wave my hands in front of my face like I'm a cat that he's sprayed with water. I want answers and I don't at the same time.

He comes over and sits on the couch next to me. We sink into the leather, each of us on a separate cushion, a third one in between. I put the magazine down on it.

"I—" He pauses. "I didn't expect you to write about Sunday."

It takes me a minute to realize what he's talking about, and when I do, I feel a roller-coaster rush that leaves me unsteady and breathless.

"I didn't say anything about . . ."

But as I'm saying it, I realize that it's an excuse, not an apology. And as far as excuses go, it's not a great one.

"I know," he says. "And I'm grateful you didn't tell people about my dad and . . ." He gestures between us. "You know."

He lets out a breath.

"I'd forgotten that you were writing an article about me," he says.

Back then, I had thought I was being so benevolent and so clever by writing around our conversation about Gabe's father. That I'd managed to have my cake and eat it too by including the titillating humble-brag about watching *Star Trek* with him, not even stopping to consider that it wasn't just the details about his father he'd hoped to keep private.

"That night, I thought that it was just you and me. Not a reporter interviewing *Gabe Parker.*" He spreads his hands, as if picturing his name on a marquee.

I look at the magazine, now imagining what it must have been like for him to read it for the first time. To discover that I'd shared something that he had never intended to share with anyone else.

"My team loved the article," he says. "They were thrilled. And you *are* a good writer, Chani."

He drapes his arms over his knees.

"It almost made it worse," he says. "That you wrote about everything—about that night—in such a way that it made me feel like

I was there again. Only, it felt like the whole world was there with us."

His hand curls into a fist. Not a tight, scary one, but solid. He looks at it.

"It made me angry," he says. "Really angry."

He shakes his head.

"The fact that I was drinking a lot didn't help, but fuck, I read that and I felt like a fool."

I know what that feels like.

"I only half remember going to Vegas," he says. "All I remember was feeling like I had to do something. Like I had to prove something to myself."

My throat is tight.

"And Jacinda . . . ?" I can barely get the question out.

"She was surprised by the suggestion, but almost immediately on board," Gabe says. "She wanted to take control of her reputation, and getting married did that. We never lied to each other about why we were doing it, but I wasn't as forthcoming as I should have been. Not for a while. But I always left the ball in her court. We'd stay married as long as it was useful to our careers. That was always the deal."

He glances down at his hand, no longer in a fist.

"Because you're right. People in Hollywood do stuff like that all the time. It's just easier—being with someone who gets what you're going through—who understands the games you have to play. Who . . ." He trails off.

"It doesn't matter. What matters is that I read your article, and I reacted like a stupid, drunken fool with a bruised ego."

"I hurt you," I say.

"Yeah," he says.

I reach out and put my hand on his. He puts his other hand on top of mine. We sit there for a while.

"I'm sorry," I say.

He looks up at me. Smiles.

"Me too," he says.

Tell Me Something Good

REVIEWS

Horowitz has done it again! A gem of a collection—like her first one, her well-known interviews are featured alongside more of her personal essays. She tackles every topic—from homophobic Hollywood to how she manages depression with jigsaw puzzles—all with her signature dry, self-deprecating humor. *—Vanity Fair*

A hilarious, occasionally weepy collection of essays and interviews. Horowitz is truly the queen of the celebrity interview—we all remember the Gabe Parker piece—and this book is a master class in the form. The perfect holiday gift for all your friends. *—O: The Oprah Magazine*

Why won't Horowitz give her readers what they really want—the true story of what happened the night she passed out at Gabe Parker's house? No one cares about her thoughts on New York or her marriage—we want to know the dirty details of the article that made her famous. Come on, Chani, give your fans what they're begging for. *—Goodreads*

Chapter 23

I DON'T ASK WHERE WE'RE GOING. I JUST GET MY BORROWED COAT, and wind my thick, warm scarf around my neck until it's under my chin. It's so snug that it could probably hold my head up on its own. I lace up my boots. It takes forever, and when I'm done, I feel a little like an overstuffed penguin, preparing to waddle across Antarctica.

There's a lightness between me and Gabe, as if we're slowly lifting away years and layers of anger. Disappointment.

I know I have to ask him about the phone call, but I wait. Not now. Not yet.

Gabe clicks his tongue and Teddy comes sauntering out of his room, treating us to a long, luxurious stretch that ends with her lying on her stomach on the floor, as graceful as any two-legged yogi.

"We're not lounging today," he tells her. "Come on."

She gives a little huff and rises, arching her back as she continues her morning stretch.

"If I'm ever late, it's because of her," Gabe says.

I give Teddy a pat on the head and she wags her shaggy tail with slow contentment.

"I think she's perfect," I say.

"Oh, she'd agree," Gabe says. "Ready?"

I get my first look at Cooper, Montana, in the daylight. The town is almost aggressively charming, with double-stacked buildings lining narrow streets, everything made of brick and stone. There are colorful wooden shutters on second-floor windows, delineating the apartments above the stores.

It's cold—a fresh, bracing cold, which seems at odds with the bold sunlight and cloudless skies. At some point last night, it snowed and the light makes the ground sparkle. My ears have already begun to hurt from the chill, so I pull the hood of Katie's coat up to protect them.

Just as I do, a man walks by wearing jeans and a flannel shirt. The sleeves are rolled up.

"Morning," he says.

"Morning," I say.

"Morning," Gabe says.

Even though I can feel the chill through my jeans, I suddenly feel overdressed and out of place.

"Isn't he cold?" I ask.

Gabe, who is wearing an unzipped coat over his sweater, shrugs.

"He's probably running an errand," he says. "No point in putting on a lot of layers if you're just running to the store."

I feel a little better.

"I guess we're not just running to the store," I say.

Gabe grins at me. "Not quite," he says.

"Are we meeting Ollie?"

"He's got other things to do today," Gabe says.

As far as I can tell, the only reason Ollie is in Montana is to spend time with Gabe, but I'm not about to make a fuss on his behalf. If Ollie wants Gabe, he can come get him.

Until then, he's mine.

"I thought I'd show you around," Gabe says. "Just the two of us."

"Okay," I say.

Teddy walks between us, a slow, relaxed amble that I appreciate, even though it also makes me more aware of her age. Of time.

The Cozy isn't open yet, but I attempt a casual glance as we pass. It's dark inside, but I can still see that it lives up to its name. The walls are lined with shelves and I can see some overstuffed chairs placed in duos around the store.

"We'll come back," Gabe says.

He takes me to a coffee shop that flips its sign to OPEN just as we walk up.

"Morning, Violet," Gabe says.

"Hi, honey," the woman behind the counter says. "Your usual?"

"Can you add an extra croissant to my order?" he asks. "And whatever drink Chani wants."

Violet waits patiently while I look at the menu.

"Earl Grey tea, please," I say.

"Earl Grey, hot," Gabe says.

He can still do a British accent.

I smile down at my hands.

We take our drinks and our croissants and continue our walk. The pastry is buttery and I let Teddy lick my fingers when I'm done. Her tongue is wide and flat like a cow's.

We pass a hardware store with bright Christmas lights decorating the doorway. The tea warms my throat and coats the inside of my chest. There's a toy store next to a jewelry store. They're both decked out for the holidays. Well. One holiday.

"Any Jews in Cooper?" I ask.

"I think you're the only one at the moment," Gabe says.

All the lights I see are red and green, poinsettia garlands and mistletoe hanging in windows. Lots of baby Jesuses in their mangers.

"Hmm," I say.

"There's a synagogue in Myrna," Gabe says. "About thirty minutes from here."

"Hmm," I say.

"I love this town."

He says it like it's the start of something more, so I turn toward him.

"I love this town," he says again. "But I bought the house in L.A.

because I don't want to live here all the time. Especially when the smallness of the place is too much, in too many ways."

He's telling me something without actually saying it.

I'm not in any rush.

There's an enormous Christmas tree at the end of the block, where the road is closed off to cars and the pavement turns to cobblestones. It's very beautiful. We stand in front of it for a while. Teddy sniffs the branches that extend outward.

"Does she live here all the time?" I ask, thinking of how his Laurel Canyon house didn't have any dog supplies.

"Naw," Gabe says.

He's kneeling and scratching her impressive neck ruff.

"I usually drive to L.A. or vice versa," he says. "Load her in the car and we just cruise down the Fifteen. She likes to stick her head out of the window. Even in the winter."

Teddy sits on my foot.

"I divide my time pretty evenly between here and L.A.," Gabe says. "I do miss seasons."

"It does seem like Montana delivers on that end."

"It does. Makes up for other things." He gestures. "A lack of synagogues and the like."

"I'm sure your family is happy to have you around," I say.

"Yeah," Gabe says. "Especially after the accident."

I turn to him. "I'm sorry about your brother-in-law."

Gabe is looking at the tree. "Yeah," he says. "That was a bad year."

I reach out and take his hand. When he links his fingers with mine, I realize that we've never really held hands before. Not like this.

It's surprisingly intimate, his palm pressed against mine, the calluses of his fingers, the warmth of his skin.

"It's not a perfect place," Gabe says. "Cooper."

I stare up at the tree.

"Neither is L.A.," I say.

I think about how it felt when I came back from New York. How I expected L.A. to feel like home again, but it didn't. How a part of me has been chasing that feeling without really knowing what I'm looking for.

"Believe it or not," Gabe says. "The tree isn't the thing I wanted you to see."

He gives me a tug and I realize we're still holding hands. That brief shock of intimacy smoothed out into something comfortable. Something familiar.

We go around the massive tree trunk, and I can smell the pine.

The town is decorated in nostalgia.

Gabe stops us in front of the one building that isn't lit up with Christmas lights and holly. It's dark, with boarded-up windows and a cracked marquee. If this was a Hollywood film, it would serve as a metaphor for the tortured hero's tortured past.

Standing back a little, I see that it's an old theatre.

"Ta-da!" Gabe says.

There's a FOR SALE sign on the window of the ticket booth, and a SOLD sticker tacked over it.

"Mazel tov," I tell Gabe.

"Do you want to go inside?" he asks.

"Is it haunted?"

He grins. "Only one way to find out," he says.

Inside, the air is filled with cobwebs and dust. It's not a movie theater, like I expected, but a *theatre*-theatre. There's a stage and a small pit for a small orchestra. There are at least three hundred seats and even two modestly sized but grandly built balconies on either side of the stage.

"I hope you didn't pay a lot for it," I say.

Gabe *tsk*s and Teddy sneezes.

"Oh, ye of little faith," he says. "Use your imagination."

"I'm imagining a lot of mice and rats using this space to stage their own rodent-positive version of *The Nutcracker,*" I say.

Even as I do, I'm looking past the layer of grime on every surface. Past the moth-eaten curtains and the well-worn carpet. Past the cracked and crumbling molding on the walls.

I can see intricately carved seats. I can see a beautifully built stage. And when Teddy lets out a short, happy bark, I can hear the incredible acoustics.

It's a perfect little theatre for a little town. With Gabe's name behind it, it could bring attention and people to Cooper. He could have as much—or as little—control over the productions as he'd like.

It could be a brand-new classic.

"What do you think?" Gabe asks.

"I think it's perfect," I say.

VANITY FAIR

POUR OUT THAT MARTINI:
Gabe Parker Talks Sobriety

[EXCERPT]

BY BETH HUSSEY

WE SIT DOWN AT THE RESTAURANT AND GABE PARKER orders a big, tall glass of water. It's his first interview since the former Bond star left the franchise in a spectacular fashion and entered rehab. Twice. And now he's ready to talk.

"I try not to trade in regrets," he says. "I'm not proud of the way I did things, but I can't regret them. Not really. Because, in the end, that's what pushed me to get help."

He's referencing the viral video that leaked from the set of his final Bond film—the one he walked off of. The production had just enough footage to get the movie into theaters, but the last of his four-film contract was terminated immediately, and no other offers have been forthcoming.

Parker is nearing forty and his career is, as of this moment, over.

There are rumors, of course, of projects in the works, but whoever hires him will do so at their own peril.

"I'll always be an addict," he says. "But right now, I'm an addict in control of my addiction."

It remains to be seen if producers will feel the same way.

—

Chapter 24

We get lunch from a nearby sandwich place and have a picnic on the stage, our meal illuminated by a ghost light on a stand. The theatre looks even more impressive from this angle.

"It needs a lot of work," I say.

Gabe shrugs, feeding some sliced turkey to Teddy.

"I have money," he says. "And a business partner who has even more."

"Ollie."

"Ollie," Gabe confirms.

"That's what this trip was always about," I say. "You and Ollie making plans for the theatre."

Maybe I should feel guilty about monopolizing Gabe's time, but I don't.

"Yes and no," he says. "That was the original plan—meet up with Ollie in L.A. while I'm doing press—and fly back to discuss our next steps."

"But?"

Gabe turns and grins at me. "Then you showed up at the restaurant with your very big eyes and your smart mouth . . ."

"And my bad questions?" I ask.

I'm still a little salty about that even though I know he's right.

He reaches over and pats my hand.

"If it makes you feel any better, your questions have gotten a lot better."

I roll my eyes.

"Thanks," I say. "I only ask questions for a living."

Gabe chews. Swallows.

"About that," he says.

"About how I'm bad at what I do?"

He ignores my goading.

"Whatever happened to the dragons?" he asks.

My hand—which was on a journey from the bag of fries to my mouth—freezes. I know what he's talking about. *The* story. The only piece of fiction I've ever had published.

Something I've been thinking about more and more these days. A certain type of creative torture. Teasing myself with something I can't have.

"I hate to tell you this . . ." I try for casual. Light. "Dragons don't exist."

"Ha," he says. "You know what I mean."

I eat my fries, not really wanting to answer.

"It's not what people want from me."

"Are you sure about that?" he asks.

"Are you my therapist?" I ask.

The sharp words echo in the amazing acoustics.

"Just someone who thinks you're talented," Gabe says, effectively cutting my anger off at its knees.

I breathe out.

"Can you imagine what my agent—what my editor—would say if instead of writing the third collection of essays they've been asking for, I told them I wanted to write fiction? Not even *literary* fiction, but a book about dragons and witches and fairy tales."

I don't have to imagine it. I already know their response.

They all thought I'd been joking. So I said that I had.

"I imagine," Gabe says, "that if they're the right agent and the right editor for you, then they would at least want to read what you came up with."

I want to tell Gabe that he doesn't know what he's talking about. That he doesn't understand what it's like to build a career on a certain type of image, and that changing that could mean losing everything.

Except, he *does* understand.

It isn't a joke to him.

"Jeremy didn't think it was a good idea," I say.

It feels pathetic to say it out loud—that I let my ex-husband tell me what I should—or shouldn't—do with my career. But no less pathetic than letting *anyone* tell me what to write.

"Well, if *Jeremy* didn't think it was a good idea," Gabe says.

His tone is as dry as a desert.

"He's a successful writer," I say.

"So are you."

I'm looking at my sandwich as if it might contain the answers to life instead of just turkey, avocado, and cheese.

"I'm scared," I say.

I've never admitted that out loud. Barely admitted it quietly to myself.

"Yeah," Gabe says. "It's scary."

He leans back on his hands, legs extended out in front of him, an entire theatre at his disposal.

"What's the worst that could happen?" he asks.

I discover that Jeremy is right. About everything.

He had been drunk that night. He apologized afterward, said that he didn't mean it, but we'd both known that after that point, our marriage was irreparably broken.

It was a party for his friend—in New York, practically everyone we knew was a friend of his—a brownstone gathering in Brooklyn to celebrate a book release. All the writers we knew were "serious" writers, who wrote "serious" books like Jeremy's.

He'd been struggling to finish his second novel—the one that was already way overdue.

"These deadlines are creativity killers," he always said. "They're the reason I can't write."

He'd been working on it for years. I'd published dozens of articles by that point as well as my first collection and was working on my second.

"It's not the same," he would always say when I tried to encourage him to think of the deadlines as motivation.

He'd been in a sour mood all day. He didn't want to go to the party.

"The book isn't even good," he'd said.

It was getting great reviews, and even though Jeremy's book had gotten the same, he was jealous. He was convinced everyone else was getting the attention he deserved.

"You'll get it when your next book comes out," I'd said.

"That's never going to happen," he'd said. "I can't just churn out words like you. Everything I write is carefully crafted."

He said things like that a lot, and he had laughed when I told him I was thinking about writing fiction.

"Oh, you're serious?" he'd said afterward. "I'm sorry, I just didn't think that was the kind of writing you could do."

He'd laughed even harder when I told him what kind of books I wanted to write.

"I'm just being honest," he'd said.

We'd arrived at the party and he'd gone straight to the open bar. Three whisky sodas later, he started getting rude, and I was trying to shepherd him out the door when the host cornered us, with a young woman with big glasses and red lipstick trailing behind him. She reminded me a little of myself when I was younger. Eager. Bold.

"A fan of yours," the host said.

Jeremy had lit up.

"I love your work," the young woman had said to me.

"Thank you," I'd said.

"For fuck's sake," Jeremy had said.

We'd both turned to him, with different forms of surprise. He'd waved a drunken hand as if to say "carry on."

The young woman had blinked, and turned to me, affixing her smile back in place. "I just wanted to say how much I enjoyed your book."

"Thank you," I said.

Jeremy had snorted, but we'd both ignored him.

"And your article on Oliver Matthias was really beautiful," the young woman said. "You're so good at making someone larger than life seem normal and relatable."

"That's very nice of you." I'd been flushed with pride.

I was accustomed to people coming up to Jeremy at parties like these, listening as they told him how much his novel meant to them. And although I'd feel a twinge of jealousy, I was mostly happy for him.

I had figured he would feel the same.

I had been very, very wrong.

"And can I just say"—the young woman leaned forward, her voice going low and conspiratorial—"your Gabe Parker piece is probably my favorite celebrity profile *ever*."

"Thank you," I'd said.

"Of course it is," Jeremy had scoffed.

"I hope this isn't too forward," she went on. "But I'm a writer as well, and I was wondering if I could just ask you about—"

"She fucked him," Jeremy blurted out. "*Obviously*."

My heart had dropped like a broken elevator.

"What?"

"Obviously. She. Fucked. Him," Jeremy said, each word like a weapon.

The poor girl was beyond flustered.

"I, uh . . ."

"That's what you were going to ask, wasn't it?" Jeremy had demanded. "You wanted to know if anything happened between the two of them, and Chani here was going to give you the same bullshit line she always does about how nothing happened but everyone knows that's a lie. Everyone knows what you did, Chani, and everyone knows it's the only reason you have a career at all."

I had never been more horrified.

"I'm so sorry," I said to the young woman, who took that chance to get the hell out of Dodge.

I turned to Jeremy, but he wasn't done.

"You're not better than me," he'd said, and walked out of the party, into the rain.

I'd stayed with Katie that night and Jeremy had called when he sobered up, apologizing profusely. He was under stress. He was drunk. He was sorry.

But he never said that he didn't mean it.

The worst part was that I already knew. I knew what people thought of me, of my writing, and it ate away at whatever pride I might have been able to have in my work. I had just hoped that my own husband didn't believe what everyone else did.

But he did.

And I wasn't sure he was wrong.

"Chani?"

I look at Gabe. At the reason I have a career.

"Lost you there for a second," he says.

"Sorry," I say. "Just remembering something."

"Anything you want to share?"

"No," I say.

Film Fans

THE PHILADELPHIA STORY REVIEW

[EXCERPT]

By Chloe Watson

DEPENDING ON WHO YOU ASK, *THE PHILADELPHIA STORY* is the best romantic comedy ever made. Or it's an actors' showcase with several questionable story lines.

Oliver Matthias's latest adaptation of the classic play turned film turned musical (because we can't forget *High Society*) clearly intends to honor the first school of thought while addressing the second.

He very nearly succeeds.

Although he's able to update the extremely problematic father-daughter relationship, plus address the casual domestic violence sprinkled throughout, Matthias never truly nails the zaniness of the original.

Credit where credit is due, though, the casting is impeccable.

There was outrage when it was announced that disgraced former Bond Gabe Parker would be playing C. K. Dexter Haven. The internet exploded with think pieces about how casting a recovering alcoholic to play a recovering alcoholic was lazy and exploitive.

We should all know now that Oliver Matthias, in his infinite wisdom, knew exactly what he was doing when he chose Parker. Parker's C. K. Dexter Haven is droll, debonair, and pitch-perfect. While the rest of the cast is superb—Benjamin Walsh as Mike Connor is a true revelation—it's Parker who steals the show.

Chapter 25

I AGREE TO HAVE DINNER WITH GABE AND HIS FAMILY. WE DON'T talk any more about my writing or Jeremy. As we lock up the theatre, Gabe tells me that he and Ollie are planning to spend the next several months renovating, hiring staff, and planning their first season.

"We want to open next fall," he says.

"Ambitious," I say.

He shrugs. "I don't have much else going on."

It's a topic both of us seem to be avoiding—the future.

"No movies in the pipeline?" I ask.

"I think everyone's waiting to see how *The Philadelphia Story* does before I'm officially welcomed back to Hollywood," he says. "You get into *one* drunken, viral argument with your shitty director and suddenly no one wants to work with you. Unless, of course, you might make money for them."

There's that desert-dry tone again.

"You should have just stuck with the old standby of anti-Semitic insults and referring to female officers as 'Sugar Tits' and you'd be welcomed back with open arms and awards," I say.

Gabe snaps his fingers. "Dammit, I knew I'd played it wrong. Where's your phone? Let's get something on film."

And just like that, we've once again sidestepped the conversation I'm not ready to have.

It isn't until he stops, breath visible in the cold air, that I realize we've been walking down Main Street in silence.

"Here we are," he says.

We're outside of the Cozy. With the setting sun and the lights inside ablaze, it lives up to its name.

There's a bell above the door—a sweet, old-fashioned one like what Meg Ryan had in *You've Got Mail*—and it jingles when we enter, announcing our arrival. There are Christmas carols playing softly over the store speakers.

"Be right with you," a voice comes from the back.

"It's just me, Mama," Gabe says.

Mama. He calls his mother Mama.

It smells of apples and cinnamon, warming me along with the well-heated store. There's a little cart by the door with a carafe, mugs, and a sign that reads HELP YOURSELF.

"Want some?" Gabe asks.

He pours before I can answer—apple cider—and passes me a cup. On the bottom shelf there's a bin for dirty mugs.

It all feels strangely familiar, even though I've never been here before.

"The store is beautiful," I say.

Gabe grins.

"It is pretty nice, isn't it?" He looks around, one hand on his hip, the other holding a mug, looking very much like a man who likes what he sees. "I think we're going to use the same contractors to renovate the theatre."

"Do you help out when you're in town?"

He nods. "I like the store at night the best. When I'm here, I'm usually the person fulfilling the online orders—I'll put on some music or a podcast and really go to town. If you think I'm good on the screen, you should see me assemble a shipping box in under a minute."

"You're in charge of sending out the online orders?"

He gives me a knowing smile. "I am. I always know who's ordering from us."

Which means that he probably knows how many times I've ordered books from here. Which is often.

Thankfully, I don't have a chance to respond because a woman with Gabe's green eyes, and his dimple, emerges from the back of the store. Her expression lights up when she sees us.

"Is this her?" she asks.

"Mama, this is Chani," he says.

His arm is around my shoulders, almost as if he's presenting me. Which, I suppose, to an extent, he is. The moment feels significant and it scares me.

I know Gabe is thinking about what will happen beyond this weekend. I know he wants to ask.

I'm grateful that he hasn't because I don't have an answer. Not yet.

"This is my mother, Elizabeth."

"It's so nice to meet you," I say, holding out a hand.

A hand which she ignores, wrapping me up in a hug instead. I hold the hand with the mug of apple cider awkwardly out behind her.

"We're so glad you're here," she says. "Gabe talks about you all the time."

Gabe makes an awkward coughing sound behind me.

"Not *all* the time," he says.

I look back at him.

"A lot, though," he says, and gives me that grin.

I glance at Elizabeth and she's giving me the same grin.

"The store is beautiful," I say.

Her smile grows.

"Thank you so much," she says before looking at Gabe with the kind of "hung the moon" eyes that only a mother would have for her child. "We're very lucky here."

Gabe shuffles his feet, embarrassed but pleased.

Teddy is drinking out of a bowl that was clearly left out just for her.

"Would you like a tour?" Elizabeth asks. "Lauren and Lena are on their way. I thought we'd eat at our place tonight."

"I'd love a tour," I say. "And thank you so much for including me in your family dinner."

Elizabeth waves a hand.

"We're just happy to finally meet you," she says. "I was starting to think Gabe would never get his act together."

"They think so highly of me," he says.

Elizabeth loops her arm through mine and pulls me through the store. Teddy and Gabe follow.

"Each bookshelf has a name," she says, pointing to the large colorful signs. "When people ask for a book, we tell them to go to the Ursula K. Le Guin shelf—if it's in the sci-fi section, for example—instead of just telling them a number."

I'm listening, but mostly I'm just taking it all in.

The walls are lined with floor-to-ceiling bookshelves, so tall that there are some *Beauty and the Beast*–style rolling ladders to help readers get to the out-of-reach volumes. Spread throughout the store are more shelves, but none of them go above my shoulders, which keeps the space from feeling too crowded. There are overstuffed leather chairs tucked away in every corner, and I imagine that if the store was open, each of them would be cradling the butt of an avid reader. There's even a little table next to most of them, presumably for readers to place their mug of apple cider on.

The whole store feels welcoming and warm.

"Ta-da," Elizabeth says, stopping in front of a shelf full of books and covered with colored labels.

THE COZY RECOMMENDS is written across the top.

And there are my books. Right in the middle. The place of honor. And beneath them is a handwritten sign: RECOMMENDED BY GABE.

Smart, funny, addictive nonfiction, the card reads in what I assume is Gabe's writing—blocky and a bit uneven. *You'll be thinking about it long after you've put it down.*

"We're big fans here." Elizabeth beams at me.

I think I say "thank you" as I touch the shelf—and Gabe's words—quickly, briefly, like they're precious artifacts.

I feel unbalanced. Emotionally wobbly.

I can't look at Gabe.

"Would you like me to sign them?" I ask.

Elizabeth claps her hands together. "Would you? That would be just wonderful." She gives me another quick, impulsive hug. "I'll go get you a pen. You can sit at the counter. Oh, could we take a picture?"

"Sure," I say, charmed and overwhelmed.

Elizabeth lets out a little sigh of happiness and hurries out of sight.

"You don't have to do that," Gabe says.

His voice is low but he's moved closer to me so I feel the heat of his breath on the back of my ear.

"Smart and funny?" I ask. "Addictive?"

"You disagree?" he asks.

I don't have an answer.

"You've read them," I say instead.

"I thought we'd established that I've read everything you've written."

It's one of the hottest things anyone has ever said to me.

I turn slowly toward him. He doesn't move back and my gaze is level with his lips. They wear a wry smile.

I look up, my eyes locking with his.

"You're a great writer," he says.

I revise my previous thought. *That* is probably the hottest thing anyone has ever said to me. Mostly because it's Gabe. Mostly because I can feel tension stretching between us, pulled taut like Saran wrap. Mostly because if I just move forward a step or so and move upward four or five inches, my mouth will be on his mouth, and ten years later, I still haven't forgotten how good that feels.

"Here we are!" Elizabeth says, and Gabe takes a step back to let his mother through.

She has a bouquet of pens fisted in her hand and she pushes them all at me.

"I didn't know if you had a preference, so I just brought you the ones we had."

"Thank you." I find a simple ballpoint. "This will do fine."

She smiles at me, and it's such a great smile, so warm and open and loving, that I realize I might do just about anything to keep it on her face.

No wonder Gabe bought his mother this store. She seems like a wonderful person to make happy.

I settle behind the desk and begin signing the books she puts in front of me. Their stock is much larger than I expected—usually when I go to sign at independent bookstores, I'm lucky—and grateful—if they have half a dozen of both books combined.

The Cozy has at least thirty copies of each.

The day my first book came out, Jeremy insisted that we go to as many bookstores as we could so I could sign copies. It started out poorly. Our local bookstore didn't have it, neither did the one in the next borough. The thought had been a kind, encouraging one, but Jeremy had assumed that everyone got a rollout like he did. He thought my book would be stocked everywhere.

In total, he ended up finding three places across Brooklyn and Manhattan. We went to each of them and he introduced me as "the brilliant debut author Chani Horowitz," which wasn't meaningless since quite a few booksellers recognized him. Afterward we went to my favorite Italian restaurant, a little cash-only place with homemade limoncello and vegetable lasagna.

It's one of my favorite memories from our marriage.

But even then, Jeremy had never looked at me the way that Gabe is looking at me now. With an expression of immense pride. And awe.

It should make me feel good.

It doesn't.

Because all I can think about is what Jeremy said that night.

"It's the only reason you have a career at all."

"It" being Gabe. The assumption that I'd slept with him. The tawdry nature of my article. The public's obsession with the private lives of celebrities.

I'd taken full advantage of that when I was twenty-six. I'd made excuses for it. I needed the work. It was a good story. I was entitled to tell it.

I feel differently now.

It isn't just that I now know how Gabe felt about it—that he'd been surprised and hurt by what I'd chosen to include. It's that Jeremy's words have since congealed each and every uncertainty that has been swirling inside me since the article was published.

It was one thing to ignore it when strangers online or shitty up-and-coming actors were telling me that I was an unprofessional, lying slut. It was another when the person I'd slept next to every night for almost seven years believed it too.

My career—my success—wasn't because I was a good writer. It was because I'd latched onto Gabe like one of those suckerfish that follow sharks around, gorging themselves on their castoffs.

And if I tried to disengage, I'd starve.

It feels like that now—sitting in a bookstore that Gabe owns, signing books that he's promoting.

Would I ever know if my work was good enough on its own?

Would I ever know if *I* was good enough?

The bell above the front door jingles. Teddy—who had positioned herself at my feet—perks up, head cocked, ears raised.

"We're here," a female voice says from the front of the store.

Teddy rises and follows the sound.

"We're back here," Gabe says. "Signing books."

"Hi, Teddy Bear," another voice—a younger one—says. "Are you a good girl?"

"Signing books?" the first voice asks as it approaches. "Oh. Right."

Gabe's best friend is the spitting image of him. Dark hair with artful grays streaked throughout, a strong jawline, and that wholesome, sturdy Montana vibe. She's wearing jeans and flannel. The scarf around her neck looks handmade.

"Hi," she says. "I'm Lauren. Gabe's sister."

I stand and hold out my hand.

"Chani," I say.

I feel like I should quantify myself as well, but what can I say? I'm Gabe's interviewer/fangirl/friend/who-the-hell-knows-what?

"This is Lena," Lauren says, putting her hands on her daughter's shoulders.

"Hey," she says, looking at the floor.

Her dark hair is pulled back in a braid that's coming undone around the ears, loose hair against her neck, which is extended like a giraffe's. It's clear she's going to be tall, and also clear that right now she hates it. Her shoulders are pulled forward, like they're trying to hide her.

"Hi," I say.

"I'm hungry," Lena says when her grandmother comes out of the back room.

"Me too," Gabe says, and I can sense he's trying to offset his niece's rudeness.

I don't mind. I might be ancient by Lena's standards, but I can still remember what it was like to be her age. It sucked.

"Of course, you are, honey," Elizabeth says, coat in hand. "Let's go get some dinner."

We take two separate cars to the house that Elizabeth shares with Lauren and Lena. It's a beautiful two-story Victorian with blue shutters and trim.

"I bought it for them after Spencer died," Gabe says. "Lauren didn't want to stay in the old house, and I think it's been nice to have my mom around."

I nod as if I can understand what it's like to lose a spouse or a parent.

"I'm sure they're grateful for your help and support," I say.

It sounds so bland, so meaningless.

"I was in a bad place when he died," Gabe says. "It wasn't my worst, but it was pretty close. I managed to pull myself together for the funeral and for a few months after, but it didn't keep."

His hands are still on the wheel.

"It's true what they say," he says. "That you can't get sober for other people. Because if that was true, then I would have been able to do it for them. For him."

Lauren's car pulls into the driveway, and we sit there, watching as the three women go into the house. Gabe doesn't move. It's quiet and dark, and I see the lights come on inside.

"We all grew up together. Me, Lauren, and Spencer. He was in my grade, but the three of us were pretty inseparable. Until him and Lauren . . ."

Gabe lets out a breath.

"Spence knew my dad," he says. "Which isn't nothing. Him and Lauren were, like, disgustingly in love, but even if they hadn't been, even if they'd never gotten together, losing him was a bit like losing my dad again."

There's a sheen to his eyes, a deep, weighted sadness. I sense that he's kept these thoughts inside and now they're spilling out, maybe unintentionally. I don't know what it's like to be in his shoes, but I know that sometimes you just need someone to listen. So I do.

"She was the same age as me, you know," he says. "Lena was. When her dad died."

I didn't know. At least, I hadn't made that connection.

"It's weird," he says. "Not the right word, but . . ."

He gives himself a shake.

"Lauren and my mom have each other. They know what it's like to become an only parent overnight—it's not exactly the same, but it's similar, I guess. They can talk about it. They *get* it."

He runs his hand over the back of his neck.

"I thought I could be that for Lena. That there would be this understanding between us. This bond. And it was that way at first. We talked a lot. We got really close. But . . ." He lifts his shoulders, holds them, releases them. "I fell off the wagon, and broke whatever connection we had. She doesn't want to talk to me anymore. She doesn't want to talk to anyone."

His guilt is palpable, and Teddy lets out a soft, mournful little woof from the backseat, pushing her nose against Gabe's arm. He reaches back and scratches her neck.

"She's a teen girl," I say. "I think their genetic disposition is to be silent and surly for at least two years, maybe three."

Gabe smiles a little at that.

"Yeah," he says. "I know. I keep reaching out, hoping that she knows I'm here for her."

"I'm sure she does," I say.

"Still hurts, though. Still feels like there's something more I should do."

I think about reaching out for his hand, but already this moment is so intimate, so raw, that I keep the impulse to myself.

"Give her time." I offer platitudes instead. "All you can do is be there when she's ready."

He lets out a breath.

"Yeah," he says.

As if she knows we're talking about her, Lena steps out onto the porch. She's taken off her shoes and jacket, so she's standing there, in the dark and the cold, in her socks and T-shirt, her jeans ripped at the knee, well-worn everywhere else. Throwing out her arms, she gives a look of exasperation so spot-on that it's hard not to be impressed.

Having effectively made her point, she turns and goes back into the house.

"I guess the food is ready," Gabe says.

Dinner is all homemade, from the lasagna to the garlic bread. Conversation is stilted, mainly because of some unmentioned fight that seems to have occurred between Lauren and her daughter.

Lena sulks at one end of the table, arms crossed, eyes on her dinner plate. She's smack-dab in the middle of what will probably be her most awkward years—years I remember well. Her features haven't quite settled into her face—everything looks just slightly out of place. Her thick eyebrows slouch downward over dark brown eyes she must have gotten from her father, while the lower half of her face obviously comes from her mother's side. Everyone at the table—besides me—has the exact same nose.

It is clear that this dinner is a special kind of torture for her.

She stabs her lasagna while avoiding all attempts to include her in the conversation.

"Lena is a big reader," Lauren says. "Practically came out with a book in her hand."

Lena grimaces but doesn't say anything.

"The two of us have always been at about the same reading level," Gabe says. "When she was little, she would read *me* stories before bed."

He's joking, of course, but Lena doesn't even acknowledge it.

"What kind of stories are your favorite?" I ask, not really expecting a response.

Sure enough, I don't even get a blink.

"Sometimes people send me copies of books they want me to read," I say. "Before they're released. I could send you a few, if you'd like."

"Oh, that is so generous of you," Elizabeth says. "Wouldn't that be nice, Lena?"

"We own a bookstore," Lena says.

It might have been funny if it wasn't so awkward.

The only living creature at the table she devotes any warmth to is Teddy, who has settled herself at Lena's side, licking her arm, as if to say "you're okay." Or perhaps Lena dipped her elbow in bacon grease just before coming to dinner.

"Gabe says that you're working on a novel," Lauren says to me.

"Not quite," I say. "I'm still mostly doing nonfiction."

"She's extremely talented," Gabe says. "She could write whatever she wanted."

I can feel a blush spread upward from my chest.

"Gabe," his mother says. "You're embarrassing the poor girl."

"Oh, I know," he says.

He holds my gaze while he takes a big bite of lasagna, grin affixed to his face. I roll my eyes, but the heat lingers.

I catch a knowing glance being exchanged between Lauren and Elizabeth. They've been nice, so nice to me. I like them.

Like with Ollie, I'm worried I'm going to disappoint them.

It isn't until we're halfway into our meal, and I've just put a very large forkful of very good lasagna into my mouth, that Lena says something directly to me.

"I know who you are," she says.

It's an accusation.

"Lena," Gabe says.

"What?" She shoots him the look that all teenagers have in their arsenal.

The look that says that if you were to drop dead right there, she wouldn't even care.

Even though I don't have a teenager of my own, I *have* stood in front of a room of mostly men who, despite having never written a book in their lives, were convinced that they were destined to become the next great American novelist, and who didn't have a question, really, but more of a comment.

I can withstand a baseline of disrespect from virtual strangers—I've practically trained for it.

"You're the reporter," Lena says.

"I am," I say.

"I read the article."

"What did you think of it?" I ask.

I can sense everyone at the table sucking in a breath.

"Lena," Lauren warns, but I wave her off.

"It's fine," I say. "Gabe didn't like it either."

"That's not true," Gabe says as his mother and sister turn to glare at him.

"Trust me," I say, "I've heard far worse. One time I was signing someone's book for them and they told me I was overrated. A reviewer once wrote that I wasn't pretty enough to be so angry. My favorite, however, was the ten-paragraph email I got that broke down everything that was wrong with the first essay in my first collection and informed me that I should expect more of the same type of criticism for each following chapter. He had also attached an invoice for the work he'd done and an address where I could send the check."

Gabe coughs back a laugh.

Lena's eyes are round, surprised.

"You can't hurt my feelings," I tell her. "And it's okay if you didn't like it."

"It wasn't terrible," she says, her face red. "Just, like, whatever, okay?"

She pushes away from the table and her chair falls back on the floor. Teddy is immediately on her feet, tail between her legs.

Lena is out of the room before anyone can say anything.

I feel terrible.

"I'm sorry," I say. "I didn't mean—"

"It's not you," Lauren says. "After her dad died, people were calling the house all the time. Lots of reporters. Not all of them were nice."

"I'm sorry," I say again.

Lauren shrugs. "It's part of the trade-off, I guess. Gabe gets paid a bunch of money to do very little and people want to know about him and his life."

"Excuse me," Gabe says. "I do not get paid a bunch of money to do very little. I get paid a *ridiculous* amount of money to do very little."

Lauren reaches over and puts her hand on his.

She looks tired.

There's a buzz and both siblings check their phones.

I watch as Lauren reads the screen, her cheeks growing pink.

Gabe stabs his dinner as she shoves her phone back into her pocket.

"Again?" he asks.

"It's fine," she says.

"I'll tell him to stop."

But she shakes her head.

"I don't . . . mind," she says.

I can tell this surprises Gabe, but he doesn't say anything—he just sits back, arms crossed.

"Gabe," she says. "I can handle this. I am older than you, remember?"

"And he's younger than you," Gabe says. "Younger than me. Probably younger than Chani."

Now I'm very, very curious.

"Who is this?" I dare to ask.

The siblings exchange a look, before Gabe makes a "tell her" gesture.

Lauren lowers her head and her eyes.

"Ben Walsh," she says.

My eyebrows go way up.

"Ben Walsh," I say. "*Benjamin* Walsh?"

Lauren's cheeks have gone bright red.

"He's . . ." I struggle to find the words.

"A decent actor," Gabe offers.

"Very handsome," I say. "Like, painfully handsome. The kind of handsome where you can't even look at him directly without feeling a little light-headed."

Lauren lets out a choking little laugh.

"I'm *right* here," Gabe says.

This time it's Elizabeth who reaches out and pats his hand.

"You're very handsome too," his mother says.

"So, Ben Walsh . . . ?" I prompt, unable to help myself.

I also kind of like seeing this faux-jealous version of Gabe.

"He's been sniffing around Lauren ever since she came to visit *The Philadelphia Story* set," he says.

"Sniffing around?" she says. "I'm a person, not a lost steak. Don't be a macho asshole."

Gabe looks appropriately cowed.

"Sorry," he says. "It's just . . ."

"You don't like him, I know," she says. "You've made that perfectly clear."

The humor has been sucked right out of the room. Lauren gets up from the table.

"Excuse me," she says. "I'm going to go check on Lena."

Once she's gone, Elizabeth shoots Gabe a look.

"What?" he asks. "She said she wasn't interested."

His mother shakes her head and disappears into the kitchen.

"Benjamin Walsh?" I ask, now whispering for some reason. "Really?"

Gabe sighs. "Yeah." He runs a hand through his hair. "Let me guess, you loved him in *Mighty Kennedy*."

"No, I mean, yes, of course," I say, because who hadn't loved Benjamin Walsh in *Mighty Kennedy*?

Benjamin Walsh is the Irish Hawaiian version of Gabe. At least, Gabe from ten years ago—with all the drinking and carousing included. Handsome, talented, and a modern-day surfer bro. His casting as Mike Connor in *The Philadelphia Story* had been against type, just like Gabe had been as Bond.

He's also thirty-two if he's a day.

Gabe's sister is over forty.

She has the famous Parker family looks, but not in the way that would disguise her age. She looks like a handsome mother of a teen, not a dewy thirty-something. She's clearly smart and interesting and funny, but that's just not how things are done in Hollywood.

Suddenly I have a lot more respect for Benjamin Walsh.

"Of course," Gabe says, looking wary.

"He's been texting your sister?"

Gabe nods. "Thinks she's amazing—which she is—but I know his type."

"Oh?" I ask.

"Models," Gabe says. "Young actresses. He was flirting with Lauren when she came to visit, but hooking up with Jeanine the rest of the time."

Jeanine Watterson was the actress who had played Liz. She was probably twenty-five.

"I know," Gabe says. "It's none of my business."

"I suppose you know better than anyone how us everyday folk need to be protected from the big, bad movie stars," I say.

"If anyone in this room needs protecting," Gabe says, "I don't think it's you."

I give him a look. He gives it right back.

We sit there, in the quiet dining room, listening to the muffled sound of conversation coming from upstairs, or the other side of the house. It's hard to tell. Grandmother. Mother. Daughter.

"Well," Gabe says. "You do know how to clear a room."

"Thank you," I say.

"I think dinner is over," he says.

"I think you're right," I say.

THE JAM—NEWSLETTER

EXPAT

RELATIONSHIPS ARE LIKE COUNTRIES. FRIENDSHIPS, families, marriages. Any deep, meaningful relationship tends to form its own customs. Its own language.

I was married for longer than I should have been. The country I founded with my husband was full of inside jokes, of little unseen intimacies, of shared habits. We had our morning routine down pat.

He was always up first. He liked to write in the morning and I liked to sleep in. He'd get up before the sun, head to his office by way of creaky floorboards, and work for hours on his typewriter. That sound—the squeaking of steps, the metallic *clink* of keys—made its way into my early-morning dreams more often than not. Sometimes it was images of tiny mice hammering away at a tiny ore mine. Sometimes it was my grandfather on a rocking chair he never owned on a porch he never sat on.

We'd eat breakfast together. He'd tell me what he'd written, and I'd tell him the dream it inspired. Once in a while my dreams would make it into his work. A character in a short story, a lithe, innocent young thing (there are always lithe, innocent young things in his fiction), took mushrooms with the charming professor she admired so much, and hallucinated a row of hedgehogs tap-dancing unevenly.

I liked seeing my dreams in his work. I found it strangely thrilling to see them in literary magazines, just as it's almost more exciting to find my name listed in the acknowledgments than to hold my own book in my hands.

My husband thanked me in his first novel. Called me "his muse."

I doubt I'll get a mention in his second one. The one that will be dedicated to his soon-to-be second wife.

I don't say this to shame him or her. She's not the reason our country fell apart.

All marriages, just like all countries, have conflict. Sometimes patriotism is strong enough to overcome it—weighing what is shared against what could be lost—but sometimes, the conflict highlights that the country itself was founded on unsteady ground.

xoChani

Chapter 26

WE'RE EVENTUALLY REJOINED BY LAUREN AND ELIZABETH, the latter offering dessert, but it's clear that this part of the evening has come to an end.

I'm nervous as we drive away—Gabe's expansive truck seeming to shrink with each passing mile. I'd been offered wine at dinner but I'd declined.

Neither Gabe nor I say anything on the ride back to his apartment.

I rest my hand on my chest, my fingers against my throat where I can feel my pulse chattering. Both Gabe and I know what's going to happen next. It feels inevitable and impossible.

And I want it. I want it *so* bad.

But just as he's about to turn off the truck, I reach out and stop him.

"Gabe," I say.

"Uh-oh," he says. "That sounds serious."

"I just said your name."

"I know," he says. "But in a serious way."

He's joking, but not really. He has a worried look to him. I can't really blame him. We're so close and yet . . .

"We just need to talk about the call," I say.

He wrinkles his brow.

"The call."

He seems so confused that for a moment I think there's the possibility I just imagined the whole thing.

"You called me," I say. "The night before you went to rehab."

"Which time?" Gabe asks. His tone is dry, but I can hear the shame beneath it.

"The first time," I say.

I hadn't known any of that at the time, of course. Things between Jeremy and me had been fine, but not good. We were in couple's therapy. I could only sense his resentment at that point, bubbling under the surface, but hadn't known the root of it.

It had been fall.

I'd gone to a movie by myself, had just gotten out of the subway and was heading home when he called. Seeing *Gabe Parker (Team L.A.)* show up on my phone had been a shock. After the interview, I'd hoped for a call, a text. There were even times I'd go back and read the few messages we'd exchanged, but after the Broadway incident, I was convinced I'd never hear from him again.

Still, I'd never been able to bring myself to delete his contact information.

"Gabe?"

"Chani," he'd said.

It hadn't been right, though. The pronunciation was fine, but it was drawn out and sloppy and I could tell just from those two syllables that he was extremely drunk.

"Gabe, are you okay?"

"Chani, Chani, Chani," he said. "Hel-lo."

"Hello," I'd said.

"You're still in New York, right? New Yooooooooork. New Yoooooooork. Hell of a town!"

It had been surreal, listening to Gabe Parker drunkenly sing to me from wherever he was.

"You sound like you could use a glass of water," I'd said.

"Well, I am thirsty," he'd said.

I'd heard the clink of ice and liquid, but I'd been pretty sure it wasn't water he kept drinking. He'd coughed a little, and my heart had felt like a wet rag being rung out. Heavy and tight.

"Chani," he'd said.

"Yes," I'd whispered. "Gabe, I'm here."

"God. Your name. Your eyes. Like that cat, you know? Tick tock, tick tock." He'd laughed. "Bet you don't even remember. But I do. Remember Woody Allen? I met him, you know? Well, sort of. I saw him at a thing. Didn't meet him. Didn't want to meet him. Asshole. Asssssssssshole."

I'd heard him take a long drink.

"Whoops," he'd said. "Time for a refill."

"No," I'd said. "That's not a good idea."

"You know what's not a good idea?" he'd asked.

There was a long silence.

"Gabe?"

"Huh?"

It had been easy to picture him—handsome eyes, heavy and hooded.

"Did you see it?" he'd asked.

"See what?"

"You know." He'd sounded annoyed. "You know."

"The play?" That had been the last time we'd seen each other.

"Noooooo." The word had been long and drawn out. "Bond. I bet you didn't. You don't like Bond. I know. I read about it."

"Gabe—"

"You were nice. Wrong, but nice. I shouldn't have been Bond. You know it. The world knows it. They should have picked Ollie. I'm wrong. I'm all wrong. I deserve this. I deserve it all."

At the time, I hadn't known what he was talking about. It wasn't until afterward, when I checked Twitter and discovered that "Gabe Parker" was trending, that I saw the Ryan Ulrich video.

"You need to drink some water," I'd said. "Please? Just one glass?"

"We were a good team, though," he'd said. "Running Pyramid.

You were good. You got it. You got me. Dream team, right? We haven't played in so long. It's been soooooooo long. You know? You know."

He paused and for a moment, I thought that he had hung up.

"Gabe?"

"Data was your favorite, right? Yeah. Yeah. He was. I like Data. But all these human feelings he wanted? Overrated. Over. Rated. Who needs them?"

I'd sat down on my stoop. It had been cold, but I didn't go inside. The last thing I'd wanted was for Jeremy to ask who I was talking to.

After a while, it seemed as though Gabe had forgotten I was even on the line with him.

"I've read everything," he'd slurred. "Evvvvvverything. All the words. I'm not as smart as he is. Not as smart, but I *can* read. Not just scripts. Books. I read books. Lots of books. You should see the books. I could send them to you. All of them. I could fill your whole house with books. I could buy you all the books. You'd be like that princess with the library and all the books."

My fingers had gone numb from the cold and I'd kept switching my phone to the other ear so I could put my free hand in my pocket.

"Chani," he had whispered. "Chani, Chani, Chani."

"Gabe."

"You'll call me back, right? You have to call me back. I just . . . you have to, okay?"

"I will," I'd said, even though I was sure he hadn't heard me.

There had been a long silence and that's when I'd realized he'd hung up.

"Wow," Gabe says after I finish telling him.

The look on his face now—that surprise and shock—makes it clear that he doesn't have the same recollection of that call that I do. He seems to have grown older at the memory. Sadder.

"You kept begging me to call you back," I say.

"I thought I'd dreamt it," he says. "I was drunk. So fucking drunk that night and I wanted to call you—I always wanted to call you when I was in a state like that, but I never did."

"Except that one time."

"Except that one time." He glances over. "I was probably an embarrassing mess."

I pinch my lips together. "A little," I say.

He scrubs a hand over his beard.

"Jesus," he says. "Did I make any sense?"

"Sometimes," I say.

"I'm sorry," he says.

"It was nice to hear your voice," I say.

He smiles at that.

"What happened the next morning?" he asks. "Did you call me back?"

"Jacinda picked up," I say.

"Oh," Gabe says. "Shit."

"Yeah," I say. "Shit."

My hands had shaken a little when I called back the next day. I'd waited until Jeremy had left the apartment, watching him walk down to the end of the block, counting to ten after he was out of sight.

The phone rang three times and then it was a female voice that answered. A British female voice.

"Is Gabe there?" I'd managed to ask.

"No," Jacinda Lockwood had said, her voice tart. "He's in rehab. No phones allowed."

"Oh," I'd said.

Part of me was relieved because he had been so drunk the previous night that it had been worrying. The other part was selfishly disappointed that I wouldn't be able to contact him.

"I just have one question," I ask now.

"Hit me," Gabe says, clearly still embarrassed.

"Who's Tracy?"

"Tracy?"

"Just before Jacinda hung up, she called me Tracy," I say.

"Don't call again, Tracy," she'd said.

Gabe sits there for a moment, and then he laughs, his palm hitting the steering wheel. It breaks the tension—heavy and somber—hovering over us.

"You're Tracy," Gabe says, shifting onto one hip, digging his phone out of his pocket.

He unlocks the screen, scrolls for a moment, and then turns it for me to see. It's a contact for Tracy Lord. The main character from *The Philadelphia Story*.

"Call it," he says.

I do, and there's a buzzing in my pocket.

I've just called myself.

I stare at the screen and let out a surprised huff of a laugh.

"You put me down as Tracy Lord in your phone?" I ask.

Gabe grins. "It seemed clever at the time."

We both burst out laughing. I laugh until my lungs hurt, crying just a little at how utterly ridiculous this whole thing is. Gabe leans his head back against his headrest, turning to look at me.

My breath catches.

Because this is it. There are no more secrets, no more forgotten moments. I'm vulnerable and exposed. Brand-new. Ready.

He's watching me. Waiting.

"Let's go inside," I say.

PUBLISHERS WEEKLY

Interview with Chani Horowitz

[EXCERPT]

THOUGH HOROWITZ STUDIED FICTION AT THE IOWA WRITERS' Workshop, she's mostly known for her nonfiction. Her debut, *Tell Me Something I Don't Know,* is a collection of her latest work, and out in paperback this Tuesday.

Though there are several personal essays, Horowitz's claim to fame is her celebrity profiles, most notably the one she did on Gabe Parker a few years ago, which went viral.

"I never expected the reaction I got," she says. "You never do."

I can't help pushing back on that a little. She didn't think writing about going to a premiere with a movie star and then passing out at his house the following night wouldn't be exactly the kind of story our celebrity-hungry culture would jump all over?

"I didn't," she insists. "Sure, there are times when you think that something might break through, but you just never know."

I ask if she'll ever write a follow-up.

"When it comes to interviews like that, I'm at the disposal of the interviewee," she says. "I don't seek out subjects."

It's clear that she doesn't want to talk about Gabe Parker, but I can't resist asking the question that everyone has been asking since the article came out.

"Nothing happened," she says with a smile. "Don't I wish, though?"

Chapter 27

TEDDY LEAPS OUT OF THE TRUCK WHEN WE ARRIVE, SNIFFING around the back of the building until she finds a place on the snow to squat and pee. I'm wearing my coat, but Gabe's is draped over his arm. He doesn't seem to notice the cold.

It's only seven, but dark as midnight. It gets dark early in Montana, so I've been told.

Still, I can see the mountains—white-tipped and rolling—like a frothy wave in the distance.

When Gabe puts his hand on the small of my back, I lean into it.

"Okay?" he asks.

"Okay."

Once inside we knock the snow off our boots, and Gabe cleans out the frozen globs that have formed between Teddy's toes.

I hold my coat against my chest as Gabe starts a fire. I'm still standing in the entryway when he finishes. He comes over, takes my coat, and hangs it up.

"Chani," he says.

"I'm fine," I say, because I don't know what else to say.

"We don't have to . . ." he says.

"I . . ."

The room warms. Gabe puts his hands on my arms, his thumbs stroking my biceps as if I'm a scared animal he's trying to soothe.

It's not entirely incorrect.

"I'm not in any rush," he says.

He's not talking about tonight. He is, but also, he isn't.

I push back. Move away. A few inches.

That tight, scared, panicky feeling presses against my ribs. My confidence falters.

"The last time we did this . . ." I gesture between us.

"Yeah," he says. "About that."

There's something in his voice that makes me stop. He sounds embarrassed, and I don't know why.

"About what?"

"About what happened between us on the couch," he says. "I'm sorry."

"Sorry?"

We're getting into weirdly intimate territory. We've talked around that weekend but we've never talked about what actually happened. Or didn't happen.

"I shouldn't have . . ." He rubs his hand across the back of his neck. "It's just, I felt like such an idiot."

Apparently, the call wasn't the only thing we still needed to discuss, only this time I'm the one in the dark.

"Why?"

"Because," he says as if I know what he's talking about.

"Because *what*?"

Then, to my complete astonishment, I watch as a flush spreads across *his* cheekbones.

"You know," he says.

"I don't," I say.

He looks up at the ceiling. For a moment, the only sound is the crackling fire, the room nice and warm and cozy.

"That night," he said. "When we were . . . when things got . . ."

I'm staring at him, and he's staring at the beams overhead.

"We were kissing and you were, you know, underneath me, and it was really hot, and then . . ." He trails off. "You *know*."

I don't. I don't know. It's clear that whatever memory I have of that night is not the same one he has.

He glances down, catches the expression on my face.

"Come on," he says. "Are you really going to make me say it out loud?"

"I don't know what you're talking about," I say.

"You don't know that I got so turned on that I came before we could go any further?" he asks.

My mouth falls open. It is quite literally the last thing I expected him to say.

"You *what*?"

He throws his head into his hands. The fire pops.

"Oh god," he says. "Oh my god."

My eyes are practically bug-shaped.

"Oh my god," I say.

"Jesus *Christ,*" he mumbles into his fingers. "I thought you knew."

"I didn't," I say. "I thought . . . when I told you to stop . . . I thought you were annoyed but okay about it."

"I *was* annoyed," he says. "At myself. For being too drunk and out of control. For acting like a horny teenage boy. For getting off and then not getting you off."

Suddenly our awkward interaction after the fact takes on a whole different meaning.

"You wanted to—?"

"Very much," he says.

"Well," I say. "I didn't know."

His face is still flushed and it's adorable. My heart feels like it's contracting and expanding at the same time.

"I don't know whether I should be relieved that it's all out there or horrified that I just told you," he says.

"It's kind of charming," I say. "That you wanted to, but couldn't."

"Hold on," Gabe says, his hand up. "I still could have."

The indignation in his voice makes me bite back a laugh.

"But you just said . . ."

He moves toward me. My laughter quickly cuts off, my mouth

going dry at the look in his eyes. We're no longer joking about something that happened ten years ago. We're not joking at all.

"I would have needed some time, but that wouldn't have been a problem. It won't be a problem." His voice is a low growl. "It's *not* a problem."

I swallow. Hard.

It's not just about us talking about something that happened back then. It's about what's happening now. Between us.

Back to what has felt inevitable since I accepted this assignment.

"It's not a problem?" I ask, even though I know I'm poking the bear.

I'm wobbly and nervous and not one hundred percent sure that this isn't a terrible life-altering mistake, but I also know that this is *it*.

Gabe might not be in a rush, but all of a sudden, I am.

After all, it's been *ten* years.

He looks at me.

"It's not a problem," he says. "With you, I . . ."

"You . . . ?"

"I want you," Gabe says. "I've wanted you. Since the first moment."

It's so simple and direct.

"Yeah," I say. "Okay."

He blinks.

"Okay?"

I nod.

"Okay."

We stare at each other for a moment, the tension crackling between us. Then, as if it's nothing, as if it's something we do all the time, Gabe reaches out and puts his hand on my elbow. It's enough to make me unfurl, his arms coming up around my back, holding me against his body, my chest pressed to his.

Then he leans his head down and kisses me.

It's soft, soft the way a first kiss is soft. New. Tender.

It isn't our first kiss, but maybe there's some rule about fresh starts and clean slates that applies to people you haven't kissed in a decade.

My head goes back because he's just *that* tall. His palm is firm on my back, holding me there, and I think of how he dipped me in the club, how I trusted him then and how I have to trust him now.

Trust that he won't drop me.

One hand unwinds itself from behind me, his palm tracing up my arm, curving over my shoulder before it displaces my hair to get at my jaw. And *wow*. Nothing has ever felt as good as the brush of his fingers against that sensitive skin along the side of my neck.

His lips are still on mine, resting there, not kissing but not not-kissing. Like a placeholder. A promise.

He draws his thumb against the curve beneath my chin and I sigh.

It changes everything.

We collide into each other, as if we were at opposite ends of the room, racing into each other's arms, instead of already wrapped up like a pair of horny octopuses. *Octopi?*

That hand on my cheek moves my head into position, tilting it into Gabe's palm so our lips can meet like puzzle pieces. My tongue is in his mouth as my hands reach under his shirt, and none of it is enough.

This isn't what happened ten years ago. There's no fumbling now. No hesitation. We're not going to stop. We're going to go *all the way*.

Still cupping my head, Gabe's other hand careens down my back, right into my jeans, bypassing everything underneath and gripping my ass with a possessiveness that's unbearably sexy. He tugs upward and I climb him, wrapping my legs around his waist.

We're older now, and it's clear that both of us know exactly what we want and there's something so very hot about that. About that knowledge. That history. That experience.

He's solid and strong and I can feel his muscles tense and adjust to my weight as he carries me across the living room and into his bedroom. It feels almost like a movie until he trips and all but throws me onto the bed, falling in after. I smack my head on his collarbone, and he grunts as he holds himself back on shaking arms, then laughs as I pull him down against me.

We kiss, our hands moving up and down, finding fabric and occasionally skin, moving, moving, moving, like we're trying to start a fire. My legs are trembling.

Gabe is having difficulty with my shirt.

"I just . . . these fucking . . . goddamn buttons," he mutters, his fingers fumbling, the backs of his hands haphazardly brushing against my breasts, making me wiggle, which in turn makes it even more difficult to get the shirt undone. "Can I just . . . please . . . can I . . . ?"

I don't exactly know what he's asking but I don't exactly care.

"Okay, yeah. Yeah."

He gives me a grin, equal parts wicked and boyish, and before I really realize what's happening, he grips the sides of my shirt and pulls. Buttons scatter, the fabric rips. And my shirt is gone.

"I've always wanted to do that," he says.

I'm breathless with how much I liked it. Gabe stares down at me like I've just given him everything he's ever wanted.

"They're just breasts," I say for literally no reason at all.

He looks up, and shakes his head, long and slow, his hair falling across his forehead.

"There's nothing *just* about you," he says.

If I hadn't already been literally swooning beneath him, that would have done it. My entire body feels itchy and crackling and desperate. I'm ready for more. I'm *so* ready.

We remove clothes. My jeans. Gabe's shirt. My shirt.

It's like high school, but better—that sweet, hot anticipation of kissing, kissing like you're the first people in the world to discover it, like there's no possible way other people are doing it like this, because if they were how in the hell would anyone ever get anything done.

I let my hands wander. I'd gotten a chance with his chest ten years ago on his couch in Laurel Canyon, back when he was fighting fit—on his Hollywood Bond diet, lean but muscular, his torso as waxed as my kitchen floor.

The muscles are still there, but he's nowhere near as chiseled as he was. The six-pack isn't as prominent and he even has the tiniest of love handles on his sides. And his chest. His chest is covered with a sprinkling of hair, his shoulders unreasonably broad.

I love all of it.

I love how his chest hair tickles my palms, the same way his beard is rough and soft as he rubs it against my chin. I love feeling the way time has passed through his body, the way we've both changed. This Gabe feels more real to me than the one I basically dry-humped on his couch ten years ago.

And this is the Gabe I want.

"Take off your pants," I murmur as his hands skate along my sides, tracing my hips.

Laughter sputters out of me as Gabe rears back, attacking the buttons on his well-worn jeans as if they were on fire. He flings them across the room and comes back down against me, kissing thc remaining humor from my lips.

That need—*his* need—is enough to make me shake.

Because this is Gabe. Not just Gabe Parker the Movie Star, though it must be acknowledged, but *Gabe*. I'm feeling too many things at once, and for a moment I'm overwhelmed, stepping outside my body and looking down on our forms entangled on the bed and wondering, *How the fuck did I end up here?*

I know that if we do this, I'll never get over him.

He stops, pulling back to look at me, his eyes searching my face.

I'm in love with him.

But I can't say it. I can't.

Instead, I take his face in my hands and kiss him. Sweetly and then less sweetly. He's a quick study and not a fool, so it doesn't take long to ratchet both of us back up to that burning, taut point of desire we'd been climbing toward.

Dragging my hands down the length of his spine, I hook my fingers into the waistband of his boxer briefs and begin to push them down. He shifts to help me, leaning back enough that he can do the same for me, removing my bra and my underwear.

Then he's on me again, kissing me hard.

I think of the dumb joke from all those years ago. *What's my perfect weight? Me with Gabe Parker on top of me*.

If that isn't the whole damn truth, though.

Gabe's mouth finds my ear, each touch of his like he's discovering something new.

"Please," I beg. "Please, please, please."

I don't even know what I'm begging for, but thankfully he does. He drags his hot, perfect mouth downward, nipping my collarbone, his beard coarse against my stomach.

Then the weight of him, the heat of him, is gone. He wraps his long, beautiful hands around my ankles and pulls me toward him, my feet hanging off the edge, his palms hot on my legs.

"Can I?" he asks.

I nod, my heartbeat like a drum throughout my entire body.

The sight of him there, kneeling in front of me, is the hottest thing I've ever seen.

But then he actually touches me—his thumb circling the inside of my knee, the stubble of his beard brushing against my inner thigh—and I know that every sexual experience I've ever had in my life pales in comparison to the way it feels when Gabe puts his mouth on me.

His tongue is hot and wet and eager as he drapes my leg over his shoulder. And I can tell he's making a point down there. Making up for what happened ten years ago.

It's the tremble, though, that makes my heart feel like it's a vibrating anvil. The slight shake of his hands when he touches me, the groan he let out when he first knelt on the floor, the way his fingers tighten around my hips, holding me as if he's afraid I might disappear.

My head is against the mattress, my arm over my eyes. My other hand is in his hair, and it's so soft against my palm. I want to capture everything, hold it in my memories forever.

Gabe's tongue stokes a forest fire of need inside me, burning brighter and brighter. I dig my ankle into his shoulder blade, toes curling.

"There . . . Please . . . Gabe . . . Please . . ." I'm a broken record, unable to verbalize anything but the same words over and over again. "There. There. *There*."

I squeeze my eyes shut like I'm standing on a twenty-foot-tall diving board, about to hurl myself off the edge.

I realize I'm coming a half second before it happens—that moment after leaping, when your heart is still in your throat and there's nothing but air around you.

Maybe I scream his name. Maybe it's all in my head.

When I come back to reality, Gabe is there, leaning over me, his hair sticking up every which way and a bead of sweat sliding down his brow. He's laughing, but his arm, planted next to me, is shaking.

I stare up at him, both shocked and spent.

"Good?" he asks, and I want to kiss that cocky smile right off of him.

But hell if he hasn't earned it.

"Good," I say, my throat raw.

His hand comes up to cup my face, and I lean into it, lean into the kiss he gives me, at first gentle, his smile imprinting on my own. My desire feels like a wave, still and settled one minute and then, in the next, a rising swell.

The kiss goes from soft to desperate and this time it's Gabe's fingers in my hair, almost as if he's bracing himself.

"Gabe," I murmur, his lips still against mine.

"Mmm," he says, the sound strained and distant, as if he's reciting baseball statistics or math equations or whatever men do when they're too turned on to function.

"Now," I urge him. "Now *please*."

His forehead is damp against mine as he nods, his hand flailing outward, searching. It returns with a condom and lube. His head rears back as he applies them, touching himself, and for a moment,

I'm able to admire the gorgeous stretch of his neck, the hard swallow he makes as I reach out to feel him.

"Don't," he chokes out, stilling my hand. "I . . . you . . . can't . . ."

I shift beneath him, making space for his body, my hips cradling his, feeling the length of him against me.

"Fuck," he groans. "Can I . . . can we . . . please . . . ?"

I grip his shoulders.

"Yes," I say. "Yes, please *yes*."

With a hiss of pleasure, he notches himself against me and pushes.

His voice is gravel, swearing and praising as he advances, thick and deep and slow inside of me. I might have responded, but my breath, my voice, is gone, my entire being focused on the place where our bodies are coming together.

His arms are braced on either side of my shoulders. I don't know where he gets the strength because I'm having trouble remembering how to breathe. I wait for him to start moving. *Need* him to start moving.

But he stays still, releasing one long, gusting exhale.

"Gabe . . ." I finally manage to choke out. "Don't . . . stop . . . Please . . . don't . . ."

Before I can say it again, he's responding, easing slowly back and then pushing forward, deeper.

"Yes . . ." My head goes back. "I need . . . yes . . ."

The words hiss out between my teeth as he tilts his hips and thrusts again. Hard. Perfect.

My words are gone then, lost in the cacophony of groans and panting coming from a place deep inside of me. Sounds that Gabe matches, his own head shaking back and forth as our bodies meet over and over again, almost as if he can't believe this is actually happening.

I rake my nails down his back and he growls, tucking his head against the crook of my neck, biting and kissing, his hips moving faster. We're both chasing the same thing, racing toward it together.

"Yes." He takes my earlobe between his teeth. "Yes."

It's a request. A command.

Somehow, he's able to balance himself on one arm, his other hand snaking between our bodies. His fingers are slick. He leans back slightly, just enough to change the angle of everything, just enough for him to go even deeper, just enough for him to drag his thumb hard and firm against me.

Just enough.

"Chani." His breath is burned into the side of my neck. "*Chani.*"

My name on his lips is *perfect*.

"Fuck, I'm . . ."

Words seem to escape him. His palm slides against mine, pressing my hand against the bed, our fingers entwined. Gabe holds on to me like we're finding our way out of a storm. I'm aware of nothing but where our bodies connect. Hands. Hips. Lips. There's a shudder and at first I can't tell if it's me or him, but then I'm lost. I explode like a star.

It takes a long time for him to stop shaking. For the room to stop spinning. And when he does and when it does, he leans back and pushes the hair out of my face, his thumb tender against the side of my cheek.

I close my eyes as he kisses me.

My entire heart feels like it's sitting at the base of my throat. Heavy. Tight.

"It's you," he says.

THE RUMOR MILL

RENEWING OLD BONDS

GABE PARKER IS PLANNING HIS COMEBACK. THE FORMER Bond star is already getting some Oscar-worthy buzz for his upcoming role as C. K. Dexter Haven in Oliver Matthias's remake of *The Philadelphia Story*.

The infamous actor was spotted out and about in L.A. this week, and was captured having lunch with writer Chani Horowitz, who—as most fans will remember—rose to infamy of her own for her deeply personal profile of Parker almost a decade ago.

Horowitz wrote about spending the weekend with Parker attending premieres and after-parties. Most memorably she recounted passing out at Parker's house after a private party he held. Despite being photographed together at the premiere of *Shared Hearts* both have denied anything unprofessional ever happened.

Their representatives have confirmed that Horowitz is indeed writing a follow-up to her first article, but the cozy pictures of them at lunch insinuate what people have suspected for years—that despite Horowitz's juicy profile, there was plenty that she left out.

Fans are dying to know—what really happened that night?

Monday

BROAD SHEETS

GABE PARKER:

Shaken, Not Stirred—Part Four

BY CHANI HOROWITZ

GABE PARKER HAS A VERY NICE GUEST ROOM.

It's got a big bed and clean, crisp sheets and lots of pillows. I'm sure you're all wondering what it's like to sleep in, but I'm going to disappoint you because I didn't. Sleep in it.

I was more than welcome to, of course. Gabe Parker, at all times, was a consummate host, while I was an embarrassing, sloppy mess that pushed the limits of professionalism multiple times.

I can only hope he doesn't hold it against me.

But in that moment, I was too embarrassed to face him.

Which is why, while it was just barely light outside, I snuck out of Gabe's house, hailed a cab, and sent myself home.

Now, there's something I should have mentioned at the beginning of this article.

I've never seen a James Bond movie. I've never read any of the books. I know that Sean Connery played Bond and so did Pierce Brosnan and a bunch of other people, but that's the extent of my knowledge about the canon.

Some might say this should disqualify me from writing about the next—and most controversial—Bond. They might be right, but it's too late. The article is already written and if you've gotten this far, you've already read it.

Even though I'm on the outskirts of Bond culture, I still know enough about what he represents as a character. He's masculinity personified—smooth, suave, debonair. He always gets the girl—and the martini. He's an icon, and he's far bigger than the man who plays him.

Knowing this, I can say with all confidence that Gabe Parker is the Bond we need. He might even be the Bond we deserve.

—

Then

Chapter 28

I COUNTED TO ONE HUNDRED.

When I was certain that Gabe was in his room, that he was probably asleep, and that the front door was far enough away that he wouldn't hear it open, I gathered my things. My shoes, my purse, my jacket.

I didn't put any of them on, flinching when the guest bedroom door creaked as I opened it. I held my breath but no sound came from the other side of the house.

I couldn't stop the swell of embarrassment that hit me each time I thought about Gabe's face—how he had looked when he came back into the room after I'd turned him down. It was as if every emotion—every feeling—had been wiped clean. As if that moment had never even happened.

It had felt like a slap in the face, but one that I'd needed.

I'd needed to be reminded of who I was. Who *he* was.

Sleeping with him would have been the biggest mistake of my life.

My bare feet were silent on the hardwood floor and the front door opened without a sound. I pulled it closed until I heard the soft, muffled *click* of it locking behind me. It felt final. Even if I wanted to get back inside, I couldn't.

I carried my shoes until I was out of his front yard. I sat on the curb and pulled them on. As I walked to the bottom of the hill, the sun was just beginning to light the sky—a hazy amber that made the houses around me glow.

I called a cab and went home.

Now

Chapter 29

I'M WOKEN BY SUNLIGHT IN MY FACE AND A BUZZING FROM MY phone.

I stretch my arms wide and find nothing. The sheets are wrinkled, the bedding pushed back like a dog-eared page. I can hear Gabe in the other room. He likes to whistle to himself in the morning.

It's strange that I know this, and not strange at all.

The air beyond the comforter is cold and fresh. It makes me want to stay in bed all day. Rolling over, I bury my nose in Gabe's pillow. It smells warm and like the spot behind his ear.

I'm pretty sure the tightness I feel in my chest is happiness.

I find my phone and blink at the screen.

My agent sent me the link to the Rumor Mill post.

Everyone *is going to read your article,* she writes.

I look at the pictures—clearly shot on someone's cellphone from a table or two away. I hope they got good money for them.

The photos themselves are fairly innocuous. Nothing like the shots that had been circulating of Gabe and Jacinda in Paris all those years ago. Gabe and I seated on opposite sides of a table. Not touching. It's mostly Gabe's face and half of mine, shot from over my shoulder. We look, for all intents and purposes, like two people having a conversation.

There's one shot of him greeting me, but even that is innocent, Gabe's hand on my elbow.

The thing that makes all these images worthy of a post, worthy of attention, is the look on Gabe's face.

He looks like a man in love.

I put my phone, facedown, on the bed.

Gabe comes into the bedroom, with tea, without a shirt. He stops in the doorway and I don't blame him because I can *feel* the expression on my face. It's heavy. Stormy.

He looks where I've put my phone.

"Bad news?" he asks.

I exchange my phone for the tea. He sits on the edge of the bed, his thumb scrolling through the pictures.

"Okay," he says.

There's a tinge of confusion in his voice. I can see that he doesn't exactly understand what he's looking at and why it has resulted in me doing an imitation of a sad theatre mask.

"Okay," he says again. "This isn't ideal, but we can make it work."

"Make it work," I echo.

Gabe nods, but he's not actually listening. He's thinking. Problem-solving. And I can tell that this isn't the first time something like this has happened.

Of course not.

"We'll call my management. We'll put out a statement."

The mug is hot against my hands, burning the delicate whorls of my fingertips.

"A statement," I say.

I'm fully parroting him, but he doesn't seem to notice.

The tightness doesn't feel like happiness anymore.

It's that quicksand feeling again. Like I'm being pulled under and I know that no matter how hard I struggle, I'm still going to drown, reality pressing in around me.

I put the tea on the side table with a *thunk*.

"I need more time," I say.

I'm not in any rush, Gabe had said.

"We had ten years," Gabe says now, and this time the ironic twist to his words isn't funny at all.

"That's *not* what I mean," I say.

"I know." He looks a little chastened. "But we don't really have that luxury. It's better if we put out a statement now than say nothing and have paparazzi stalking us when we get back to L.A."

Paparazzi.

They say that you should never read the comments.

I made that mistake after the first Go Fug Yourself article. The comments had been fine there, but once it went viral, appearing on websites where posts weren't monitored, the claws had come out. People were incensed that I had gone with him to the premiere. It was almost a personal affront that I'd been allowed to stand next to him on the red carpet. After my article came out and there were whispers about how he'd fucked me to get good press, the vitriol increased. People were furious that I dared to be so unattractive and still get Gabe's attention.

My very presence near Gabe had apparently created a tear in the fabric of the universe. Up was down, right was wrong, cats and dogs living together, total anarchy.

People had felt entitled to tell me that. In comments. In reviews. In emails.

To them, I was nothing more than a bad writer who had slept her way into the spotlight. I was the walking, breathing stereotype of a female reporter. And the worst part is that there's truth in it all. How unprofessional I've been. How reckless. How selfish.

And *now*? That reaction would be *nothing* compared to the backlash I'd get if the world discovered the truth. If this thing between Gabe and me went public.

I'd be proving them right, and revealing myself to be a liar.

I'm sinking.

"No," I say.

"No?" Gabe looks at me, then back at the phone. Frowns. "You want to say something else?"

"I don't want to say anything."

"Okay," he says, the word slow and drawn out.

He's confused.

"I can't do this," I say.

"What?"

"I. Can't. Do. This," I say, enunciating each word like an asshole.

He looks as if I've slapped him.

"Are you fucking serious right now?"

His voice is quiet but hard.

"Gabe," I say. "I'm sorry if you thought differently, but—"

"Stop," he says.

I can't.

"Maybe something could have happened back then. But it didn't. You made your choice; you ran off and married Jacinda while the whole world gossiped about whether or not I'd slept with you—"

"Enough," he says.

The sharp lash of the word stops me.

He's furious.

"I've held my tongue, but this is ridiculous. Yeah, I shouldn't have gone to Vegas with Jacinda. Yeah, I should have called. Yeah, I could have done things differently, but the thing that you keep forgetting, Chani, is that you left."

"What?"

Gabe points a finger at me.

"You. Left."

I'm clutching the sheet in my hands.

"When I woke up that morning, you were gone," Gabe says. "You left in the middle of the fucking night. No note. No text. Nothing. You know what I thought? I thought, well, she probably got exactly what she wanted—a couple of good sound bites and a good story to tell her friends about how she hooked up with a celebrity."

My knuckles are white.

"Well, maybe you were right," I say. "Maybe that's all this is."

"I know it's not," he says.

"We barely know each other."

"Chani," he says, but I keep talking.

"Collectively, we've spent maybe six days together," I say. "That's nothing. You can't know someone in six days."

"Can't you?"

I shake my head.

"I know you," he says.

"No, you don't," I say. "And I could write about all of this. About last night. About your family. About your relationship with your niece. About your sister and Benjamin Walsh. This could be my story."

It makes me sick just saying it out loud.

Gabe is silent for a long time.

"Then do it," he says.

"What?"

"Go call your editor," he says, extending a hand toward the living room. "Write that article."

We stare at each other, playing the weirdest game of chicken ever.

"No?" he says. "I thought so."

I scowl at him. "Don't be smug just because you think I'm a decent person."

Gabe shakes his head. "I don't understand why you're being like this," he says.

"Because this was a mistake," I say.

"No," he says. "It wasn't a fucking mistake. *Isn't*. Ten years ago, maybe, but that was one we made together. If anyone is making a mistake right now, it's you. On your own."

I'm out of bed and pulling my clothes on.

"Chani," Gabe says.

His hand is on my elbow, but I shake it off.

"You don't understand," I say. "You don't understand at all."

"Then tell me," he says.

I shove my legs into my pants, not looking at him.

"You know what happens at my book signings?" I ask. "People don't come to learn about my writing technique or my interviewing process. They don't want to know about craft or publishing. They buy their book and get in line and every single one of them asks me what really happened between the two of us."

"So what?" Gabe says. "You think I don't get asked about my Bond outburst or my drinking problem or half a dozen other personal things that people feel entitled to know about? You know how it is! It's part of the job."

"It's not the same," I say. "You can recover. No matter what—no matter the scandal, no matter the narrative—at the end of the day you still get to be Gabe Parker. Look at what's happening now—you've already been forgiven. Your career is on the rise again. You still get to be judged on your work. On your talent."

"Chani—"

I shake my head.

"I'll always be known for writing that article. And this will just prove everything that's been said. That I'm a fraud. I'll always be the girl who fucked Gabe Parker and lied about it. Who thought she was good enough. And no one will *ever* forgive me for that."

"That's bullshit," he says. "*You* wrote that article. *You* decided what to include. Take some responsibility. Stop acting like a victim."

Anger rears up inside of me. It builds like a tsunami, overwhelming every other emotion.

"Fuck you, Gabe," I say.

I pull my sweater on with such force that I get rug burn on my chin.

"I wish I'd never written the fucking thing," I say.

"You know what," Gabe says, "me too."

Chapter 30

I DON'T BOTHER TYING MY BOOTS.

Teddy scrambles out of her dog bed as I pass, her tail wagging. I grab my coat, laces flapping. I hear Gabe coming out of the bedroom.

"Chani." His voice is muffled beneath the shirt he's putting on. "Chani, wait."

I leave my scarf behind.

I leave my purse behind. All my things.

All I have is my jacket, unlaced boots, and my phone.

I know Gabe is probably going to come looking for me, so I duck into an alley and hide. It's ridiculous and pathetic, but I don't know what else to do.

I stay there, crouched alongside a dumpster until my ears go numb from the cold.

Then, I lace my boots up. Slowly. Carefully. I think about calling Katie, but that's not the person I end up dialing.

"Hello, darling," Ollie says.

He's far more awake and far less surprised than I would have expected for this kind of call at this point in the day. It's barely seven.

"Tired of Gabe already?" he asks.

"Something like that," I say.

"Hmm," he says. "Shall I come get you?"

"Please," I say.

I have to step out from beyond the dumpster to give him directions. I wait on the sidewalk, chilled and stupid, half expecting to see Gabe appear from around the corner. When Ollie arrives, it's in a very nice car that smells brand-new. Cooper is quiet, just beginning to wake up as we turn away from Main Street.

I'm certain this place is magical when it's snowing.

I have that feeling of not belonging. What it was like in New York. What it's been like in L.A.

I'm wondering if I just don't feel at home in myself anymore.

Ollie takes me to a diner at the other end of town and doesn't say anything until we've both ordered and have cups of tea set in front of us.

"I think you should give him another chance," Ollie says.

"You don't even know what he's done," I say.

"Don't I?" he asks.

He glances at his phone under the table. Half paying attention to me.

I clear my throat. He smiles and puts his phone facedown on the table.

"Sorry. Continue," he says with a benevolent wave of his hand.

"I don't want to talk about it," I say.

I'm a terrible liar.

"I assume this is about the pictures," he says.

"You've seen them?"

He nods. "Not your best angle, but not bad. Your hair looks good."

I glare at him. He sips his tea.

"Then you know what it looks like," I say.

"That Gabe is smitten with you?" he asks. "Yes, but I didn't need paparazzi pictures to tell me that."

Despite all that's happened I blush.

"He's a movie star," I say as if that explains everything.

"Eh," Ollie says. "Is he, though?" He stretches, wingspan extending beyond the diner booth. "*I'm* a movie star. Gabe is, well, Gabe is a recovering movie star. And a friend. And business partner."

"Ollie," I say. "You know what I'm talking about."

"I know that being a movie star doesn't insulate a person from having feelings just like everyone else," he says. "We *are* capable of feeling things. Like friendship. And love."

I ignore him.

"I didn't ask for this," I say.

"And Gabe did?" he asks.

"It's not the same," I say.

"No," he says. "But I don't think you're giving him enough credit."

I put my head on the table. I'm so tired.

"He's been paying attention," Ollie says. "To you. To your career."

"Then he knows how people see me," I say, my words muffled behind my hair.

"Yes," Ollie says, and lets out a dramatic sigh. "The cost of fame."

"Not worth it."

But even as I say it, I don't know if that's true.

It feels different than it did ten years ago. *I* feel different.

"Perhaps not," Ollie says. "But I do like having the jet."

"At least you got a jet out of it," I say. "I just have a reputation. 'Will write in cxchange for sexual favors.' "

There's a long pause.

"Did you really think that Gabe got Dan Mitchell fired because he was jealous of Dan's youth and vitality?" Ollie asks.

I lift my head. He raises an eyebrow.

"The bloody fool came back from that interview *bragging* about you," Ollie says.

My stomach does the same sickening twist that it did when Dan had generously offered me the enormous privilege of sucking his dick.

"Oh," I say.

I hate that even though I know—*I know*—that I didn't do a damn thing to deserve that grotesque overture, I still feel a twinge of guilt. Of embarrassment.

I'd never told anyone, but I wasn't really surprised that Dan had. I just hadn't thought he would have said something to Gabe.

Business has begun to pick up in the diner and the door jingles behind me, bringing with it a whoosh of cold air that hits the back of my neck and makes me shiver.

"He knew Dan was running his mouth," Ollie says. "He knew it was a lie. That you wouldn't—"

"Wouldn't I?" I ask.

I hadn't done what I'd done with Gabe because of the story, but the whole thing had never been some innocent, youthful misstep. Gabe was right—I wasn't the victim. I'd known what I was doing and I'd known that it was ill-advised.

I'd been there to do a *job*. Not Gabe.

"Chani."

Gabe.

He's standing at the end of our booth, looking nervous. I look over at Ollie who shrugs and takes a sip of tea.

"Business partner," he says. "Friend."

"Can we talk?" Gabe asks.

Most of my anger has dissipated, exposing the emotion I was trying to avoid. Fear.

"Okay," I say.

There's shame too.

"I'll eat your breakfast for you," Ollie says.

As we walk out of the diner, Gabe hands me my scarf.

"You forgot this," he says.

"A few other things too," I say.

He nods.

The heat is on in his truck, so I don't even need my scarf. I keep it balled up in my hands.

We drive back to his apartment and park outside. From this direction, I can see all the way down Main Street. Where I have a view of the mountains but also the church spire and a water tower and what appears to be an old hotel in the distance. Cooper is quiet and cold, a thin layer of snow covering every surface like icing.

I turn away from this view, away from Gabe, and find myself looking at the dumpster I'd hid behind like a coward.

"I could see you," Gabe says.

I look back at him. "What?"

He points—to the dumpster and then up.

"From my living room," he says.

There's a window above the alley. *His* window. Which meant that Gabe watched me duck behind a trash can to avoid him. Watched me crouch there like an old-timey burglar all because I couldn't have an adult conversation about an adult decision without my flight impulse kicking in.

Teddy isn't in the truck, so I imagine her in the apartment, looking out the window.

My face and neck are so hot that I have to unzip my jacket. This whole thing keeps getting more and more embarrassing and stupid.

"Ollie texted you," I say.

"I texted him," Gabe says. "When you left."

I nod.

"Déjà vu," he says.

"It's not the same," I say.

"I know."

I keep futzing with my scarf, scrunching it into a ball so it fits in the palms of my hands and then releasing it to expand in my lap.

"I didn't want it to happen this way," he says. "When I said we'd have time, I thought we would. I thought that I could do what I'd done with my father—that I could keep you, that I could keep *this,* out of the watchful eye of the press. That this could be something I didn't have to share. At least not right away."

I know it's not his fault.

"I never thought I deserved Bond," he says. "Even before I found out about Ollie."

Outside the truck, snow has begun to fall—fat, fluffy flakes caught and buffeted around by the chilly air.

"Every article, every think piece about how ill-suited I was for the role, how *wrong* I was, I could have written myself," he says. "Even in rehearsals, I was always two seconds away from quitting."

I hear him shift, hear the squeak of the seat as he turns toward me.

" 'I can say with all confidence that Gabe Parker is the Bond we need. He might even be the Bond we deserve.' "

I start crying.

"I thought you hated the article."

"Not all of it," he says. "And I never hated it."

My hands are open and my tears are gathering there, in the curve of my palms.

"You were good," I say.

"You were right," Gabe says.

"You had Dan Mitchell fired?" I ask.

His jaw tenses.

"I'd like to think I would have done it no matter what," Gabe says. "That if I heard him saying things like that about any woman, I would have done the same thing—would have thrown all my weight behind getting him fired." He lifts a shoulder. "But it was you he was talking about."

"Why?" I ask.

"Why what?"

"Why me?"

He takes a moment.

"I think it was the short story," Gabe says.

"The story?"

"I think that's where it started," he says. "When I read your story."

"It's not that good of a story," I say.

"I guess I really like dragons, then," he says. "Because by the time you walked up to my front door, talking to yourself, I think I was already halfway infatuated with you. It wasn't just the story, I don't think, though it was good. It was the *way* you wrote it. The way your brain worked. I liked that. A lot."

The confession leaves me breathless.

"What you're feeling," he says. "The doubt? It never really goes away. Not really. I'll never know if people go to see my movies because they like me, or because they think of my personal life as a never-ending car wreck that they're hoping will show up on-screen."

He looks at me.

"I should have asked," he says. "What you wanted. From this trip. From me. From us."

Us.

"The funny thing is," he says, "I think we would have been a mess ten years ago. If you'd stayed. If I'd called. But now . . ."

The wind has picked up. The truck is warm, and it feels a little like we're inside a snow globe.

"I can't change how people see you. I can't change the fact that you're right about what they'll say about us. About you. The world is unfair. They'll forgive me and punish you. People will be cruel and they will be relentless and there will be times when there won't be anything I can do about it. I can't get all the Dan Mitchells in the world fired. I can't promise that I'll be worth it."

It's so quiet in the truck.

"Chani." His voice is rough.

I look up at him.

"I want to be worth it," he says.

I'm crying again.

"But you have to decide what *you* want."

Simple as that.

Gabe continues. "You can take the truck and go to the airport. Ollie's plane can get you back to L.A."

There's a jangling noise and he puts his keys on the dash.

"Or you can come home with me," he says. "It's your choice."

He opens the door, letting in the cold and the snow, which settles onto the seat he's vacated. The world feels muffled once he's closed the door and I watch him walk away, his figure blurred by the snow.

My choice.

My heart is pounding, high up in my chest, almost like it's trying to claw its way out of me. Ten years ago, I counted to one hundred. I waited until it was quiet.

It's quiet now. So quiet.

I'm alone with my thoughts and my feelings and they are at war with each other. I want to run again. I want to take Gabe's truck and go to the airport and fly back to L.A. on Ollie's private jet and write the article and lie to everyone about what happened this weekend.

I slide across the seat and put my hands on the wheel. It's warm. I can still feel what Gabe left behind. The warmth from his hands. The smell of his hair.

It would be easy to leave.

I think of everything that will be said if I stay. Of the articles, the comments, the smug confirmation that I'm exactly as unprofessional and undeserving as people thought.

But I realize—for the first time in a long time—that I don't care.

I don't care what people will say.

I know what I want.

I take the keys off the dash.

The wind fights me as I shove the door open, my scarf once again left behind.

I run into the white flurry of snow and hit something. *Someone*.

Gabe's arms come around me. Steadying me for a moment before letting go.

There's a bark and I realize that Teddy is with us too, her tail whapping against my leg as she circles us.

"I was coming to get you," I say.

"Me too," he says. "I forgot something."

He takes my hand.

My heart goes up even higher in my throat. I'm afraid it will fall out onto the sidewalk if I try to say anything.

"In the midst of my very dramatic and completely unnecessary cinematic gesture, I forgot to say the one thing I should have said first." Gabe looks at me.

My breath fogs in the air between us.

"I love you," he says.

Our fingers are entwined, our palms pressed together. I imagine that I can feel his heartbeat there, but I'm pretty sure it's just my own, beating harder and faster than ever before.

"I love your clever mind. I love your hair and your butt. I love how fucking brilliant you are, how bold and how brave. I love that Teddy loves you. And I'm pretty sure that my family loves you too. I love your ideas, your stories. And mostly I love your very big eyes and your very smart mouth."

I swallow my heart down.

"And my dumb questions?"

He smiles at that. His hand is on my elbow.

"Everything," he says. "I love everything about you."

I let my heart settle in my chest. Where it belongs.

"I love you too," I say. "Everything about you."

Then I plant my face directly into the spot where his neck meets his shoulder. I get it very wet. He lets me cry, the two of us standing there in the snow and the cold.

"Stay," Gabe says when I'm done.

"Here?"

"Wherever," he says. "With me."

"Okay," I say.

I wipe my nose on my sleeve.

"How are we going to make this work?" I ask, thinking of the logistics of our lives.

"We'll figure it out," he says. "At least, we owe it to her to try."

I look down at Teddy, whose mouth opens and unfurls her tongue in the perfect doggy grin. She barks and nudges my hand.

"That's true," I say.

Gabe puts his hand on my cheek, his thumb rubbing the drying lines of tears, flaking away the salt there. He kisses the spot, softly. Then, with his hand on my chin, he kisses me. My arms go around his neck and it's not so cold anymore.

"Chani," he says.

I love the way he says my name. And this time, there's a question there. A question I finally have an answer for.

"Yes," I say. "*Yes*."

BROAD SHEETS

Bringing the Big Show to the Big Sky

[EXCERPT]

BY GABE PARKER-HOROWITZ

I'VE BEEN GIVEN THIS ARTICLE, THIS SPACE ON A PAGE, TO promote the theatre I'm launching in my hometown. I know I'm supposed to talk about the season we have planned for the fall, starting with a production of *Angels in America*. I'm supposed to write about things coming full circle and second chances and new starts and all that. Maybe toss out a brilliant metaphor or life lesson or something.

But it's fair to say that I'm not much of a writer. And yes, I'm aware that there are people who would argue I'm not much of an actor either.

I'm also not going to talk about my drinking or my recovery or even my latest movie and how well it was received. Okay, maybe I'm going to talk a little bit about that.

Mostly, though, I want to write about a question.

It's a question my wife asked me when we first met. About success. How I defined it.

I didn't have an answer for her then, but I think I do now.

It was easy, when I was younger, to think of success in terms of the roles I was getting, the money I was being paid, the perks that were being lavished on me. I was successful because I was famous. Because I was *known*.

It's a funny thing when the world thinks it knows you. Or, when you think what the world knows is who you are.

Acting, for me, was an escape. When I stepped onstage or in front of a camera, I knew who I was. I was more comfortable playing pretend than I was being the person that existed when the lights were off.

I felt safer in the fantasy.

I'm sure it will surprise no one to learn that alcohol helped maintain that. When I was working or when I was drunk, I could ignore the voices in my head—and in the media—that told me that no matter what roles I got, no matter how much money I was being paid, no matter what perks were given to me, it would never be enough. *I'd* never be enough.

It took fucking up on a global scale, it took rehab, it took divorce, and it took losing the thing I'd used to define myself to realize I didn't want that anymore. To paraphrase the indomitable Tracy Lord, I realized that I didn't want to be successful. I wanted to be loved.

But when you're focused on feeding something that can never truly be satiated, you miss what you're actually hungry for.

Ten years ago, I wasn't able to answer the question. I wasn't ready.

Now, I'm ready.

Success is starting a theatre where I'm beholden to no one but my co-founder and staff. Success is being present for my family—physically and emotionally. Success is being Bond and then not being Bond.

It's stepping off the stage and feeling like *I'm* still there. That I deserve to be there.

Mostly, though, it's her. It's us.

It's the stories she reads me late at night, when she's spent all day writing and isn't sure that any of it is good (it always is). It's mornings waiting for the hot water to boil so we can have tea and coffee and talk about what comes next. It's feeling like every day is the perfect day, even if the whole day isn't perfect, but finding the moments that are. Being so proud of her that I could burst.

It's knowing that this isn't a fantasy. It's real life.

—

Acknowledgments

WRITING IS INTIMATE AND NERVE-RACKING AND A LITTLE embarrassing. Thank you, dear reader, for the opportunity to be vulnerable with you.

Endless thanks to Elizabeth Bewley, who in addition to being a wonderful human being is also a damn good agent (dare I say, the *best* agent?) and who saw something in this book before it was even finished. Elizabeth, I'm so lucky that you're on my team.

I'm beyond grateful for my editor, Shauna Summers. It's incredibly rare to find someone you immediately click with on a creative level. Shauna, what a gift it is to work with you. There's nothing better than collaborating with someone so sharp and insightful. I can't wait to do it again.

Thank you to the entire team at Penguin Random House. Thank you to Lexi Batsides and Mae Martinez. Thank you to Kara Welsh, Kim Hovey, Jennifer Hershey, Cara DuBois, Belina Huey, Ella Laytham, Barbara Bachman, and Colleen Nuccio. Thank you to marketing and publicity goddesses Morgan Hoit, Melissa Folds, and Courtney Mocklow, all of whom share my love of a good spreadsheet. And to everyone else who touched this book with their talents.

This book had several early champions—friends and colleagues whose support I cherish. Thank you, Tal Bar Zemer, Katie Cotugno, Zan Romanoff, Maurene Goo, Robin Benway, Sarah Enni, Brandy

Colbert, Margot Wood, Jessica Morgan, Alisha Rai, Rachel Lynn Solomon, and Kate Spencer. You're all as talented as you are beautiful (and you're all very beautiful).

Thank you to my parents for taking me to the library whenever I needed to refresh my stacks of paperback romances. Mom and Dad, you never put restrictions on what I was allowed to read, therefore the sex scenes are totally your fault. Thank you.

Adam and Abra, I wouldn't trade you for any other siblings on the planet. I definitely haven't tried to.

John. You're better than any romance hero I've ever read (or written). Because you're real. And you're spectacular. I love you.

PHOTO: © JOHN PETAJA

Elissa Sussman received her BA from Sarah Lawrence College and her MFA from Pacific University. She is the author of three young adult novels, and *Funny You Should Ask* is her debut adult novel. She lives in Los Angeles with her husband and their two dogs, Basil and Mozzarella.

elissasussman.com

Twitter: @ElissaSussman

Instagram: @Elissa_Sussman